DEADLY WRATH

Riley Malloy Mystery, Book 6

Judith A. Barrett

Wobbly Creek LLC

DEDICATION

Deadly Wrath is dedicated to farm dogs and to farmers who grow and harvest our food and fiber.

DEADLY WRATH

RILEY MALLOY MYSTERY BOOK 6

Published in the United States of America by Wobbly Creek, LLC

2024 Georgia

wobblycreek.com

Cover by Wobbly Creek, LLC

ISBN 978-1-953870-69-8 eBook

ISBN 978-1-953870-70-4 Paperback

ALSO BY JUDITH A. BARRETT

Wren and Rascal Mystery Series
Jenna Ross Mystery Series
Riley Malloy Mystery Series
Donut Lady Cozy Mystery Series
Maggie Sloan Thriller Series
Grid Down Survival Series

Previously...

RILEY

My name is Riley Malloy Carter. I'm a vet tech, and I understand what animals tell me, which must be why people call me an "animal whisperer." When the clinic where I was working in my hometown abruptly closed, Toby, my five-year-old black and brown German Shepherd mixed with a bit of Labrador Retriever, and I moved to Barton, Georgia, to live in my grandma's old cabin. I found a new job at a fantastic animal hospital with wonderful people, but best of all, I met my sweet husband, Ben Carter, a cute, tall deputy sheriff with brown hair, greenish hazel eyes, and a smile that melted my heart. Not that we're competitive or anything, but I enjoy reminding Ben that I love him more.

While Ben was in training as a crime scene specialist with the Georgia Bureau of Investigation, we rented a house only twenty minutes from his classes, and I accepted a part time position with the local vet, Doc Ned Halsey.

I agreed to help Doc Ned's longtime friend, Nora, with the horses at her bed-and-breakfast. None of us dreamed that the Trail's End Bed and Breakfast would become the headquarters of a criminal ring, but it did. Derek, an undercover GBI agent who was also working at the B&B, led the team that broke up the ring; Toby, Diane, who was a caterer at the B&B, and I stopped the mastermind.

Ben completed his classes and field training; he's an official GBI Crime Scene Specialist. We've rented a house in the country near Jimson, Georgia, and Doc Ned recommended me to a veterinarian who has recently added farm visits to his practice. I love farm visits.

BEN

Riley is brilliant, has a remarkable talent for communicating with animals, has fiery red hair, and is the prettiest girl I've ever seen. Her talent is a little more than dog whisperer; she talks to animals and understands what they are telling her when they respond. I know it's a stretch to believe, but I've seen her in action, and it's true.

Riley is the love of my life; I wish she wasn't always the target of murderers. A talented GBI agent, who worked undercover at the bed-and-breakfast, said Riley was a natural investigator and wanted her to join his team, but thankfully, Riley said she wasn't the type to follow rules, and I heartily agreed.

Mom said some people have hinted to her that Riley and I rushed into marriage too quickly, but they abruptly change the subject when Mom dares them to tell Riley.

In case it comes up, I loved her first.

CHAPTER ONE

While Ben cleared their breakfast dishes, Riley made their sandwiches for lunch. She sighed as she cut their sandwiches on the diagonal. "It doesn't seem fair that I'm only twenty minutes from the Jimson Veterinary Clinic where I'll be working, and you have almost an hour's drive to your office."

"The regional office covers ten counties, and this house is in the center of the counties where I'll be working." Ben pulled out ice packs from the freezer and put them into their insulated lunch bags along with a bottle of water, an apple, and a plastic sack with two cookies. "It's going to be cold today, babe; do me a favor and wear long johns since you'll be going on farm visits."

Ben wrapped his arms around Riley; she snuggled against his chest and sighed as she listened to his heart beat.

"Do you think it would be okay if I text you during the day?" he asked.

"I'd love it; you won't feel so far away."

Ben scratched Toby behind the ears, kissed Riley, and grabbed his warm jacket, lunch bag, and thermos of coffee before he dashed out the door.

Toby padded to the living room and flopped down in front of the gas fireplace while Riley started another pot of coffee before she opened the three-ring notebook with the recipes from Ben's mom. After Riley found the slow cooker recipe for her small pork roast, she scanned the kitchen for an electrical outlet close to a counter surface.

She set the slow cooker on the stove top and plugged it into the outlet next to the stove. She pulled out the meat from the refrigerator, placed it inside the slow cooker along with chicken broth and spices, and set the dial on the slow cooker to medium.

"Next, laundry, and I guess I better put on long johns. I hate being cold."

Toby opened his eyes but didn't move as Riley gathered the laundry. After she started the washer, Riley packed a backpack with Toby's water bowl, a container of water, and a few treats for the day then hurried to the bedroom and added layers to her clothing.

Riley slid her pistol into the waistband holster then put on her warm jacket before she slipped Toby's backpack over one shoulder and her backpack over the other shoulder.

After she picked up her work backpack that she had stuffed with a change of clothes, her vet apron, and her lunch, Riley and Toby went outside. A gust of wind from around the corner of the house added to the intensity of the frigid morning air and took away her breath; she pulled up the neck of her jacket to cover her mouth and nose. Riley started the car's engine, then immediately turned down the fan that was blasting out cold air from the vents.

"I didn't expect it to be so cold this soon; at least we'll be on the road long enough for the heater to warm up."

The frost on the still-green grass alongside the road sparkled in the bright sunlight. "We should get a small thermos so Ben can have hot soup or chili with his sandwiches for lunch."

Toby yipped.

"We'll stop at the grocery store on the way home this afternoon to pick up a small thermos, potatoes, and green chiles for the pork stew. Ben will enjoy having piping hot, green chile pork stew with his lunch tomorrow."

Riley slowed as she went through the center of town. "Jimson is much bigger than I realized. There was a second veterinary clinic at the edge of town, and I've seen four boutiques, two coffee cafés, a bookstore, a craft beer shop, two banks, three restaurants, and two lawyer offices on Main Street so far. We'll have to stroll around town this coming weekend."

When Riley reached the Jimson Veterinary Clinic, she furrowed her brow as she examined the structure. "The building is really old, isn't it? From the architectural style, the clinic must have been converted from a house to commercial use quite a while ago. I wonder if the veterinarian practice owns the building or is leasing it; there are obvious signs of deferred maintenance, like the paint's peeling at the eaves, and the gutters are sagging."

After Riley parked behind the Jimson Veterinary Clinic and turned off the engine, she remained motionless in her seat with her hands on the steering wheel while she examined the building.

Toby whined.

"Don't be pushy. I was admiring the wide, well-constructed ramp that goes to the back door."

Toby yipped.

She exhaled. "I wonder if I should have asked to meet with Doctor Peterson and his staff before I accepted the position, since I've only talked to Doctor Hugo Adams on the phone, and that was just briefly after I sent my resume to the Jimson Veterinary Clinic on Doc Ned's recommendation."

Riley shivered from the cold and snorted. "That's total nonsense, because Doc Ned told me Doc Peterson was the best. I'm definitely suffering a weird case of new job nerves. Let's go in the front door. Doctor Adams said to park in the back, but I'd feel weird going in the back door like I was trying to sneak in."

The door creaked as Riley opened it and went inside with Toby on her heels. When she stopped short to inhale the surprising aroma of vanilla that was in sharp contrast to the austere surroundings of the clinic, Toby veered to avoid running into the back of her legs; Riley was startled by his sudden move and grabbed onto the metal bench next to the door to keep from falling.

A woman with short, brown hair with gray roots sat in a wheelchair at the desk; she cocked her head. "That was quite the entrance."

Riley giggled. "Thank you."

The woman grinned then shouted, "Doc Hugo, Riley and Toby are here."

After she removed her earbuds and left them dangling, the woman wheeled around the corner of the desk and held out her hand. "I'm Maureen."

"It's nice to meet you." Riley shook Maureen's hand and peered at the melted wax in the electric warmer on Maureen's desk.

"I would have preferred candles, but the fire marshal told me he'd shut us down if I did, so I make do with my electric warmer."

"Vanilla is a comforting aroma and makes the clinic inviting; I think it's brilliant; clients and patients must find it calming."

"That's my goal. Our senior veterinarian is Doctor Wesley Cooper; he came here as a brand-new veterinarian twelve years ago to work with Doc Peterson to learn the ropes then stayed on as a partner; he drops off his kiddos at school before he comes in, so I'm sure you'll meet him this afternoon when you return from the farm visits. Our other vet tech is Lisa; she's on her way here; you'll probably meet her before you leave."

Riley furrowed her brow. "What about Doctor Peterson?"

Maureen chuckled. "That old cuss hired Doc Hugo then retired and went on a cruise with his wife. He must have been planning that cruise for a long time. I'd be miffed at him, but I've been nagging him to retire for at least five years, so it was probably my fault."

"How long has it been since he left?"

Toby put his chin on Maureen's knee, and she rubbed his face. "You're such a good boy, Toby; I'm so glad you're here."

Maureen shifted to glance at Riley. "Doc Peterson retired almost three months ago."

A man who was nearing middle-age strolled down the hallway. He wore jeans and a white lab coat over a red and gray plaid flannel shirt that had the obvious fold lines of a shirt that had been recently purchased but never washed.

Toby trotted to him before Doc reached the receptionist's desk.

Doc Adams glanced at Toby then shook hands with Riley. "It's a pleasure to meet you, Riley; Doc Ned and Julie Rae think a lot of you."

Riley briefly frowned at his carefully manicured fingernails then cleared her throat. "You know Doc Julie Rae?"

"I went to school with her; she's brilliant, isn't she? Ready for a tour? The rest of our team will be here soon."

As Doc Hugo led Riley toward the exam rooms, Maureen said, "Don't forget you'll need to leave for your first farm visit in a half hour."

"Thanks; I haven't quite gotten used to the travel time between farm appointments. We'll make it a quick tour."

After he showed Riley the third examination room, Doc Hugo said, "I joined the practice three months ago. Before we moved here, I worked at one of the largest animal clinics in the Atlanta area for twelve years. We had fifteen veterinarians, and the practice specialized in dogs, cats, and other small mammals." Doc Hugo beamed. "It was fairly upscale, so a small town practice is an enormous change. I've never worked away from a clinic until now, but my wife's family lives in a county north of here on a farm with two horses, chickens, and goats, so I'm a natural to include farm animals."

"That's great; I learned a lot from Doc Ned and Doc Julie Rae. One thing I learned is that I love taking care of horses; I think cows are a little harder."

"Is it because they have a tendency to have more complex issues? When my wife's dad told us there was a vet here who wanted to retire and needed someone to take over his practice, we knew it was for us; we've always wanted our kids to be closer to their grandparents, so here we are. Last month, Wesley and I decided we could expand our business if one of us took over the office visits, and I've been wanting to try my hand at farm visits. I'll show you our trauma and x-ray rooms; they're in the back."

Riley examined the x-ray equipment. "This is nice."

"We upgraded two months ago. We don't have a kennel, but I think we should; I heard Julie Rae handles patients that require overnight care. That might be something we will consider, but we'll need to find a larger facility and maybe hire a third vet."

On their way to the breakroom, Riley asked, "Where are you looking for your new building?"

"We're looking close to town because this is our base for our customers."

When they reached the breakroom, Riley said, "You have a lot planned; that's exciting."

"I'm thinking it will be a simple transition."

"Ha!" Maureen's voice carried to the breakroom.

Doc Hugo cleared his throat. "Maureen keeps me honest."

"Somebody has to." Maureen chuckled.

Doc Hugo shrugged. "She's definitely up for it. I'll remember to check the acoustics before I approve a new building. Care for some coffee? I haven't had my quota for the morning yet."

"Coffee sounds wonderful."

A slender woman with streaks of gray in her dark brown hair was out of breath as she hurried into the breakroom. "Hi, Riley; I'm Lisa." Her dimples deepened when she smiled.

Riley returned her smile. "It's nice to meet you."

"You too; maybe we'll have a chance to talk when you finish your farm visits this afternoon." Lisa put her lunch into the refrigerator. "I've been in a rush all morning because my husband and his brother decided late last night to leave early this morning for the farmers' meeting that is being held near Atlanta. Thank goodness I went to the library last week to research the government reports they would need; I was up half the night pulling together relevant data for them. While he packed a few things this morning, I fixed them sandwiches and snacks. I have to dash; Doc Wesley, Maureen, and I always have a meeting first thing in the morning to go over the day's schedule." Lisa's dimples returned. "Although I don't know why we bother, because our days never go as planned."

Riley chuckled. "Sounds typical to me."

"You're late again." Doc Hugo sniffed as Lisa hurried to the door.

Lisa stopped, slowly turned to face him, and put her hands on her hips. "You're out of line," she growled, then left the room.

After Riley joined Doc Hugo at the break table, he asked, "Will Toby be going with us? Maureen said she heard Toby occasionally went with you and Doc Ned on farm visits."

"You don't mind if he goes along? I'll ask him what he'd like to do. What types of visits do you have planned?"

"You're going to ask him?" Doc Hugo snorted and sipped his coffee.

"Yes." Riley narrowed her eyes. "Why?"

Doc Hugo smirked. "Just sounded strange. The first farm visit is in the next county. A farmer called me at home last night; he found two dead calves in a pasture, and a few of the cows that had grazed in the same pasture yesterday weren't doing well last night; he's worried he has a toxic weed on his property. I told him we'd be there this morning to check the pasture. I'll show you how to do that."

"Doc Ned trained me on the typical toxic weeds, but I'm sure there is more I could learn," Riley said.

"It can't be all that hard. The second one is about five miles from here; they have mules on their farm. I ordinarily prefer for Maureen to group each day's appointments to be geographically close to each other, but I juggled my schedule to examine the pasture. She'll have a fit, but I'll give Maureen our revised schedule before we leave, so she'll know where we are if an emergency arises."

"That's great; I'll let Ben know he can call Maureen if he can't reach me."

"That's what my wife does."

As they headed to the receptionist's desk, Doc asked, "I'm guessing since you've been on farm visits, you packed a lunch."

"Doc Ned said it's a timesaver."

"My wife didn't understand why I'd rather eat on the side of the road instead of sitting at a table in a café until I told her I'd get home two hours later if I didn't have my lunch with me."

"She sends you to work with gourmet lunches, Doc, because she wants you to eat healthy," Maureen said. "Riley, I think Toby's staying with me, aren't you, boy?"

Toby yipped.

Riley raised her eyebrows. "Then it's settled; Maureen, you have a bodyguard for the day."

"Don't be too impressed, Riley." Maureen chuckled. "I bribed him with the promise of a roll and stroll to the dog park for our lunch break and extra treats when we got back." Maureen's eyes twinkled. "Roll and trot might be more accurate, but roll and stroll sounds more trendy."

Riley giggled. "I think you had him at dog park."

Riley glanced at the earbuds that dangled above Maureen's shoulders. "What kind of music do you like?"

"My earbuds are old school, but I like them because I can pop them out and not lose them. Have you ever talked to someone then realized they were wearing earbuds, and you have to start over? I'm super vigilant about removing mine. I enjoy listening to our local radio station and podcasts while I work when no one is around."

"Maureen invented multitasking," Doc mumbled.

"And I'm the best," she said.

While Riley knelt next to Toby and stroked his back, Doc Hugo headed to the back door.

Riley asked, "Can I have your cell phone number, Maureen?"

"I should have thought of that." Maureen opened her top desk drawer, pulled out a card, and handed it to Riley. "Here you go; I have yours because it was on your resume."

Riley waved as she rushed to the back door then caught up with Doc Hugo before he reached his truck. Before she climbed inside, she glanced at her phone as it buzzed a text from Ben.

"Leaving the office for my first assignment. Loved you first."

Riley grinned and returned his text. "Same. Love you more."

As he drove through town, Doc said, "I never had a specific vet tech work with me at the clinic in Atlanta. It was hard at first to adjust to Lisa because she's more experienced than the vet techs in Atlanta; they were mostly straight out of school, so I did a lot of things myself. Lisa mostly works with Wesley. Doc Ned told me you have a talent to understand animals, but he added I might not fully grasp what that meant until I met you; he was exaggerating, wasn't he?"

"I don't think anyone really understands right off. I never thought it was unusual because my grandma always talked to animals and understood what they told her. When I went to school, I was surprised when people made fun of me."

Riley side-glanced at Doc as she continued. "I felt sorry for those kids because I thought something was wrong with them. When I told Grandma what they said, she said little kids understand animals, but they forget as they become older. I thought that was really sad; I'm glad I never forgot."

Doc snorted then sped up when he reached the highway. "I was interested in your choice of words when you said Toby would be Maureen's bodyguard. Is that what he usually does?"

"I guess he does in a way, but he enjoys being at the front desk and greeting the patients, so it made sense to me when he said that was what he wanted to do. Can you tell me more about the farm we'll be visiting?"

"John Winston is a fourth generation farmer; John manages the cattle, and his wife and their son manage the cropland. The Winstons are well known for being innovative; John Junior was the first in the area to use equipment that planted seeds without disturbing the soil."

"He's smart; no-till farming is not only cheaper because it requires less labor and fuel, it also saves the soil and nutrients."

Doc Hugo grunted. "I'd never heard of it until I moved here; I'll have to remember that you're not a city girl."

Doc pointed at the large sign, "Winston U-Pick Blueberries," before he turned onto the wide driveway. "My father-in-law told me a lot of farms replaced their tobacco fields with blueberries years ago; Mrs. Winston was one of the first in the area to implement an agritourism farm with You-Pick and a small shop at the farm to sell produce."

They passed a small wooden building with a sign, "Winnie's Market" and a graveled parking area in front of the building.

Doc Hugo continued past the old farmhouse and stopped next to an off-road utility terrain vehicle that was parked in front of a barn.

The cows in a corral behind the barn bellowed as Riley and Doc climbed out of the truck.

"The cows are mourning the dead calves," Riley said.

Doc cocked his head. "Really? They sound angry to me."

"They are."

A wiry man who wore a seed company ball cap came out of the barn and strode to Doc's truck.

"Good to see you, Doc, and this must be Riley."

After they shook hands, Doc said, "Sounds like your cows are pretty unhappy."

"They think they are free-ranging cows and too good for hay, but I can't let them roam right now. I'll show you where I found the dead calves last night. My wife called the sheriff after I went out at first light this morning; he'll be here later. We'll take the side-by-side, and I'll show you what I found."

As they rode along the fence line, Doc said, "Pastures are looking good. I don't see any toxic weeds; do you, Riley?"

"I would need to walk the pasture to tell," Riley said.

Doc Hugo sniffed; Mr. Winston glanced back at Riley and nodded. When Mr. Winston slowed, Riley leaned forward to peer at the pile of branches with a few leaves next to the fence that was less than ten feet from the road with only a shallow ditch between them.

"Is that a burn pile?" Doc asked.

"No, someone threw them over the fence."

Mr. Winston stopped next to the pile. "Most of the branches have been stripped of leaves, and there isn't any fruit."

Riley jumped out of her seat to examine the branches; after she leaned close to a branch with leaves and sniffed, she gasped. "These are wild cherry trees. The calves died of cyanide poisoning."

Mr. Winston paled. "These limbs were gathered from somewhere else and thrown over my fence..." His voice broke. "Why? To kill my cattle?"

"I'll check the cows as soon as we get back; are any other calves ill?" Doc asked as Riley returned to her seat on the UTV.

Mr. Winston straightened his back. "Hang on, Riley."

He sped over the rough terrain toward the barn; the UTV rolled from side to side, hit a bump, and went airborne. John grunted when the vehicle landed. "Didn't expect that. The two calves I have left seem fine; they're runts, so they probably couldn't have gotten past the larger calves or the cows who circled the branches to nibble at the leaves."

"How many cows are sick?" Doc asked.

"One still isn't quite up to par; three others have improved since last night."

Doc pulled out his phone; after he did a quick search, he called the clinic. "Maureen, do we have any thiosulfate?"

Doc frowned. "Thanks."

Doc hung up. "We don't have any thiosulfate; Maureen mentioned garlic water. Do you have any idea what she was talking about, Riley?"

"It's a home remedy frequently used as a substitute for thiosulfate. Grandma peeled and crushed fresh garlic cloves, dropped them into boiling water, and simmered the mixture for fifteen minutes."

"You sound like my wife," John said.

"John, does your wife have any fresh garlic?" Doc asked.

John stayed focused on his driving. "Always; my wife is a garlic water expert. She was up half the night mixing garlic water for the cows, and she kept me busy carrying out bucketfuls to the barn. For the record, I'd thought she had totally lost it."

"Do you think the garlic water made a difference?"

John exhaled. "I guess it did, but I'm glad we don't have a dairy farm; the milk would be awful."

Doc shrugged. "What do you think, Riley?"

"It's what Grandma and I did when the goats got into the peach trees."

John nodded. "Your grandma was smart. Peach pits release cyanide when they're chewed, and ruminants like goats and cows process their food multiple times. It would take a strong concentration of garlic water, though; just ask my wife."

Doc Hugo furrowed his brow. "John, as close as the calves were to the cherry branches when they collapsed, I didn't think they had a chance of surviving."

After John parked at the barn, Doc said, "I'd like to talk to the sheriff; I won't be long. If you want to go ahead, I'll join you in a few minutes."

As John and Riley strolled to the corral, he said, "I didn't know anything was wrong at first because the cows frequently trickle back to the barn, but all of them are always back by dusk. When the last few cows showed up, they were stumbling as they walked, and their breathing was labored. I thought they'd gotten into a toxic weed. While my wife rushed to take care of them, I realized I was missing two calves and went to find them."

"Why did she give them garlic water if she thought it was just a toxic weed?"

"She didn't; I did. She said the cows were too well-fed and smart to eat toxic weed, so it had to be something that was as toxic as dried red maple leaves or something similar that they'd never encountered before."

As John and Riley approached the corral, an older cow grunted, and the younger ones cleared a path for her as they moved away from the fence.

"What's going on, old girl? Do you have something to say?" John asked.

The cow stamped her feet and lowed; Riley's eyes widened.

John scanned the rest of the cows. "I know you'd tell me what you saw if you could."

The old cow mooed.

Riley stroked the old cow's head as she whispered, "Have you ever seen them before?"

The cow moaned before she strolled to the gate.

"Doesn't sound like she feels very well, but she looks fine." Doc joined them. "What do you think, Riley?"

She bit her lip then cleared her throat. "The corral seems a little small for them."

John furrowed his brow. "They haven't touched the hay I put out for them; we'll move them to a pasture that isn't too close to a road."

"I don't see any particular problems; we can come back by this afternoon," Doc said.

"Hate for you to make a special trip; why don't I call you if there's any change?" John asked.

"Sounds good; just call Maureen."

After they were in the truck and back on the road, Doc asked, "I got the feeling there was something you didn't want to say in front of John. Was there a problem?"

"Two men threw the branches from the back of their truck over the fence, and the young ones rushed to the branches. The men watched while the little ones ate the leaves. The cow recognized one man because he has been at the farm a few times."

Doc Hugo side-glanced at Riley; his voice dripped with sarcasm. "Right."

Riley rolled her eyes and pursed her lips as she gazed out her side window. *Don't ask if you don't want to know, Doc.*

She shrugged. *His loss.* "What's our next visit?"

"Nothing unusual; it's a bi-annual visit for vaccinations and checkups for mules."

"I don't have any hands-on experience with mules. Are their vaccinations the same as horses?"

Doc Hugo slowed as he turned at an intersection. "They are, but that's only because there are no protocols developed for mules and donkeys. The assumption is that any adverse reactions would be the same."

Riley shook her head. "I've heard that, but I'm not convinced it's true just because it's what everybody says."

"I don't have any reason to doubt it."

Riley turned away to hide her inadvertent eye roll. *Maybe you should.*

CHAPTER TWO

A few minutes later, Doc Hugo pointed at the upcoming cotton field on their left. "There's another cotton field being harvested; all this is new to me."

She nodded as she gazed at the monster harvester with an enclosed cab as it lumbered along and stripped the plants of open and unopened bolls on its way to the end of the field.

Riley scanned the cotton fields, pastures, and pecan orchard as they rode in silence. *Feels like home to me.*

When Doc Hugo slowed to make a right turn at a driveway, Riley peered at the cows and two donkeys in the nearby pasture.

After Doc Hugo parked near the barn, a woman who wore a blue denim jacket over denim overalls and had pulled back her long, silver hair into a ponytail rushed out of the house to greet them.

"Our harvester broke down; my husband took the mules to pull it closer to the barn, so he and our hired hand could work on it." She smiled. "Those mules love to work; it makes them feel important. You want to check the donkeys, Doc? I'll call them to the barn."

The woman smiled as she turned to Riley. "You must be Riley; I'm Rachel. I met your mother-in-law at a baby shower two or three years ago, and we've kept in touch. Melissa is a wonderful person, isn't she?"

"She really is." Riley returned her smile.

Rachel buttoned up her jacket and flipped up the collar as protection against the wind. "Let's go to the barn, and I'll show you my donkey calling skills. We may get the entire herd because we have very nosy cows."

As the two of them headed toward the barn, Doc Hugo said, "I'll be there in a minute; I have a text from the office."

"Melissa told me about your talent with animals; I understand our donkeys. My husband is a kind-hearted man, but he shakes his head when I tell him what the donkeys told me; unfortunately, I don't understand the cows or mules."

"That's exciting; I'm not surprised when children understand animals, but I've never met a donkey whisperer."

"Sometimes I think the cows are trying to tell me something, and I apologize to them because I don't understand. My husband tells his farm workers I'm eccentric, but I don't think it hurts to be polite, do you?"

"Not at all, and I'm sure the cows appreciate it."

When they reached the barn, the woman put her thumb and index finger up to her mouth and whistled. The donkeys trotted to the barn, and the cows followed them.

"Good girls," Rachel cooed and rubbed the donkeys' faces. "Go into your stalls, and I'll give you a treat." She turned to the cows. "Sorry, but y'all will have to wait out here while the doctor does his business."

The cows mooed then turned back to graze in the pasture.

Rachel opened the gate to the barn; while the donkeys strolled to their stalls, Doc Hugo strode into the barn.

"Did you have any concerns about the donkeys?" Doc Hugo asked.

"Not at all," Rachel said.

He quickly examined and vaccinated the donkeys. "They're doing fine."

Rachel's cell phone in her bib pocket buzzed. She read the text and frowned. "We'll have to reschedule the mules' checkups. We have a second piece of equipment that was in the same field as the harvester, and it has a problem too; my husband, his workers, and the mules are going to be busy for most of the day."

Doc Hugo furrowed his brow. "Sorry to hear that; just call Maureen when you're ready, and she'll schedule us to return a day or two later. Is there anything we can do before we leave?"

"No, but thank you so much for asking."

Before Doc Hugo started the truck, he said, "Maureen wants us to squeeze in one more farm before our next scheduled visit, but it's about thirty miles away, so we'll be having a late lunch unless we eat on the road. What do you think?"

"I don't mind a late lunch; eating while we travel is fine too. What's the problem?"

"Sick horse."

"Any details?" Riley narrowed her eyes. *Doc Hugo is annoying.*

"Off her feed and listless."

"Do you know how old she is, or if this is a recent problem?"

Doc snorted. "Why don't you call Maureen with your questions, and I'll concentrate on driving?"

Riley glared at Doc while she pulled out her phone from her backpack then called the office; after she counted ten rings, she hung up.

"No answer; Maureen mentioned going to the dog park. Doesn't anyone else answer the phone?"

"We close for lunch; the phone should have rung over to voicemail. I'll look at that when we return to the office."

Riley sent Maureen a text. "How is Toby doing?"

Maureen replied, "Great. We're at the dog park. We have new friends."

Riley returned her phone to her backpack. *At least someone is having a good day.*

Doc Hugo pulled into an abandoned gas station. "I thought about trying to find a roadside park, but the wind has come up. It's too miserable to be outside. I usually eat in my truck because if it's not windy, it's buggy."

Riley pulled out her lunch while Doc Hugo opened his door and left it open while he climbed out of the driver's seat and opened the back door to retrieve a small cooler. She zipped up her jacket when the wind gusted from the north and blew the driver's door wide open.

Riley shook her head. *Doc's lucky the wind didn't swing that door hard enough to mess up the hinges.*

After he jumped back into the truck and slammed his door, Doc said, "It has turned much colder than I expected; my jacket's not warm enough for this weather. I'll call Maureen after I eat to see if she can reschedule the rest of today's appointments."

"Tomorrow's going to be colder."

"Maybe the forecast is wrong." Doc took a big bite of his sandwich.

Riley sighed and poured a cup of coffee to go with her sandwich. *Doc's contrary attitude wears me out.*

While they ate, Doc asked, "Do you always carry a thermos of coffee?"

"Not always, but I try to when it's cold."

"I never paid much attention to the weather all the years that I was in Atlanta because I was never exposed to the outdoors when I went to work," Doc said. "I parked in covered parking with a covered walkway to the clinic, so I went from my garage at home to the clinic and back to my home garage."

"It's a lot different here, isn't it?"

"I don't see how people stand it; it's a lot colder and lonelier." Doc tapped his fingers on the steering wheel. "I guess I'm used to the city noises and traffic."

Riley nodded as she sipped her coffee. *We are definitely different; Jimson is city enough for me.*

Doc Hugo's phone buzzed a text. After he read it, he exhaled. "Maureen said a cow is having trouble delivering a calf; the farm is near here."

Doc replied to the text then started the engine. After he did a U-turn, he glanced at his phone when it buzzed. "I asked her if Wesley was available to come to the farm and help; he isn't, so I'm on my own."

"No, you aren't, Doc. I can talk you through it," Riley said.

"Thanks for the offer, but I'm sure I'll be fine; it's probably not as difficult a delivery as everyone is making it out to be."

"You don't really want a vet tech, do you?" Riley asked.

"That's a strange question; I wouldn't have hired you if I didn't want a vet tech."

"Good; then I'll assist you." Riley's voice hardened.

Doc Hugo slammed the heel of his hand on the steering wheel. "We've got a complicated delivery ahead of us; you need to stop being so negative."

How am I being negative? Riley side-glanced at him and cleared her throat. "How can I help you?"

"Just stay out of my way." Hugo gritted his teeth. "I'll be fine."

Riley bit her lip. *Stay calm; don't snap back.*

After she slowly exhaled, Riley said, "I won't let the calf die."

"Oh, you won't, will you?" Doc Hugo growled, "Just stay in the truck. I don't think this is working out."

Riley raised an eyebrow. "You're right, Doc."

Riley's phone buzzed a text. "Maureen said to step on it, Doc. The cow is in distress; I can talk you through it."

"I thought you said cows were too complex."

"No, I said they're harder than horses; that doesn't mean I don't have experience with a delivery."

"Right."

Same obnoxious tone. Riley narrowed her eyes as she turned to her side window. *I wonder how long it would take me to walk back to my car.*

"A walk would do me good," Riley mumbled.

"What?"

"Just thinking out loud; I'm used to Toby ignoring me."

"I'm not used to having anyone around."

Riley nodded. *That's obvious.*

After Doc Hugo parked his truck, a tall man ran from the barn toward them.

Doc Hugo's chuckle was hollow. "Doesn't look like this will take long. I'll come get you if I need you."

Doc grabbed his medical bag from the back seat; the man motioned for Doc to hurry, and the two of them ran to the barn.

Riley pulled out her shoulder length gloves and vet apron from her work backpack. While she had put on the apron and tied it around her waist, the man raced to the house. As Riley neared the barn, the cow bellowed.

When she went inside, Doc Hugo was standing in the middle of the barn with his arms crossed. "We're going to see how quickly Wesley can get here. I don't see a calf at all."

"I'll bet it's breech." Riley hurried to the cow then whispered, "We need to help your baby." Riley felt the abdomen. "Doc, you'll need to push back the calf so you can straighten the legs."

"We're waiting for Wesley," Doc Hugo said.

Riley put on her shoulder-length glove. "Doc, I'd do it myself, but my arms are too short.".

"It will kill her; I won't do it." Doc Hugo shouted as he stormed out.

Riley stroked the cow's back. "I'm sorry, but I'm going to have to see how far away the baby is."

Riley reached inside the birth canal up to her shoulder. "I think I found its rump with the tips of my fingers, but I can't push the calf back."

Tears ran down Riley's face. "This is maddening."

The farmer rushed into the barn. "Doc went to his truck; I guess he needed to get something. Are you okay, Riley?"

Riley brushed away the tears mixed with sweat from her face. "The calf is breech. I can feel the calf moving, but my arms aren't long enough to push it back so its legs can straighten."

"Shoot, is that all we need to do? I've done that a hundred times. I don't know why I thought it was more complicated than that."

The man removed an apron from a hook and pulled out a pair of long exam gloves from the pocket. "Here we go, girl; we'll have that baby in no time." He patted the cow's side then stepped into position behind the animal.

His face reddened from the strain as he pushed. "Stubborn little cuss doesn't want to move," he grumbled.

Riley stood next to the cow's side; she stooped and lifted the cow's heavy belly to help keep the calf from slipping back as the farmer pushed and lifted its rump so the calf's legs could straighten.

"There's one leg," the farmer grunted.

Riley knelt under the cow and pushed up to help lift the calf.

The farmer grunted. "A little more, Riley."

Riley squatted and pushed the cow's belly upward with her shoulders.

"Okay, hold it; don't let it drop."

Riley's legs quivered from the strain.

"Got the second leg, Riley; hang in there," the farmer said.

Riley groaned. "I can feel it moving lower into the birth canal."

"Boy or girl?" the farmer asked. "I think it's a girl who wanted to make a grand entrance."

Doc Hugo rushed into the barn and froze at the doorway.

Riley grunted from the strain of keeping the calf from slipping back. "I think it's a boy who didn't see any reason to change."

She collapsed when the weight was suddenly gone; Doc sprang to help her up.

The farmer grinned. "We got us a baby, Riley, and it's a boy; you called it."

After Riley stood and straightened her back, she shook off Doc's hand from her elbow.

Doc asked, "What can I do, Riley?"

Riley forced herself to remain quiet as she helped the cow turn in the narrow stall so she could take care of her baby.

After Riley and the farmer backed away to give the new mama space, Riley exhaled. "Is Doc Wesley coming?"

"We don't need him now," the farmer said. "Mama will take it from here. Thanks for lighting a fire under me, Riley; you missed all the action, Doc."

"I guess I did; I didn't reach Wesley." Doc glanced around the barn. "Is there anything else you need for us to do?"

"That's it." The farmer put out his hand to shake with Doc then quickly withdrew it when Doc gaped at the farmer's glove.

The farmer chuckled. "Guess you and I need to clean up a bit, Riley."

Riley smiled. "Yes, sir."

After she washed at the utility sink, Riley removed her vet apron and folded it. "You ready, Doc?"

When they were on the highway that led to town, Doc said, "I don't think I'll ever be suited for farm visits. I'm more comfortable in the more orderly, clean environment and routine of the clinic."

As they neared the town limits, Riley asked, "What about the appointment for the sick horse?"

"Send Maureen a text to cancel the rest of the farm visit appointments."

"It's still early; shouldn't we at least..."

"Are you going to text Maureen like I asked?"

"I really think..." Riley's eyes widened as Doc Hugo pulled onto the shoulder and pulled out his phone.

After he sent the text, he pulled back onto the road. His phone buzzed with a text, but he ignored it.

"Aren't you going to ask Doc Wesley if he wants to take over the farm visits?" Riley asked.

Doc Hugo growled, "You really overstep your bounds, don't you?"

Riley furrowed her brow. "No, I don't really think I do, but I agree some people prefer the more predictable work in a clinic, and others thrive on the challenges of farm visits."

When Doc Hugo parked at the clinic, he said, "You don't have to be here early tomorrow."

"I'll ask Maureen to call me for farm visits."

Doc Hugo snorted as he opened his truck door. "You didn't seem like the quitter type."

Riley shrugged as she gathered her backpacks. "But here we are."

The two of them went into the clinic; Doc went straight to his office and slammed the door.

When Riley reached the receptionist's desk, Toby grinned, and his tail went into high gear. Riley knelt next to him and stroked his back.

Maureen raised her eyebrows. "I just got a strange text from Doc; he's in his office, right? That's weird. First, he canceled all the appointments, and now he wants me to reschedule the appointments, but I'm a little worried about the sick horse; I'll talk to him about it before I reschedule. We started off the morning with a trauma that was followed by an appointment that was more complicated than we expected. Doc Wesley and Lisa are almost caught up and are close to back on schedule with appointments, but they worked through lunch. What a day."

Maureen pushed back from the desk then stopped. "This was a shorter day than usual for Doc. Is he feeling okay? Was it a rough day?"

"The delivery was a little dicey, but the cow and her calf are fine." Riley rose. "Thanks for everything; I know Toby enjoyed his day. Call me for any farm visits. Ready to go, Toby?"

"We had three already scheduled tomorrow, but with the two from today that I rescheduled, it will be a busy day," Maureen said. "The first one is at nine. If you're here at eight, I'll give you the folders for review."

Riley bit her lip. "Sounds good; let me know if there's any change in the schedule."

Maureen smiled. "What are you going to do with all your extra time today?"

Riley returned her smile. "We still have boxes to unpack, so I won't be bored at all."

"Lucky you." Maureen grinned.

Lisa came out of an exam room with a patient and a client. She handed the folder to Maureen. "Follow up in two weeks."

Lisa peered at Riley. "You're back early; take a break with me?"

"Well, I was..."

Lisa glared.

Riley continued, "Just about to take a break."

When they went into the breakroom, Lisa closed the door. "Doctor Hugo is a jerk." She grinned. "Want to argue with me?"

Riley giggled. "Sure, but we'll have to pick a different topic besides Doctor Hugo Adams."

Lisa gazed at Riley. "Don't judge the office by him; Doc Wesley is great."

Riley sighed. "We'll see what works out, but I can't work with Doctor Adams."

"See how smart you are? It took me two full days before I realized it was him, not me. I'll talk to Doc Wesley in the morning. My husband needs the one report he forgot to take with him; unfortunately, I have the data on a flash drive that I have here, but the report is on my laptop at home. I'll have to leave now, so I can email it to him. Don't give up on us."

Riley exhaled.

When she reached Maureen's office, Maureen bit her lip. "Whatever Lisa said goes double for me. I'm going to have a little chat with Hugo Adams." While she rolled toward Doc Hugo's office, Riley and Toby left.

After they were in her car, Riley sent Ben a text. "Short day. Quick stop at the store then heading home."

On their way to the grocery store, Riley asked, "Are you glad you stayed with Maureen?"

Toby growled then whined.

"It was good you were there then; the man sounds sketchy. I would have thought anyone asking for directions to a farm would have gone to the gas station too. Was the dog park nice?"

Toby yipped.

"I'm happy to hear that; my day was not pleasant at all. Doc Hugo isn't used to working with a vet tech. He's out of his element when it comes to farm visits, and to top it off, he's a jerk. Remember how I burned myself out with taking classes? Evidently, I have a low burn out tolerance level now because I'm completely done with that irritating veterinarian after half a day."

After Riley parked at the grocery store, she asked, "Are you going to stay in the car?"

Toby yipped.

"I don't blame you; it gets downright chilly, especially when the wind blasts around a corner."

Riley pulled out her wallet and shopping list from her backpack and locked her car doors.

She stopped at the produce section and picked up a bag of potatoes and a bag of onions then headed toward the second aisle. While Riley examined the cans of green chile in her effort to find her favorite brand, Rachel joined her in the aisle.

"What's your favorite brand?" Rachel asked.

Riley grinned as she pulled four cans off the shelf. "This one; I have a pork roast in the slow cooker; I'm making my version of green chile stew for supper."

"Do you add a dollop of sour cream and fresh cilantro?"

"Hadn't thought of that, but it sounds good; I'll pick up both of them. Did the mules get the equipment back to the barn okay?"

"They're still out. My husband found a third piece of equipment that isn't working. I think it's sabotage, but my husband said I'm paranoid."

"Why sabotage?"

"My husband takes pride in how faithful he and his crew are with inspection and regular maintenance of the equipment; three major pieces of equipment completely failing in one day? My sabotage-o-meter went off the charts."

Rachel peered at the contents in Riley's grocery cart. "Are you planning tortillas with your green chile stew? That's the best brand." Rachel pointed to the tortillas across the aisle on the bottom shelf.

"Hadn't thought of it, but what a great idea."

Rachel beamed. "Glad I could help. I'll call Maureen after I get home to schedule that follow up for the mules; I'll see you later this week."

Riley nodded; as Riley picked up a package of tortillas, Rachel rolled her cart to the next aisle.

Riley's phone buzzed a text from Ben. "See you around six."

She replied, "We're on our way home."

Riley rolled her eyes at Ben's text. "Call me when you can."

After Riley picked up fresh cilantro and sour cream, she diverted to the freezer section; after a few moments of indecision, Riley selected a pint of rocky road ice cream then hurried to the checkout line.

The cold air took away her breath when she stepped outside. She rushed to her car, hurriedly popped open the trunk, and shivered as she slid into the driver's seat.

"Ben wants me to call him. It's getting colder; I didn't see a thermos, but there's a hardware store right after the gas station. Surely they'll have one. I'm putting on my coat before I get out of the car next time."

Riley called Ben.

"Why are you going home so early? Do you feel okay?"

"Doc Ned's friend retired, so I was working with a different vet who has taken over the practice. Doctor Hugo Adams and I didn't get along. He's incompetent and has never worked with a vet tech. I'm not sure if I was fired, or I quit."

"Did he do or say anything out of line?" Ben growled.

Riley exhaled. "No; his superior attitude got on my nerves, but worse was he abandoned a cow and her unborn calf that was in distress during labor. I wasn't strong enough to turn the calf. If the farmer hadn't been experienced with turning a breech calf, the cow and her baby would have died. Doctor Adams canceled the rest of the day's farm visits, and we returned to the office. When I told Maureen to call me for farm visits, he called me a quitter. I don't even know how he came up with that."

Ben scowled. "I can't believe any vet would abandon a cow."

"He tried to play down her condition, but I'm positive he was over his head."

"I'm sure you'll find another position with a practice that appreciates an outstanding vet tech, but you don't have to work unless you want to, and you definitely don't have to work where you're unhappy."

Riley bit her lip as her eyes welled up. "Thank you, honey; I appreciate you."

"We'll talk more later. I loved you first."

Riley heard Ben's smile in his voice; she smiled. "I love you more."

When Riley went inside the hardware store, her eyes widened at the narrow aisles that were packed with hardware items and camping supplies. "Can I help you find something?" The gray-haired man who was behind the counter asked; his gold front tooth gleamed as he smiled.

"I need a small wide-mouth thermos."

"For soup and chili? I've got just the thing; follow me."

The man scurried to the middle aisle then continued to the back of the store; Riley half-ran to keep up with him.

He pointed to the thermoses and beamed. "Here you are: small, medium, and large. Take your time; holler if you have any questions."

Riley furrowed her brow. *I would have enjoyed hot soup today, but I won't be going on a farm visit any time soon.* Riley shrugged and picked up one small and one medium thermos. *Maybe Toby and I will go hiking when it isn't too cold.*

The man's eyes twinkled when Riley put the two thermoses on the counter. "Couldn't decide, or is this a his and hers?"

"His and hers." Riley smiled.

The man nodded. "Excellent choice."

After Riley paid for her purchase, she held her breath as she rushed to her car with her head down. When she closed the door, she exhaled. "It's getting colder, Toby, but I got exactly what I wanted."

As soon as they went inside the house, Riley turned on the gas fireplace then carried the groceries into the kitchen. The aroma of the pork roast filled the air.

When Toby moaned, Riley giggled as she pulled out potatoes and prepared to peel them. "I feel the same way."

After she put the pot of potatoes on the stove to boil, she sat at the kitchen table and pulled off her boots; Toby laid down on the rug near the fireplace.

Before she opened her laptop, her phone rang; Riley glanced at her phone and smiled. It was Claire, her closest friend, confidante, and the office manager at Doc Julie Rae's clinic.

"I just realized I should have texted, not called; are you busy?" Claire asked.

"No, Toby and I are home; are you at work? What's going on?"

"I'm sorry to say I'm sitting at my desk; everybody's cranky today. I'd like to go on record that it is actually not my fault that it's Monday."

"You just described my day. I thought I was too burned out for classes, but I might be wrong. I'd rather be taking classes than dealing with a temperamental narcissist with a streak of misogyny."

"Ouch. We don't like the vet. You have options. We will always welcome you here; you're only two hours away, and you can commute or stay at our house during the week. If you're serious about classes, aren't there a couple of online classes you could take, or would you rather be more social and attend classes in person?"

Riley sighed as she propped up her feet. "I think I just want to be irritable for now. Do me a favor: ask Doc Julie Rae if she knows Doctor Hugo Adams."

"I'll do that; tell me about your house."

"It's old and small, but it's fine for the three of us. It has a gas fireplace in the living room, which is my favorite, and an electric stove, which in not my favorite. There is an ancient shed in the side yard that is almost half the size of the house. The shed has a beautiful wood floor; Ben thinks it might have been a workshop because it has a wood stove in one corner. He checked out the chimney and the stove and said it's operational; he calls the shed his man cave. We also have a small shed; Ben put his chain saw and our tools in it."

"I can't tell Thad about Ben's man cave; he'd be jealous."

"He should probably look at the shed before he gets too jealous. I know you called for a reason. Is everything okay there?"

"Call Pia later today, but don't tell her I told you to. That's why I called you. I can't talk much longer, or I'll fall into a trap that might sound like gossip. Thad and I have an agreement that I would not say anything to you if he would stop poking at Pia."

"Okay, I'll call Pia. When should I call her? Will I be mad at you after I talk to her?"

"Text her when you're on your pretend break and tell her to call you. You won't be mad at me, but if you are, I'll have to gossip about you, but we'll have to talk about it first, so we can come up with something juicy. That's it; my lips are zipped. Call me later, so we can gossip about his royal highness, the doc we don't like. I'll talk to Doc Julie Rae about Doctor Hugo Adams and get back to you when I can. I'm going to hang up on you now because I'd like to be the dramatic one for once."

Riley giggled when Claire disconnected; Toby raised his eyebrows. "Claire is a good friend; I feel much better even though it sounds like her Monday is a close match to mine."

Riley filled the tea kettle with water, then put it on the stove. "After my tea steeps, I'll text Pia."

CHAPTER THREE

When Riley sat on the sofa with her cup of tea in one hand and her phone in the other, Toby curled up on the floor at her feet.

Riley sent a text to Pia. "I'm on a break; why don't you call when you're free?"

It wasn't long before her phone rang. "I'm hiding in the restroom. Zach and the new guy can fill in for me; they need to get used to extra work."

"New guy? Is he any good? What's his name?"

"His name is Josef with an f, not a ph." Pia lowered her voice. "I don't want anyone to hear this: he's actually almost as good as Zach."

"Wow, that's great. Do you like him?"

"No, but I don't like anybody right now except our sweet black lab, Jordy, and maybe that obnoxious preteen of mine, Jackson, or is obnoxious and preteen redundant? How's your new job?"

"A preteen, so far."

Pia laughed. "You caught me off guard; tell me about your obnoxious day."

"The veterinarian that Doc Ned knew isn't here; he retired and went on a cruise. The vet that I worked with today has absolutely zero experience with farm visits, and it showed, although he tried to bluff his way through his lack of experience. He also has never partnered with a vet tech, so he doesn't have any use at all for me."

"What are you going to do?" Pia asked.

"I'm not sure if I was fired or I quit, but Doctor Adams decided we would return to the office early this afternoon and asked the receptionist by text from his office to reschedule all the farm visits. Before I left the clinic and came home, I told her to call me for farm visits, but I don't think there will be any."

"You're taking your break at home? That's brilliant. Wait, he texted the receptionist from his office? What a preteen."

"Exactly." Riley sipped her tea. "It's nice to know you understand."

"I have news that will brighten your day; nobody knows except Tom, and he realizes I'm not quite ready to tell anyone other than you." Pia lowered her voice to a whisper so soft that Riley had to strain to hear her. "We're going to have a baby."

Riley whispered, "I'm squealing inside, so I won't hurt your eardrum; how exciting. Can I ask questions?"

"Sure, but I won't have the answers; I have a doctor's appointment next week. Tom said I should tell the office because I'm being so hormonal, but he apologized for his bad timing."

"Bad timing?"

"Having the nerve to say anything other than I was wonderful within my hearing range."

Riley rolled her eyes. "Why are you being so hard on him?"

Pia snorted. "I'm sorry you aren't here, so you could see me flip my hair while I tell you my rage hormones are on full throttle. I don't see much of Zach or Josef at work these days, but Doc Thad irritates me no end."

"Sounds about right. Zach would teach Josef to lie low, and Doc Thad has always had a knack of getting on your nerves."

"I should get back to work; thanks for listening. I'll let you know when the news is official."

After Pia hung up, Riley said, "Pia and Tom are going to have a baby, Toby. Don't you know Jordy and Jackson will be excited?"

Toby whimpered.

"No, put that idea out of your head; we won't have a baby for at least two years."

Toby closed his eyes while Riley sent a text to Claire. "Talked to Pia."

Riley answered her ringing phone.

"Did she tell you? None of us are supposed to know," Claire said.

"How did you find out then?" Riley asked.

"Pia has always been a little high strung, but she's been off the charts for about a month. Everybody has noticed, and even some of our clients have asked me when she's due. I can't wait until she tells us, so I can give her unsolicited advice."

Riley chuckled. "Are you sure you want to do that? You know it will set her off."

Claire sighed. "You're right; I'll have to be subtle."

After she hung up, Riley drained the partially cooked potatoes and added them to the slow cooker.

She scanned the living room. "This small house doesn't feel like home yet. I'll unpack a few boxes; maybe I'll find some things that will transform the living room into something less generic and more like us. I'm not crazy about the electric stove, but at least we have the gas fireplace and creaky wood floors, which helps a little."

After she opened the first box, she sighed. "Kitchen stuff; might as well empty the box."

Toby followed her as she carried the heavy box to the kitchen then set it with a thud on the table. Riley opened all the cabinet doors so she could put the items in their new place with similar items. Before she reached the bottom of the box, she frowned. "It's getting dark; I need to turn on the overhead light."

Riley glanced out the window at the black sky in the west. "I didn't know we had a storm coming our way. We probably put the box with the kerosene lanterns on the carport, but I don't know where the candles are."

When Riley went out to the carport, an unexpected gust of wind blew a swirl of leaves into the kitchen. "I think this is the box, Toby; I'll check it inside."

Riley added the box from the carport to the kitchen table then leaned against the door to close it.

Her phone buzzed a text from Ben. "Dangerous storm headed your way. Where are you?"

"Home."

"Hall closet is the best place to take shelter if the storm gets worse."

"We'll be fine. Be safe."

Riley exhaled in relief when she opened the box and saw the jug of kerosene and the two lanterns. She carried the box to the front porch where she was sheltered from the wind coming from the west; after she filled the lanterns and spilled only a little onto the grass, she carried them into the house and put them on the kitchen counter then brought in the box and the jug of kerosene.

She bit her lip. "I need a butane lighter; I don't remember unpacking them."

Riley opened the kitchen drawer that was closest to the back door. "Ah ha. Ben did."

She put a butane lighter next to the lanterns and peered outside. "It's getting darker." Riley shrugged. "I might as well continue unpacking; it's more productive than staring at the dark sky to see if it's getting darker."

As she worked her way to the bottom of her first box of assorted kitchen utensils, baking pans, and tea towels, Riley said, "This must have been one of our last packed boxes from the variety of unrelated items I'm finding."

The last item she pulled from the box was their new weather alert from Ben's mom. Riley rolled her eyes. "Toby, if I'd remembered we had this, I never would have thought to look for it in a kitchen box. I would have expected it to be with the emergency lanterns or candles wherever they are."

Riley opened the box and smiled. "Of course, Mom would have made sure batteries were included."

After she inserted the batteries, Riley turned it on and listened to the weather then put it on alert. She pulled up a map of the region on her phone and grabbed a spiral notebook from her computer bag and did a quick sketch of their county and the surrounding counties then added the counties west of them.

"I don't really know the area, Toby; my rough map will give me a better idea of where we are in relation to any alerts."

Toby yipped.

Riley smiled. "Thank you; I do have a good idea once in a while, don't I?"

She brought another box from the bedroom to the kitchen. While she unpacked the box, a strong wind rattled the windows and a heavy downpour slammed the side of the house.

"This is awful." Riley shuddered.

Toby whined.

"It is noisy, isn't it?" Riley sat on the floor and stroked his back while the storm raged. "It's a terrible storm, but tornados don't happen in cold weather, do they?"

Toby put his paw on her knee and whimpered.

"I wish Ben was here too." Riley was startled by the shrill sound of the weather alert signal.

While the announcer listed the counties under a tornado warning, Riley jumped up, checked the drawer next to the back door, and pulled out a heavy flashlight as the lights flickered then went out.

"We're under a tornado warning; maybe it's just a little tornado."

Riley turned on the flashlight then returned to Toby and sat next to him on the floor. "I should have thought of a flashlight earlier, Toby; I must be tired because I'm not thinking straight. The low pressure of the storm must be slowing me down, and honestly, I'm terrified of the two of us being in a tornado alone. I wish Ben was here, but I don't want him here because that means he would have to drive through this terrible storm."

Riley dropped the flashlight and wailed as she hugged Toby; her tears soaked her shirt as she sobbed.

Toby barked; Riley continued to sob.

When Toby's bark became more insistent, Riley shook off her panic. "What? Ben?"

Riley rushed to the front door. When she opened it, the driving wind all but blinded her. Toby pushed past her as she staggered outside against the wind. She held onto the porch support column while the wind buffeted Toby as he made his way to the driveway and barked.

"Ben?" Riley screamed.

Ben appeared next to Toby and grabbed his collar. Small hailstones pelted them as they rushed toward the house.

When they reached the porch, Ben wrapped his arm around Riley; she let go of the column and grabbed onto his belt with her arm around his waist. Ben kept a tight grip on Toby's collar, and the three of them struggled into the house. Ben kicked the door closed behind them.

"We're about to get hit hard. The closet," he shouted over the roaring storm as he snatched up her flashlight on the way.

After Ben closed the closet door, they sat on the floor. Riley was squeezed in between Ben and Toby as the weather radio sounded its shrill warning until it was drowned out by the roar of a freight train as it barreled toward their house.

Ben put his arm around Riley; his mouth tickled her ear. "I'm here, babe; we'll be okay."

Riley exhaled at the calmness in Ben's voice. Tears slipped down her cheeks as she nodded and wrapped an arm around Toby. *We're together.*

When the house shuddered on its foundation and the walls heaved like living beings taking giant breaths, Ben pushed Riley onto her side to lie on the floor next to Toby then covered the two of them with his body.

Riley covered her ears and cringed at the deafening sound of debris that slammed into the side of the house. Ben tightened his grip on her, and she froze in terror as the house groaned and an earsplitting sound of ripping metal was followed by an explosive shock wave. Riley gritted her teeth to keep from screaming when the sudden intensity of the storm's roar became so overwhelming she was certain her eardrums were going to rupture.

After a few minutes that seemed like hours, the terrifying, tumultuous storm moved away and left behind the sound of a quiet rain shower.

Ben knelt next to Riley and helped her sit up. "If that was the roof, it's gone, but we're okay, babe."

Ben turned on the flashlight. "Stay here; I'm going to see what's left."

Toby rose when Ben did and stood next to him; Riley struggled to her feet. "Don't go without us; we want to see too."

Ben frowned.

Riley' mouth quivered. "I have to be a little clingy for a bit."

Ben traced her lips with his fingertip then kissed her. "We're safe, and we're all together. Here's your flashlight; I have the one I grabbed from my glove box."

"I'm sticking with you."

Ben exhaled. "Okay, but stay close; you too, Toby, because we don't know how stable the house is."

When Ben opened the door, he swept his flashlight toward the living area.

Riley gasped. "The living room looks like a war zone."

Ben stepped out of the closet and swung the light around the room. "Sure does, but the living room walls look intact; all the debris must have come through the windows. The ceiling looks okay, but I can't tell how stable anything is."

"Will we have to climb over the rubble to get to the front door?" Riley asked.

"I'll check the kitchen; maybe we can go out the back door or the side door to the carport."

"The hall looks clear; I'll check the bedrooms," Riley said.

"I'll go with you before I check the kitchen," Ben said.

When they came to the bathroom, Ben said, "The bathroom is fine."

Riley slipped past him to examine their bedroom. She exhaled. "Our bedroom looks like the living room."

Before Ben joined Riley at their bedroom door, he glanced into the second bedroom that was next to the bathroom. "The guest bedroom is okay."

"Do you suppose we could get to the closet?" Riley asked.

Ben stepped into the bedroom as far as he could then exhaled. "Forget it; the closet door is smashed open, but it's too tight for me to get in there."

Riley crouched down, slipped past him, and into the closet. "It's not too tight for me."

Toby whined.

"I'm okay, Toby; you stay with Ben."

"I can stand up just fine." Riley swept the closet with her flashlight. "There's nothing wrong with the closet. All our clothes are dry. I'd forgotten we had our sleeping bags in here. I'll pass them out to you."

Ben mumbled, "That's not what I had in mind."

Riley rolled her eyes. "Here are the sleeping bags. I'll going to fill your duffel bag with as much as I can."

Riley stuffed Ben's uniforms into the duffel bag then added their shirts and jeans. Riley shoved the duffel bag through the opening. "Why don't we keep underwear and socks in the closet?"

Ben pulled out the bag from the opening. "I don't know; maybe we didn't expect a tornado to crash into our bedroom?"

A branch in the bedroom that had been precariously balanced slid to the floor with a crash. Riley jumped.

Ben's voice was strained with urgency. "Come out now, babe. This debris isn't stable, and I'm afraid you'll get trapped."

Riley pushed an oversized tote bag from the closet before she crawled out as quickly as she could. When she was in the hallway, she pulled out two sweatshirts from the tote. "I stuffed the tote with sweatshirts and jackets for both of us."

While she pulled the first one over her head, then zipped up the second one, Ben picked up the duffel bag and one of the sleeping bags.

"Bring the tote bag and the sleeping bag, and we'll leave them in the guest bedroom; maybe we can hug the living room wall to check the kitchen," Ben said. "I'll go first; just because you can squeeze into the kitchen doesn't mean I can."

Toby yipped.

"I wasn't going to argue," Riley said.

"We thought you were." Ben slid toward the kitchen with his back against the wall.

After Riley and Toby joined him, Ben whistled under his breath in relief. "The debris didn't come into the house as far as I feared."

"I'll feed Toby then dish up green chile stew for our supper."

"I'll be right back." Ben hurried out the back door before Riley could quibble.

"He got me there, didn't he?" Riley measured Toby's food then poured it into his bowl. While he ate, she pulled out a bottle of water from a lower cabinet and filled his water bowl.

Riley wiped dust off the kitchen table and set out placemats, cloth napkins, and spoons. While she ladled stew into bowls, Ben came inside.

"I was soaked earlier, but now I'm soaked and cold; I need to change," Ben said.

Riley smiled as she pointed to the tote bag. "Help yourself. No underwear or socks, though. We need to update our emergency supplies."

While Ben stripped and changed into dry clothes, Riley pulled out the tortillas, sour cream, and two bottles of water from the refrigerator.

"The table looks nice, babe." Ben hugged her.

She returned his hug. "We're celebrating surviving the storm. I didn't think..." Riley bit her lip.

"We have a roof over our heads." Ben joined Riley at the table.

While they ate, Riley said, "I didn't expect a tornado that was so strong."

"I guess the conditions were just right, or just wrong, depending on your point of view."

"I vote just wrong. What was that loud ripping noise?" Riley asked.

"That was the carport. It's completely gone. Your car has quite a few dings from the hail and a crack in the windshield on the passenger's side."

"What about your truck?"

Ben snorted. "My truck is halfway down the driveway; a tree had fallen across the driveway and blocked it, so I left my truck and ran to the house."

Riley gaped at Ben. "That must have been terrifying."

Ben shrugged. "I didn't have time to think about anything other than making sure you and Toby were safe."

Ben pulled out his phone and frowned. "The low temperature tonight will be thirty-eight degrees. That's colder than last night. I'm glad we have a bed and the sleeping bags."

He served himself more stew. "This is the best green chile stew I've ever had. If we set the pot outside overnight, it will be as cold as if it were inside a refrigerator."

Ben dipped the last of his tortilla into the stew. "The shed wasn't touched. I could start a fire in the woodstove in the shed in the morning. We can heat our leftover stew for a hot breakfast."

"I came across some packets of instant coffee when I was unpacking yesterday. I stuck them into the cupboard with the coffee."

"Coffee with breakfast sounds like a regular feast."

After they finished eating, Riley furrowed her brow. "I should text Mom and tell her we're okay; I'll ask her to text Claire."

"Good idea. I'll text my boss, Graham."

Riley picked up her phone and snorted. "Honey, Hugo Adams told me he knew Doc Julie Rae, and I mentioned that to Pia. I have a text from Pia that says, 'Doc says HA is a loser. Stay away from him.'"

"Too bad you didn't know that when he called you. You could have saved yourself a day of aggravation."

Riley nodded as she sent a text to Ben's mom. "True, but it definitely confirms I'm not working with him anymore; not that there was any doubt."

Riley received a reply from Melissa and shook her head. "Ben, your mom dropped into protective mode;

she's ready to come here and help me pack, so we can move back to their house. I always thought you got that from your dad."

While Riley sent another text to Melissa to assure her they were fine, Ben grinned his crooked grin. "I got the double dose. What did you tell her?"

"I told her you can't leave your job because you love it."

Ben furrowed his brow. "That's true, but why does it sound like I'm..."

Riley interrupted him when she kissed his open mouth; he wrapped his arms around her and returned her kiss.

After he released her, Riley sighed. "I needed that."

"So did I." Ben kissed her forehead. "I'll set the stew outside near the back door before I go to the shed to make sure we have dry kindling and wood for a fire in the morning."

Riley put on her warm coat that she had left in the kitchen. "We'll go with you."

When they went past the side of the house where the carport had been, Riley gaped at the concrete pad. "It's completely gone."

She stared at the side of the house as Ben shined his flashlight where the carport had been attached.

"It looks like the tornado reached down with its giant hand and snatched it away," Riley said.

When they reached the shed, Ben opened the door and shined his flashlight inside. "I was right; I thought there was kindling and a stack of wood in here. There's a lean-to next to the equipment shed with enough wood for the season."

Riley and Toby followed Ben into the shed. After Riley closed the door, she shined her light at the walls with unfinished planks that still had bark on some of them. She raised the light to examine the rough lumber used for the rafters, then swept it downward to the uneven wood floor and the cast iron wood-burning stove that sat on a protective base of bricks.

She furrowed her brow. "Honey, what do you think about..."

Ben interrupted her. "It's going to be colder tonight than it's been since last winter, and the windows are completely gone in the living room. The shed has a woodstove; if we slept here, we'd be warm."

Riley rolled her eyes as she prompted Ben. "And..."

"If I can, I'll bring the mattress from the guest bedroom here, so we'll be comfortable." He smiled at Riley and pulled her close. "You're amazing; you've been thinking this all along, haven't you?"

"Yes," Riley mumbled into his chest then reared back her head to take a breath.

"Am I smothering you?" Ben gave Riley a quick squeeze.

Riley gazed at Ben. "All the time, honey; don't ever stop."

"I'll get the fire started then go back for the mattress."

Toby yipped, and Riley growled, "I'm perfectly capable of starting a fire; have you forgotten the fireplace in the cabin?"

Ben cleared his throat. "I meant to say, you start the fire; I'll get the mattress."

When Toby grinned, Riley snickered.

After Ben left, Riley stacked a few pieces of kindling inside the stove. Her hands shook from the cold as she clicked the butane lighter she'd pulled out of the kitchen drawer. When the kindling caught, Riley exhaled.

When Riley heard a loud crash from the house, she and Toby raced to the shed door; Riley leaned against the door frame and exhaled in relief when she saw Ben with the mattress balanced on top of his head and carrying two sleeping bags.

"What was that loud noise?" she asked as he dropped the sleeping bags then set down the mattress on the wood floor.

"It was something at the house, but I don't know what. The debris is more unstable than I'd like." Ben's breathing was labored. "After I pulled out the mattress, I dragged the duffel bag and carried the tote to the kitchen. I stopped at the bathroom and stuffed the tote as full as I could."

"There's one more thing I'd like from the house." Riley rose. "There's ice cream in the freezer; It might not melt before tomorrow, but why take chances?"

She darted out the door with Toby on her heels. They raced to the back door and into the kitchen.

Riley picked up the tote Ben had brought from the bedroom and tossed in two bowls, two spoons, and the ice cream; they ran toward the shed where Ben met them halfway. Riley gasped for breath when she stopped and leaned against Ben.

Ben took the tote from Riley and put his arm around her. "Babe, you aren't a runner."

Riley took more deep breaths and exhaled until her breathing finally slowed. "I know, but I couldn't let the house collapse on the ice cream, honey."

"When we're back inside, you can sit next to the fire, and I'll fix you a bowl of ice cream."

As they strolled together to the shed, Riley said, "It was almost worth running because I'm not as cold."

"Almost." Ben smiled.

As they ate ice cream, Ben said, "My plan for tomorrow is to check my truck while the stew simmers. I put my chain saw in the equipment shed; I think I have enough gas to cut the tree into small enough pieces to move by hand."

"We'll help," Riley said. "I can drag branches out of the way."

"That's great; I want the driveway to be cleared for you before I leave, so you won't be stuck."

"Do you expect to go to work tomorrow?"

Ben exhaled. "I suspect tomorrow will be a long day, but we also have to find another place to live. Graham said he had a possibility, but I don't know where it is."

Riley finished her ice cream and smacked her lips. "I really enjoy ice cream after a spicy meal. The good news is you don't have to feel like we're limited to any specific location in your region because of me."

Riley poured a little water into a bowl and swirled it around then poured the water into the other bowl. After she swished their spoons in the water, she carried the bowl to the door and dumped the water outside.

Riley grinned as she set them on their makeshift table. "Our dishes are rinsed and ready for our breakfast. I'm surprised at how well the little wood stove warms the shed." Riley removed her coat and yawned.

Ben and Toby yawned.

Ben said, "We're all tired; I'll bank the fire."

CHAPTER FOUR

Riley woke to the aroma of green chile stew. When she opened her eyes, she blinked at Ben, who was almost nose to nose with her. He smiled and kissed her then rose from her side to stir the stew.

"How long have you been awake?" Riley stretched.

"Not long at all the second time; Toby nudged me earlier, so we went outside and picked up the box with the stew and the case of water from the pantry. After we came back, I put the stew and a pot of water on the woodstove, climbed back into my sleeping bag, and put my arm around you."

Riley nodded. "I think I remember that."

"When you snuggled against me, I relaxed and must have dozed off. I woke up just a few minutes before you did."

Riley groaned as she rose to her feet. "I'm really stiff. I'm glad we had the mattress; can you imagine how achy we'd be if we'd slept on the wood floor? What's our schedule?"

Ben put on his jacket. "While the stew simmers, I'd like to check my truck."

Riley grabbed her coat and her flashlight. "I thought you wanted to wait until daylight."

Ben nodded. "I did, but I'd like to get a good look, so I'll know what I'm up against."

As they walked up the driveway, Ben dragged the large limbs to the ditch; Riley picked up the smaller branches and pulled them to the side of the road.

When they reached the tree, Ben said, "It looked a lot bigger in the storm."

Ben stepped over the tree to check his truck; Toby followed him.

Riley examined the trunk and snorted. *I can't step over that.*

Ben walked around his truck. "All I see are a few hail dings on the hood and the top of the cab."

He climbed in, started the engine, and lowered his window. "I'll see how far I can get going back to the road."

Toby whined when Riley shivered.

"You're right, Toby; I'll be warmer if I'm moving around." She climbed over the tree and picked up branches and dragged them to the side as she walked toward the road until she heard Ben's truck returning.

"Time to head back, but I'm not running."

Toby trotted ahead and jumped over the tree.

While she was climbing over the tree, Ben parked.

On their way back to the shed, he said, "The driveway was relatively clear. There are a few branches close to the road that we might have to move for your car."

Riley shivered. "The sky is getting lighter, and the temperature is dropping; it will be daylight soon."

Ben put his arm around Riley. "Are you freezing?"

Her teeth chattered. "Yes."

When they went into the shed, Riley sighed in relief. "I was cold; it's toasty in here."

She dished up the stew into their bowls while Ben made coffee in their travel mugs he had pulled out of his truck.

While they ate, Riley's phone buzzed a text. Riley's eyes widened. "It's Maureen from the vet office."

Riley read the text aloud. "Hope you're okay after that awful storm. Call when you can."

"Why would she want you to call her? You won't work with Doctor Adams." Ben finished his stew. "More coffee?"

"No, let's tackle that tree."

While Ben used the chainsaw to cut the tree into manageable-sized sections, Riley rolled each log to the side of the road. When Ben finished his last cut, he heaved the log into the ditch.

"Next up, the kitchen," Ben said.

"What about the kitchen?" Riley hurried to keep up with Ben's stride by taking two steps to his one.

"I want to bring the duffel bag and whatever else I can carry from the kitchen pantry and cabinets here. What about the unpacked boxes in the kitchen? Do you know what's in them?"

"I don't have any idea; they're all marked miscellaneous. I gave in to the time pressure and dropped all pretense of organization."

"I love your practical side. Before I leave, I'd like for you to start your car; I don't want you to be stranded. What are your plans?"

"After you leave, I'll call Maureen before Toby and I go into town for some serious shopping: underwear, socks, water, and groceries. I can charge my phone on the way. I need to make a list; can you think of anything?"

"I think you've covered it, except I want a generator, a tractor, and maybe a UTV, but that's for later." Ben smiled. "Let's check your car."

Riley hopped into the driver's seat, and the engine started without hesitation.

"Now, the kitchen," Riley said.

They emptied cabinets and drawers and packed them into their original moving boxes. After they carried the kitchen table and two chairs to the shed, they followed up with trips from the house to the shed with boxes.

Riley cocked her head at the table, chairs, and boxes that had filled the shed. "The shed looked a lot larger last night."

Ben chuckled. "I guess we're not living in the shed permanently, after all."

"We'll just put boxes in my trunk and on the back seat; I'm not giving up my wood-burning stove." Riley put her hands on her hips and pouted then giggled at Ben's wide eyes.

Ben exhaled. "You had me going for a minute there. If you'll be okay, I'll head out. I'll let you know if the roads are clear enough for you to go into town." Ben kissed her then left.

Riley shifted the boxes on a chair to the stack on the table then sat down and called Maureen.

"Everything okay with you?" Maureen asked when she answered.

"The tornado slammed our house, but we weren't injured; we stayed in the shed last night. What about you?"

"It missed us, but Lisa's neighbor found her in their field unconscious and badly injured; the neighbor said Lisa looked like someone had almost beaten her to death. The on scene medical team immediately sent her by helicopter to the trauma center in Atlanta. Doc Hugo sent me a text first thing this morning to cancel his appointments for the rest of the week. That's about all I can say that would be polite." Maureen cleared her throat. "People are bringing in their injured pets, and we're slammed. Doc Wesley would like to talk to you. Would it be okay with you if he calls you, or are you kind of over us after Doc Hugo?"

Riley furrowed her brow. *I didn't expect anything like this.*

She bit her lip before she replied. "Doctor Cooper can call me."

"Good. Doc Wesley is nothing like Doc Hugo, but I know you'll have to decide that for yourself. We need someone who can work independently, but I'll let Doc share his thoughts."

"Thanks, Maureen; tell Doc to call me anytime."

Two minutes after they hung up, Riley's phone rang.

Doc Wesley's voice had a southern drawl mixed with the charming, South Carolina lilt with the sound of 'eye' softened to 'ah.'

"Riley, first off, I'd like to apologize for Hugo Adams' behavior yesterday. I was embarrassed when I learned how he spoke to you because that is not how we treat our coworkers in our clinic. Hugo and I agreed our rural practice is not a good fit for him, and he has left to pursue a more suitable position."

"That's good." Riley rolled her eyes. *I'll bet the discussion wasn't as polite as Doctor Cooper's interpretation.*

"If you could work with Maureen and me for a few days, I'd appreciate it. Maureen is doing her best to identify urgent patients when they come in the door, but we're struggling with all the injuries and could really use your expertise. Maureen told me to ask you to bring Toby if you can come; she said he could help her keep the patients calm."

Riley furrowed her brow; Toby leaned against her, and she stroked his chest and under his chin. "If I can get there safely, we'll come in to at least help with this morning's patients; if it isn't working out for either of us, Toby and I will head home at lunch time."

"Fair enough; we'll appreciate whatever you can do."

After Riley hung up, Toby yipped. "I'm glad you approve, but I know you're just looking forward to Maureen's treat jar."

Riley sent a text to Ben. "We're going to the vet's office to help. Doc Hugo is gone."

Riley checked the duffel bag of clothes and pulled out her blue long-sleeved scrub top with snaps down the front. "I need to layer."

After Riley checked her backpack and added spare clothes and a bottle of water, she put a bottle of water and a bowl in a second backpack for Toby.

Ben replied, "Good riddance. Roads are clear from the house to town."

"Okay, Toby; we're cleared to go."

Toby raced to the car. After Riley opened the back door, Toby hopped inside, and she set the two backpacks on the floorboard in front of the back seat.

When she passed the other veterinary clinic on the outskirts of town, the roof was missing, and the parking lot was empty. In the next block, her eyes widened at the crowded parking lot at the Jimson urgent care medical clinic that was spilling over into the road. "We were lucky, weren't we, Toby?"

She pulled into the full parking lot of the large general merchandise store. "I have to buy underwear and socks. I won't be long."

Riley dashed inside the busy store and exhaled in relief. *Everyone is in the grocery department.* She grabbed two packages of underwear and two packages of socks for Ben and herself. *I'll get groceries later.* She breezed through the checkout line because it was on the opposite side of the store from the grocery department.

She climbed into her car and dropped her sacks on the passenger side floor. "I'm glad I got that out of the way."

A makeshift barrier of a line of cones blocked Main Street. Riley weaved her way to the clinic as she followed the detours through the neighborhoods and shuddered at the destruction. "Some houses are demolished, but others are completely intact. It's so random and absolutely terrifying."

When Riley arrived at the Jimson Veterinary Clinic, the parking lot was full and vehicles were double-parked on the side street. The front door was open and a line of people with pet carriers or dogs on leashes snaked from the door and across the sidewalk in front of the building to the grassy pet walk area. *They are swamped.* She drove past the building and parked on the street a block away.

"Let's go, Toby; we're going to have a long day."

When Riley and Toby reached the parking lot, she heard the hum of a generator behind the building.

A man close to the door shouted, "Hey Maureen, Riley and Toby are here."

As Riley and Toby hurried to the door, they were greeted with sighs of relief and comments of appreciation.

A preteen boy, who was taller than Riley and had freckles and curly brown hair, stood at the door. "Welcome, Miss Riley. Miss Maureen asked me to make sure only ten people were inside at a time, so it wouldn't be too crowded for the animals."

Riley glanced at the people in the reception area that were sitting, standing, or gathered around the registration desk. Toby slipped through the crowd.

"Hey, Toby. Are you ready to go to work?" Maureen asked. "Riley, Doc's in the first exam room; tell him you're here."

Riley held up Toby's backpack. "This is Toby's."

"I'll take it." Maureen put the backpack on the floor next to her wheelchair.

Riley made her way to the exam room and opened the door. Doctor Cooper wasn't as tall as Ben, but probably outweighed Ben by at least thirty pounds. He had dark-brown skin, and his black curly hair was cut short.

He glanced at Riley and smiled. "Thank you for coming; I'll meet you in the breakroom in just a few minutes."

When Riley reached the breakroom, she put her backpack on a chair and exhaled.

Doc Wesley strode in and picked up the half-full pot of coffee. "Care for a cup? I hope you don't mind, but I called Julie Rae Sorenson and asked her about you, and she said she'd turn you loose and spend her time on the critical patients. So, how do we do that?"

"Coffee would be great. We have to triage the patients. Do you think Maureen could designate patients into three categories: those that can wait, patients for me, and critical patients for you?"

Doc Wesley raised his eyebrows. "That would work. Maureen definitely has the experience, and Lisa's nephew can help her by identifying any new critical patients that arrive; Mason has helped us at the clinic since he was six years old. Let's have a hallway meeting."

Riley gulped down her coffee even though it burned her tongue.

"Maureen, we need a hallway meeting," Doc called out.

"Be right back, y'all," Maureen said before she rolled to the hallway and stopped in front of the breakroom. Toby followed her.

"Riley suggested a triage system." Doc explained the three tier plan.

"Perfect. I have those colored sticky tabs for marking documents, and I think I have four or five different colors. Doc, I'll use red for you, yellow for Riley, and green for me because that's my favorite color."

Doc nodded. "Great; if there aren't any critical patients, I'll shift to the yellow patients. If we don't have any red or yellow patients, we'll take the green patients in the order of arrival."

"I can manage that," Maureen said. "When you're finished with a patient, I'll give you the next one, and if an emergency patient comes in, I'll send Mason to alert you."

"Let's get to it then. Do we have any critical patients?" Doc asked.

"I'm not sure if the patient is really critical, but I'd like for her to be your first patient; Mason and Toby can check those who are waiting outside to be sure we don't have any other critical patients," Maureen said. "I do have yellow patients that have been waiting a while, so I'll keep you busy, Riley. Mason and I will figure out what to do with the green patients while they wait, but we'll come up with something."

On the way to Maureen's desk, Doc said, "I'll take the trauma room. You can have the first exam room."

When the three of them returned to Maureen's desk, she gave a folder to Doc and one to Riley.

Doc called his patient, and Riley called hers, while Maureen called Mason to her desk to fill him in on the plan.

Riley's patient was a brown Pitbull. The client carried the sturdy brown dog to the first exam room. "I think Clarence's leg is broken; the rafters collapsed on us, and he was trapped for a while." The man carefully placed the heavy dog on the exam table.

"Your leg is really swollen. Do you hurt anywhere else, Clarence?" Riley asked.

The pittie whined.

"That's good; I'll x-ray your leg then splint it. After I find a gurney, I'll take you to x-ray."

"Clarence isn't too heavy; I can carry him," the client said.

"That's actually a good idea; thank you."

The man followed Riley to the x-ray room and placed Clarence on the table.

"Clarence, can I trust you to stay still on the table?"

Clarence whimpered.

"Thank you; I'm going to lay a strap over you, but that's just to remind you to stay as still as you can."

The man stepped out of the room. After Riley took the x-ray, the client carried Clarence back to the exam room.

Riley joined them with soft bandaging material and a splint. "It's a clean break, so you can walk with the splint later today if you're careful and feel like it, Clarence."

After she applied the splint, Riley said, "The swelling should be down in a few days. We'll ask Maureen to schedule an appointment for Clarence toward the end of the week, so we can check his splint."

The man carried Clarence as he followed Riley to the registration desk. "We need an appointment for follow up," Riley said.

Maureen nodded. "Here's your next patient."

Riley called out her patient's name.

At one o'clock, Riley's phone buzzed a text from Ben. "I'm swamped. How's your day?"

After her patient and the client left, Riley stopped at Maureen's desk to reply. "Swamped too, but I'm glad I came."

Maureen glanced at Riley. "Are you doing okay? I ordered soup and sandwiches from the food truck at the gas station. One of my friends is picking up our lunch."

"I have a feeling I won't have any trouble sleeping tonight."

Maureen chuckled. "It's been a right busy day, hasn't it? Mason told me he learned that we're the only vet office that is open in three counties. The good news is that people are being really patient and letting Mason know if someone urgent shows up. Here's your next yellow patient."

Riley called out the patient's name on the folder. A woman with a cat carrier on her lap rose.

"I'm worried because we have only one more day's dosage of Casper's seizure medication." The client followed Riley to the exam room.

Riley put the carrier on the exam table then unzipped the door. She gently lifted the pudgy orange cat out of the carrier and put him on the scale. "Your weight is up a little; are you feeling okay, Casper?"

Casper's meow was loud and pitiful.

"I'm so sorry, but I'm glad you're here, so we can make sure you don't run out of your medicine."

The client's eyes widened. "Is something wrong with Casper?"

"He doesn't like to have his temperature taken, but he knows it's part of the routine." Riley stroked his back, and Casper purred.

Riley smiled. "You'll see; I'm gentle and fast."

Casper closed his eyes, and Riley took his temperature. "It's normal; thank you, Casper."

Riley glanced over his file. "Your ears haven't been checked in a while. I'll take a peek."

After she examined both ears, Riley said, "That left ear is a little red. Has it been bothering you, Casper?"

Casper growled.

"I'd forgotten that he's been rubbing his ear on the carpet," the client said.

"I'll ask Doc Wesley what he'd like to do about Casper's ear."

Riley opened the exam room door. Doc Wesley glanced up then stepped into the hallway and closed the door behind him.

"Casper is here for his seizure medicine; his temperature is normal, but his left ear is inflamed. I'd like to treat it with an antibiotic. It's bothering him."

"Did he tell you that?" Doc Wesley asked.

Riley raised her eyebrows. *How did he know?* "Yes."

"Go ahead." Doc Wesley reached for the door handle then paused as he glanced back at Riley. "Doc Julie Rae told me she learned to go with the flow when she worked with you; I have a better understanding of what she meant." Doc Wesley shook his head as he went into his exam room.

Riley returned to Casper and the client. "Doc Wesley prescribed an antibiotic for Casper's ear. While you check out with Maureen, I'll bring you Casper's medicine."

After Casper and the client left, Maureen said, "I thought Casper was green, but Toby sniffed Casper's carrier and corrected me with a moan. I guess he was right, wasn't he? Mason put lunch on the counter in the breakroom; he and I have eaten. The Cuban sandwiches are cut in half. The soup is potato soup with bacon; it's heavenly. Help yourself to a bottle of water or lemonade in the refrigerator. After you eat, I'll give you the file for your next patient."

Riley pulled out a bottle of lemonade from the refrigerator and put half a sandwich on a paper plate before she sat down at the table. She sent a text to Ben. "I'm on a quick break for lunch. How's your day?"

Her phone rang as she took a bite of her sandwich.

"I just finished a barbecue sandwich from the food truck. What are you having?" Ben asked.

"One second." Riley finished chewing then swallowed. "Maureen ordered lunch for us; I have half a Cuban sandwich."

"That sounds good."

Riley nodded as she continued eating.

Ben continued, "Graham's brother has a one-bedroom, partially furnished rental about ten miles north of Jimson. It's been vacant for two weeks, but they just finished the minor repairs and touch-up painting on Friday. The utilities are still on, which is a big deal for us. We can stay there until we find something else, or if we like it, we can sign a lease. Graham is lending me a utility trailer so we can move everything we've salvaged. I'll be heading home in about an hour, but I'll stop by the cottage to take a quick look. As soon as I get home, I'll load everything onto the trailer because I'd like to be settled in the cottage before dark. When do you think you can leave?"

"I'm not sure; about the time I think we're getting caught up, more people show up, but I'll try to leave not long after you do. I'm glad you can check the cottage before we load the trailer."

"I'll make sure the heat works, and we have running water."

"Yesterday I would have said all I needed was a roof over my head, but I've updated my standards."

Ben chuckled. "I'm right there with you, babe. I'll let you know when I'm leaving. Loved you first." Ben hung up.

Riley laughed.

"What's so funny?" Maureen called out from the receptionist's desk.

"My husband loves me, and he hung up on me."

"I need to get my hearing checked," Maureen shouted.

Riley laughed even harder as she cleared the break table of her trash.

When Riley reached Maureen's desk, she said, "Ben found a place for us to stay while we look for something more permanent."

Maureen nodded. "So he loves you and hung up on you; still don't get it, but that's my problem, isn't it? Will you be close enough to work with us?" Maureen furrowed her brow.

Riley shrugged. "If there's work for me."

"Talk to Doctor Cooper before you leave; we have plenty of work for you and Toby. Here's your next patient."

Riley smiled at the folder. "Green; this is great news."

Toby moaned.

"Oh, more yellow than green? Thanks," Riley said.

She called out, "Xena."

A woman whose hair was pulled up into a messy bun and who wore faded sweatpants and a T-shirt followed a white, standard poodle to Maureen's desk.

Riley asked, "What would you like for us to check?"

The woman exhaled. "Xena isn't herself; I think she needs something for depression."

Riley quickly checked Xena's legs and abdomen. "I'm not finding any injuries. Are you doing okay, Xena?"

Xena whined.

"Oh, I'm sorry." Riley furrowed her brow as she turned to the client. "Xena is worried about the barn cats. Are they okay?"

"I don't know." The client hugged Xena. "We'll check as soon as we get home. They prefer to be outside cats, but we can fix up a shelter for them close to the house, so they can be safe, and you can check on them, Xena. Would that work?"

Xena yipped. The client smiled. "Thank you so much, Riley. Xena and I appreciate you."

After the client and Xena left, Maureen put her hand over her heart. "That is the sweetest thing I've ever heard; you're amazing, Riley." Maureen sniffled as she picked up a file. "Here's your…"

Maureen squealed in surprise at the simultaneous sound of a pop and a whack that sounded like a rock hit the front window. When the second pop quickly followed from the front of the building, Maureen covered her ears at the shrill sounds of terrified screams that came from outside. Toby and Riley raced to the door.

CHAPTER FIVE

When someone yanked open the door, Toby darted out, but Riley was blocked by the stampede of people who shoved past her in their panic to get inside the building. Riley forced her way out of the doorway against the wave of bodies and squeezed sideways toward Toby as he continued to bark.

Toby snarled and snapped as the widening crush of people threatened to expand to the area he was guarding; Riley continued in her struggle to reach Toby.

When she was closer, she saw Toby was protecting Mason who was slumped against the side of the building; a growing red blotch near his collarbone stained the front of his shirt.

Riley was knocked down as she tried to get closer to Mason. A man instantly snatched her off the ground and set her on her feet.

"What do you need, Riley? I'm John Winston."

"I need someone to make sure we aren't trampled, an ambulance, and a trauma pack."

"Gotcha."

John shouted, "Hey, Doc! We need an ambulance and a trauma pack."

A woman at the front door relayed John's message.

"John, Maureen's calling the ambulance, and Doc Wesley's getting his trauma bag," the woman called out a moment later.

When a young man who looked like a high school football player jostled him, John grabbed the young man by his collar. "Get a hold of yourself and do something useful. Find a teacher to settle down that crowd in the building and clear a path for Doc Wesley so he can get to our patient. After Doc's out here, gather a few folks to help those people who took cover by lying down on the grass; not all of them can get up by themselves."

"Yes, sir, Mr. Winston."

"Run interference for Doc Wesley," the young man shouted at two other hefty young men.

As he neared the door, the young man shouted, "Ask the gym teacher to settle down those folks inside."

Riley raised her eyebrows, and Mr. Winston grinned at the shrillness of a referee's whistle that was followed by an abrupt silence in the veterinary office. Mason opened his eyes and groaned.

The three young men moved shoulder to shoulder as they gently shifted the crowd to the opposite side of the sidewalk.

Riley knelt closer to Mason. "Are you doing okay?"

Doc Wesley hurried out of the building with the trauma kit and knelt next to Riley.

As Doc cut away Mason's shirt, Mason exhaled. "I got the breath knocked out of me when I fell; I crawled to the building, so I wouldn't get trampled and kind of wore myself out."

An elderly woman assisted by a high school girl joined them; the woman had slipped the strap of her oversized, expensive purse across her chest and carried her cane under her arm like a British Army Sergeant Major carried his baton. She pointed with her cane. "That young man shouted at me and knocked me down; I was ready to take him on for a minute there, but I changed my mind after he took the bullet that was intended for me."

"Why would anybody shoot at you, Mrs. Thornton?" John asked.

"I've been the chairperson for the county Ag Council for twenty years, and our policies are rarely controversial, so I have no idea." Her mouth twitched into a wicked smile as her eyes twinkled. "But if I had to guess, I'd say it was most likely a jealous wife."

Riley giggled, and the old woman beamed. "Thank you, Riley; not everyone gets my humor, especially my daughter. I've told her she's far too serious for her own good." Mrs. Thornton glanced around and moved close to Riley before she whispered, "Actually, I suspect whoever shot at me has a warped concept of farming."

A deputy in a brown uniform pulled into the lot as far as she could and blocked the exit when she double-parked. John strode across the lot to meet her as she climbed out of her cruiser.

A middle-aged woman who looked like an overweight, younger version of Mrs. Thornton left her car in the middle of the street as she jumped out and ran toward them; she screamed, "Mother! How did you get out of the house? You are not supposed to go out alone. Where is Goliath? Did you take him?"

Mrs. Thornton pulled out a tiny, gray kitten from her purse.

"Goliath is fine." She snorted before she whispered to Riley, "When the young man pushed me, I tucked and held onto my purse when I rolled to my other side; I didn't fall on Goliath, but the little snitch might claim I did. Don't believe him."

Riley worked hard to maintain a serious face, but a smile sneaked past her. "Yes, ma'am. Shall I take a little peek at him to make sure he's okay?"

"Absolutely." The daughter stopped to catch her breath; after a brief pause, she continued toward them at a slower pace.

"How are you doing, Goliath?" Riley asked.

Goliath mewed then hissed when Riley reached for him; she nodded and lowered her hand. "Goliath is not injured at all; he is angry someone wanted to hurt you."

Mrs. Thornton kissed Goliath on his nose, and he purred. "You sweet, brave boy," she cooed. "I'm so sorry I called you a snitch; you have my back after all, don't you?"

"Mother, why did you go for a walk?" The daughter exhaled. "Let's go home and get you and Goliath a cool drink of water."

As she helped her mother to the car, the daughter continued, "You're welcome to go for a walk anytime, but please tell me first; I might enjoy going with you."

John led the deputy to Mason. "Did you see anything, Mason?" the deputy asked. The embroidered name tag on her shirt pocket said, Contrero.

"It was all pretty fast; I looked up when I heard the first pop and saw a man in a ski mask holding a gun out his window. When he pointed it at Mrs. Thornton, I shouted at her to get down while I dove at her."

"What kind of car was it?" Deputy Contrero asked.

Mason frowned. "I don't know; I saw the ski mask, the gun, and Mrs. Thornton; the rest was a blur."

The ambulance arrived, and the crew whisked Mason away.

"Does anyone have any more details?" the deputy asked.

"I doubt it; I was here, but I didn't even see what Mason saw," John said.

"Could you help me with the timing of the incident for my report?" she asked.

"I'll do my best." John followed Deputy Contrero to her cruiser.

Doc Wesley cocked his head toward the parking lot. "It appears our parking lot is still crowded, but at least there are no cars parked in the middle of the street. Let's see what Maureen has for us."

Riley stared at the building then scanned the parking lot. "The first shot cracked the front window. I'm not sure if it was a wild shot or a warning shot."

"Warning about what?"

"I don't know; nothing connects, does it?"

Riley and Doc headed toward the clinic, but Toby stayed near the road.

"Come on, Toby," Riley said. "We're going inside."

Toby trotted to the clinic door and waited for them.

"I'm actually surprised that there are so many cars in the parking lot, aren't you? We must still have patients to see," Doc said.

When they went inside, Maureen exhaled in relief. "I heard Mason was shot; I wanted to see if he was okay, but there was no way I could have gotten through that crowd. One of my friends told me Mason was talking to you two, and neither one of you looked worried, so I relaxed."

"He was a hero; the shooter aimed toward Mrs. Thornton, and Mason pushed her out of the way," Riley said.

Maureen narrowed her eyes. "What about the shot that hit the window?"

"We don't know, but no one else was hit," Doc said.

"Maybe Mrs. Thornton wasn't the intended target," Maureen said.

Riley furrowed her brow. *That's a strong possibility, but then who was?*

"What's wrong?" Maureen asked.

"Probably nothing; what about patients?" Riley asked.

"We have eight patients left, and I know three are yellow; I haven't checked everyone else yet, but I'm certain there are no reds." Maureen handed Doc and Riley files.

Riley called out the patient's name, then led the client as he carried an old black lab with a laceration on her shoulder to the first exam room.

After the man put the lab on the examination table, he said, "Susie was trapped under a metal cabinet when our roof collapsed. It took me almost an hour to dig her out."

Riley cleansed the wound then shaved away Susie's coat from around the wound.

"I'm glad that when the metal cabinet fell, it grazed your shoulder and didn't go any deeper or break any bones." Riley examined the wound.

The lab yipped.

"That was smart," Riley said.

"What was smart?" the client asked.

"When the roof failed, and she saw the cabinet was about to fall, Susie got as flat as she could, so she wouldn't be badly hurt."

The client stared at Riley then nodded his head. "Susie's smart."

Riley inspected the wound more closely. "Let me ask Doc Wesley if he'd like to put in a few stitches."

Riley opened the exam room door.

Doc Wesley glanced at her. "Whatcha got, Riley?"

"A wound that needs a few stitches."

"Go ahead," Doc Wesley said.

Riley gathered the suture kit and supplies. "Doc Wesley said my stitches are prettier. Is that okay with you, Susie?"

Susie smiled.

"What a sweet girl you are." Riley explained each step to Susie.

The client shook his head in wonder. "I think she understands you; I've never seen her so calm in the vet's office."

While Riley tied off the last stitch, the client smiled. "Susie is so content; she looks like she is enjoying being pampered at her favorite spa. Is it okay if I take full credit for bringing her here?"

Susie yipped.

Riley giggled. "Fine with us."

Riley applied an ointment to the wound then covered it with a bandage.

"We're all finished here; I enjoyed taking care of you, Susie. Let's go see Miss Maureen."

The client carried Susie to Maureen's desk.

Riley handed the folder to Maureen. "Susie can come back on Friday, and we'll check her wound and probably take out those stitches."

"Here's your next patient." Maureen handed Riley a file folder. "Toby said green; I've given up trying to second guess him."

After an hour, the office was finally cleared of patients.

"Lisa's husband called. Lisa suffered a traumatic brain injury; her doctors have placed her in a medically induced coma. Nash said the doctors are confident they can wake her in a few days." Maureen bit her lip.

Doc said, "Riley, I don't know what we would have done if you hadn't come in to help today." He rubbed his hand across his face. "Maureen, let's get the word out we're hiring; we need at least two vet techs and another veterinarian. Should we also..."

Maureen interrupted. "You'll be here tomorrow, right, Riley?"

Doc exhaled. "I was kind of dancing around, wasn't I? What do you think, Riley? Will you stick with us for a while? Please don't judge us by yesterday and today; we're really a laid-back practice, aren't we, Maureen?"

Maureen winked at Riley. "I don't know, Doc; so far, it has seemed like a regular week to me."

Riley chuckled. "I'll be here in the morning. Ben may have found a place for us to live a few miles north of here; hopefully we'll move this evening and have a roof, heat, and running water. I'll let you know if anything changes, or if I'm running late."

Riley's phone buzzed a text. "That's probably him now." She checked her text. "Ben wants to meet me at home in an hour; that gives me enough time to clean and stock the exam rooms before I leave."

"If you'll clean, I'll restock the supplies," Doc said.

"I'll join you, Doc, so I can make a list of what I need to reorder." Maureen rolled toward the stockroom.

When she went past Hugo Adams' office, Maureen said, "That's funny; Doc Hugo left his diploma and his portrait on the wall and that book he wrote on his desk in his office. I'll bet his bookshelf is still here too. I suppose he might have forgotten about his diploma, but he'll certainly be back tomorrow to pick up his portrait and his books."

"Doctor Adams wrote a book?" Riley raised her eyebrows. "What kind of book?"

"He claimed it was a handbook on how to be a successful veterinarian," Maureen said. "He offered to sell me a copy at a reduced price, but I declined. Doc Adams told me he knew I'd never be a veterinarian, but he needed reviews; I took the high road and pretended not to hear him. He would not have been happy with my response or any review I posted. He has a whole bookshelf in his office with the shelves filled with his copies of his book."

"I'm surprised he didn't mention it to me on Monday."

"That is odd," Doc Wesley furrowed his brow. "You're really brilliant, Riley. I think you must have intimidated him."

Maureen cleared her throat. "I might have had a hand in that. Doctor Ned Halsey told me that Riley had a standing offer for a scholarship to veterinary college. I might have mentioned it offhand to Doctor High and Mighty."

"Wish I could have seen that; I miss out on all the fun," Doc Wesley grumbled.

Riley smiled. "I'd rather focus on Ben's career to give him a chance to become established. If I were going to school, he'd be limited in where he could work."

"I hear ya," Doc Wesley said. "My wife and I wanted our children to grow up in a town that had an excellent school system and decent medical facilities but with a small town atmosphere. Our former friends thought we'd return to the big city in a month, but Jimson is perfect for us; we can't imagine living anywhere else. It's all about priorities, isn't it?"

"My priority is to go home and take a soaking bath with bubbles; I'm exhausted," Maureen said.

When Riley and Toby headed toward the front door, Doc Wesley asked, "Where are you going? Didn't you park in the back?"

"We parked a block away; that was as close as we could get to the building. We'll park in the back in the morning."

Maureen shook her head. "A block away, and you still came to help; come back tomorrow." Maureen rolled toward the back door.

"Why don't I give you a ride?" Doc asked.

"We're fine; we'd enjoy the walk." Riley opened the front door.

"I'll walk with you." Before Riley could protest, Doc said, "Humor me."

As they walked toward the sidewalk, Toby darted across the street then turned and barked.

"That's not good." Riley ran across the street; Doc passed her as he raced to Toby.

Doc examined a car parked in the boutique store's lot. When Riley joined him, he pointed inside the driver's open window.

"Isn't that a pool of blood on the seat?" Doc asked.

Riley peered inside. "Looks like it, and isn't that blood on the steering wheel too?"

"Could there have been a third shot?" Doc asked.

"I didn't hear one, but I suppose there could have been because there was a lot of screaming by the second shot," Riley said.

While Doc called the sheriff's office, Riley asked, "Do you know who was hurt, Toby?"

Toby yipped.

After Doc hung up, he asked, "What did Toby say?"

"He smelled the blood when we came outside, but he didn't see anyone."

"Why don't I walk you to your car? It will be a few minutes before a deputy arrives, and there's no reason for both of us to hang around, is there?"

"Not that I know of. Are you sure?"

"I'm positive," Doc said.

Riley bit her lip. "The shed was a welcome refuge last night, but running water would be amazing."

On the way to her car, Doc Wesley said, "Maureen has always had a way with animals, but it was amazing to see the way she and Toby worked together as a team. The process became so smooth that I was certain Toby was in charge of triage, and Maureen was in charge of communication with us and the clients."

"It didn't take them long at all to work out a system, did it?"

When they reached Riley's car, Doc Wesley asked, "Will you be okay from here? Maureen's going to grill me when I get back, you know."

Riley smiled as she opened the back door for Toby. "We're only twenty minutes from the shed, and Ben will be there soon. We'll be fine."

As Riley neared the driveway, she glanced at her rearview mirror. "There's a truck behind us, Toby; if that's Ben, we've beat him."

After Riley parked in front of the shed, she frowned at the crunch of tires on the driveway. "I might be on edge, but it doesn't exactly sound like Ben's truck. Should we step into the woods in case it's not Ben, Toby?"

When Toby yipped, Riley exhaled. "Thanks; I'm glad you recognized Ben's truck."

Ben parked his truck with a trailer behind Riley's car; he jumped out, raced to Riley, and grabbed her off her feet. After he set her down, he still held her close. "Ready to move? The house has all the kitchen appliances, a bathroom, and a roof. We can decide later if we want to stay or find another house, but we have enough to be comfortable until the weekend when we can buy some furniture. Ready to load up?"

"I sure am." Riley wiggled to get loose, and Ben released her

While Ben turned his truck and the trailer to make it easier to load, Riley went inside the shed and packed smaller items.

After they had emptied the shed, Ben scanned the house. "There are too many trees down across the front of the house, but I'd like to check the back to see if there is any access to the guest bedroom; I wouldn't mind having extra linens if I can reach the closet."

When they turned the corner of the house, Ben whistled. "It's blocked by downed trees back here too. I think we have salvaged everything possible. Ready to see our new house?"

Before she climbed in her car, Riley asked, "Will we be going back through town? Should we pick up some groceries?"

"I got it covered." Ben grinned. "I was certain we'd love the house, so I made a quick stop at a grocery store on the way to the house; follow me." Ben strode to his truck and started the engine.

Riley followed Ben on the bypass around Jimson; twenty minutes later, Ben put on his turn signal, and they exited the highway. After two miles, Ben slowed then turned onto a lane of red clay that still had water in the ditches alongside it.

They passed three houses, then Ben slowed and pulled into a short, graveled driveway. Riley's eyes widened at the white cottage with purple and yellow pansies and pink and white snapdragons on both sides of the porch.

"Toby, the cottage looks like it came out of a children's picture book."

Riley parked behind the trailer, then she and Toby hopped out of the car; Ben met them at the door with a large white paper sack in his hand.

After he unlocked the door, they stepped inside.

While Ben took his paper sack to the kitchen and put it in the refrigerator, Riley gaped at the cottage interior.

"This is much nicer than I expected. The pale blue-gray walls with white trim and the white shiplap ceiling planks are a perfect contrast to the old pine wood floors. The white blinds that cover the oversized windows are perfect."

"What about that futon?" Ben asked as he joined her.

She snorted at the old futon and its frayed orange cover that was in the middle of the living room and faced the wood-burning fireplace.

"I'd rather talk about the fireplace that's surrounded by pale gray river rock and its pale gray slate raised hearth." Riley smiled. "This is perfectly cozy except for the poor futon, which has seen better days. We'll get a rug or two for Toby, a sofa, and two soft chairs this weekend, and maybe some tables."

"I thought the same thing when I first came in," Ben said.

"The tall counter that separates the kitchen from the living room is probably a breakfast bar." Riley strolled to the counter and pulled out one of the two barstools that had been pushed under the overhang of the bar. She sat on the stool. "This is comfortable; I love the blue cushions."

Riley furrowed her brow as she examined the kitchen. "Seems like white cabinets would be hard to keep clean, but I do like the gray tile on the counter tops and the bar; the backsplash is kind of unusual with the tiles of sailboats randomly scattered among the blue and white tiles. What do you think?"

Ben said, "If they were going for different, they nailed it. Come into the kitchen; it's actually bigger than it looks. There's a dishwasher and a combination refrigerator and freezer; the freezer's on the bottom. The stove and water heater are gas, and the heat is electric, but it's a heat pump, so we have air conditioning. It has a detached two-car garage, but my truck is too big; your car will fit, and I can store my tools in the garage. You'll like the bathroom, and the bedroom has a large walk-in closet."

"I think it's perfect for us. Is this about twenty minutes to Jimson? How far is it for you?" Riley peered into the oven, refrigerator, freezer, cabinets, and kitchen drawers.

When Riley turned, she saw the stacked washer and dryer in the corner near the back door and squealed. "Wow, a washer and dryer!"

She hurried to inspect the appliances and continued, "Being able to do laundry at home is a magnificent bonus; I'm so thankful we don't have to haul our dirty clothes into town to wash and dry."

Riley exhaled. "I just realized I was excited and didn't give you a chance to talk. How far is it for you?"

"We're twenty minutes from the regional office. Let's look at the rest of the house, then I'll unload while you unpack."

"Twenty minutes for you, and twenty for me. This is absolutely perfect, although I'd have been okay if it hadn't taken a tornado for us to find it."

Riley and Toby followed Ben to the short hall.

When she peeked into the bathroom, Riley said, "We definitely have a theme going here, don't we? It's okay, though, because I love the blue and white; it looks so fresh."

Ben nodded. "Now the bedroom and closet."

"A bedframe," Riley squealed. "This is magnificent."

She rolled her eyes. "I think I'm going overboard over every little detail because I was afraid we'd be living in the shed for a long time. Will the mattress fit?"

Ben smiled. "It's an adjustable bedframe, so we'll be fine."

Riley opened the closet door. "Look at the shelves along that back wall; we'll have plenty of extra storage. Doc Wesley asked me to stay on at least until he can find more vet techs, or longer if I will, but we can talk later after we eat."

"Let's get busy, so we're not working after dark and attracting bugs into the house." Ben headed toward the front door.

Riley hurried to catch up with him. "I'll put away the groceries before I unload my car."

"I'll unload your car while you take in the groceries, so you can help me with the dining table and mattress," Ben said.

After the mattress was in the bedroom and Ben adjusted the frame, he asked, "Wasn't there bedding in the bathroom?"

"I haven't checked the tote yet; I'll look."

When Riley found a set of sheets, she exhaled in relief.

Riley strolled into the living area as Ben brought in the dining chairs. "I found them, honey." She held up the sheets in victory.

"Perfect. Everything's inside. If you'll make the bed, I'll feed Toby and take care of our supper."

"Best idea I've heard all day, except the cottage, of course." Riley stood on her tiptoes to kiss Ben's chin, but he lowered his head to meet her mouth with his.

After a lingering kiss, Ben gave Riley a playful pat. "Fun later."

"You got it, cowboy." Riley sashayed to the bedroom with the bed linens. Ben wolf-whistled then strode to the kitchen to find Toby's food dish and food.

While Toby ate, Riley sat at the bar and started a shopping list.

When Ben came in from the back door with kindling and small logs, she put down her pen. "I wondered where you'd gone."

"I thought we'd enjoy a fire with a glass of wine tonight. The fireplace was a surprise to me, so I didn't pick up marshmallows at the store. We'll get by with the oatmeal and cranberry cookies from their bakery. I have fried chicken, hush puppies, and macaroni and cheese warming in the oven. The grocery store had a deli." Ben's eyes twinkled as he beamed. "It might not be the most well-balanced meal from a nutritionist's standpoint, but I figured we could get by just this once."

"I think it excels in the comfort food category." Riley smiled.

"I should probably let my supervisor know how pleased we are with the cottage." Ben pulled out his phone.

"I'll send a text to Mom and Claire."

After a flurry of texts, Riley said, "Mom and Claire want pictures. I should have thought of it earlier, but it's still light enough to take one of the front of the cottage." When Riley came back inside, she said, "I'm off the hook."

"Our food's probably warm enough to pull out of the oven."

Riley poured sweet tea and set the table while Ben pulled out their food.

While they ate, Ben asked, "What do you think about the cottage? Should I try to find something else?"

"I don't see why; it's the perfect location for us, and it has what we need to be comfortable and a few extras like the fireplace. What do you think?"

"If you're happy, I'm happy," Ben said.

After they finished eating and cleared the table, Ben put away the leftovers, loaded the dishwasher, and started a fire in the fireplace while Riley showered.

When she came out of the bathroom wearing a soft T-shirt and sweatpants, Riley said, "That shower was heavenly; I washed away all the tornado dust and grime."

She stood in front of the fireplace and sighed. "This is like living in a mansion."

Ben handed her a glass of wine. "It certainly seems luxurious after last night, doesn't it?"

When Riley sat on the futon, she abruptly slumped to one side and almost spilled her wine. Ben took her glass then helped her up.

"I don't know where you have a new sofa on the shopping list, but I think its priority just escalated." Ben handed Riley her still-full glass of wine and chuckled. "Speaking of priorities, I was extremely impressed you didn't spill one drop of wine."

Riley smiled as Ben tugged the futon pad off the frame and folded it in half on the floor. She sat cross-legged in front of the fire with Toby by her side on the pad until Ben went into the bathroom. While he showered, Riley quickly collected their dirty clothes. She put their laundry in the washer and returned to her spot in front of the fire.

After he dressed in comfortable clothes and joined them, Riley said, "If you'll drop your clothes you were wearing today into the washer, you can start it. I already put in all the dirty clothes I could find and added the detergent, so it is good to go."

Ben started the washer and carried his empty wine glass, the wine bottle, and the box of cookies to their spot in front of the fire. After he joined Riley and Toby on the futon pad, Ben gave Toby the treat he had stuck into his pocket and then poured himself a generous splash of wine.

While they munched on cookies and sipped wine, Ben said, "Tell me about your day."

"I'll tell you the short version, if you'll give me another cookie." Riley fluttered her eyelashes.

Ben laughed as he handed her the box. "Hold that thought. The washer stopped. I'll be right back."

When Ben returned, Riley said, "That will cost you another cookie, but you can have one too."

Ben set the box of cookies aside. "I have a better idea."

CHAPTER SIX

"Cinnamon rolls and scrambled eggs is my new favorite breakfast combo, honey." Riley sipped her now-cooled coffee and helped herself to a second cinnamon roll.

"The bakery at the grocery store is operated by a local bake shop that was invited to move into the grocery store when they lost their lease," Ben said. "One of the guys at work told me to stop by there on my way home."

"You definitely have the right contacts." Riley pinched off a bite of cinnamon roll then popped it into her mouth and licked her fingers. "This is better than mine because I didn't have to get up two hours early to make it."

"You didn't make your cinnamon rolls the night before?"

Riley glared at Ben. "That would have been day-old cinnamon rolls."

"Yes, but these..." Ben cleared his throat as he pushed his chair back from the dining table. "I'll clear our dishes."

While Ben loaded the dishwasher, Riley pulled out lunch meat, sliced cheese, and condiments to make sandwiches.

Ben peered into the box of cookies. "We have four cookies left; I'll put two each in our lunch bags. I'll pick up a large box this evening."

After Riley slid her pistol into its waistband holster and zipped up her warm coat, she slung the strap of her work backpack over her shoulder and picked up her backpack with her lunch bag inside it.

Riley raised her face to Ben; he smiled and kissed her. "Do you have your long johns?"

"They're in the dryer." Riley pulled them out and stuffed them into her work backpack.

"You and Toby leave first, babe; it will be easier for me to turn around the truck and trailer with your car out of the way."

When they reached the Jimson Veterinary Clinic, Riley exhaled. "I guess I was afraid there might be another crowd here today, but I don't know why there would be." After she parked, Riley and Toby hurried to the back door.

Riley smiled as the door creaked when she opened it. Toby dashed to Maureen's desk, and Riley inhaled the now-familiar aroma of vanilla.

Maureen called out, "Good morning. Doc will be here after he drops off his kiddos at school. Grab yourself a cup of coffee; I'd like to go over a few ideas I had last night when I couldn't sleep."

Riley put her lunch in the crowded refrigerator and hung up her coat before she poured a cup of coffee and carried it to Maureen's desk.

Maureen removed her headset and pointed at the closest visitor's chair. "Pull it closer and sit; you'll have plenty of time on your feet later."

After Riley sat, Maureen said, "I think we did pretty well under the circumstances, but the sheer number of green patients we had bothered me. What could we have done differently?"

Riley cocked her head. "They were outside on the lawn in a group, which made sense to me because they were close enough to the door that they didn't feel like they were abandoned. How did you keep track of what order they were in?"

"When Toby told me they were green, I gave them the next number and recorded their number and name."

"How did clients know to come in to see you? Were the people lined up outside? Did people just get in line?"

Maureen stared at her. "There wasn't a line. The people I saw through the window were gathered in small groups. I don't know how anyone knew to come in; do you suppose the people standing outside told them?"

"Must have." Riley furrowed her brow. "It was triage; we were completely outnumbered. You had the first pass; I'll bet there were people outside who were backing you up."

"You're right; several people came in and said the furniture man or the gym teacher told them to come inside for a second check, and Toby said they were yellow. I'd forgotten the man who owns the furniture store is a first aid instructor, and the gym teacher is a sports trainer."

"If we'd had a week to plan, we might have come up with something different, but I can't imagine what we could have done any better because we didn't lose any patients, and everyone was taken care of."

"Thanks for talking to me; I think I was in a panic because the full impact of the entire day's events just knocked me for a loop."

"I had a similar reaction this morning; when I got close to the clinic, I was suddenly afraid the front and back parking lots were going to be full."

Doc Wesley came in the back door and stopped to grab a cup of coffee. When he joined Riley, Maureen, and Toby at the registration desk, Doc exhaled then sipped his coffee. "You don't know how glad I was to see both your cars when I turned the corner."

Maureen chuckled. "Actually, we do. I was awake most of the night worried about whether the whole triage thing was a mistake."

Riley added, "I was afraid the front parking lot would look like it did yesterday."

"We did a good job, but it definitely took a toll on our nerves, didn't it?" Doc asked. "Now that we've survived yesterday, here's our problem for today: I got three calls last night and two early this morning from farmers. I have a solution, but we have to talk. A lot of this will fall on you, Maureen."

"That's easy; the answer is no," Maureen smirked.

Doc rolled his eyes. "Hear me out first. The veterinary clinic at the edge of town lost their roof. I called Kaitlyn early this morning, and we had a long talk. We agreed we could easily work together, and she was relieved that she wouldn't be abandoning her patients. She has a vet tech and a receptionist."

"Wait a minute, Doc. I don't mean to get ahead of you, but if you're thinking about hiring Doc Kaitlyn, she's great, and so is her receptionist, Fiona, but do we need two receptionists?" Maureen crossed her arms. "I can't work with the vet tech, Bonnie; she's competent enough, but she's trouble."

"What does that mean?" Doc Wesley narrowed his eyes.

"If you hire Bonnie, she would have to be the vet tech who works in the field; I can't work with her."

"Can't or won't?" Doc growled. "Riley has priority for any farm visits, but we have to have a vet tech at the clinic too."

"Then find a vet tech for the clinic, or hire a new receptionist," Maureen said.

"I'm not replacing you, Maureen; explain what the problem is with Bonnie and find me a couple of good vet techs to interview."

Maureen scowled. "It's personal. I'll have three candidates for you to screen by the end of the day."

Riley cocked her head. "If Doc Kaitlyn came here and her patients followed her, could one veterinarian manage the patients from both clinics while you're on farm visits?"

Doc Wesley stared at her. "No. We'd still have to hire another veterinarian. I'll call Kaitlyn; she had plans to rent a building temporarily while her clinic was being repaired. I'll let her know to go ahead with her current plan. Maureen, I'll look forward to interviewing the vet techs you find."

"We're still short a veterinarian," Maureen said.

"What about a retired veterinarian who might be interested in working two or even three days a week, so you could do farm visits on those days, Doc?" Riley asked.

"Genius." Doc strode to his office and closed the door.

Maureen exhaled. "Crisis averted; thanks for the help, Riley. Here are the folders for our morning appointments. I have some calls to make."

Toby stayed with Maureen when Riley took the folders to the break room. After Riley refilled her coffee cup, she sat at the table and read through the folders.

Toby yipped, and Riley hurried to the receptionist desk with the folders.

A tall woman who wore a short-sleeved uniform shirt with 'Reynolds' embroidered in block letters on her shirt pocket had pulled back her dark blonde hair into a casual bun. Maureen beamed when she saw Riley. "I knew Toby called you; this is my baby sister, Gina. She's the manager at the cotton gin."

Gina smiled. "I stopped by to drop off some towels. Doc Hugo told me last week he planned to set up a boarding kennel, so I offered to put out a box in our office for old towels." She pointed to the large box on the floor in front of the receptionist's desk. "Everybody loved the idea."

"We'll put them in the storeroom for now," Maureen said. "Doc Hugo left the practice, but we'll put the towels to good use."

After Gina left, Riley said, "We should probably wash them before we store them."

"You're right; do you mind carrying them out to my car for me? I've got a heavy duty washer and dryer with fancy dials, so I can sanitize them." Maureen gave her car keys to Riley.

Riley stuck the keys in her back pocket and picked up the box. "Do you want the box on the back seat or in the back of your SUV?"

"On the backseat is perfect."

Maureen's SUV was parked near the ramp that led from the back door.

When Riley returned, she asked, "Did you know anything about a boarding kennel?"

Maureen rolled her eyes. "No."

Toby yipped.

Riley glanced at the front parking lot. "Our first patient is here."

The client and an old golden cocker spaniel with a gray muzzle came inside. When the cocker spaniel stopped at the door, Toby whined, and she slowly limped toward him with her stubby tail wagging in greeting.

"Hi, Nellie; I'm Riley. Are you ready for your checkup?"

Nellie barked.

Riley smiled. "It is kind of rude to always start with the scale, but at least we'll get it out of the way. After the scale, we'll go into the first exam room."

While Nellie followed Riley to the scale, Riley asked, "Are you having more trouble than usual with your arthritis?"

Nellie moaned.

Riley nodded. "Doc will check you; he might want some x-rays, but he'll probably increase your medication a bit. Is your stomach bothering you?"

When Doc Wesley came into the examination room, Riley handed him the folder. "Doc, Nellie's doing great with her weight, but her temperature is a little elevated and her hip is bothering her again."

Doc gently palpated Nellie's hip and knee joints. "We might have a little inflammation; let's take some x-rays, then we'll see what we can do to make you more comfortable, Nellie."

After the x-rays, Doc said, "Let's see if we can knock out that inflammation first; Riley, ask Maureen to make an appointment next week for follow up, so we can see if Nellie's feeling any better."

While Riley filled Nellie's new prescription, Maureen scheduled the appointment. When Riley joined them at Maureen's desk with the new prescription, the next patient and client were waiting.

After a busy morning with a steady stream of patients, Maureen said, "Take a break for lunch, Riley. You have a little over thirty minutes before our first afternoon appointment. I apologize, but you'll be alone in the breakroom. I eat at my desk, so I can catch up on paperwork, which is a terrible practice. Doc Wesley does the same; Lisa always said she enjoyed eating her lunch alone because she didn't have to be social and could re-energize her batteries."

Riley smiled. "I'm ready to take a break. I noticed the refrigerator was pretty full. Is it okay if I toss whatever is expired or looks iffy?"

Maureen rolled her eyes. "Please do. That's been on my list for ages. Don't save any of the containers; they're all disposable. There are garbage sacks under the sink."

"I'll take whatever I pull out to the dumpster in the back."

Riley examined each item and dropped it into the garbage sack, or set it on the table until the refrigerator was empty. She pulled out a flash drive from the top shelf that had been hidden behind an out-of-date coffee creamer and sprayed the inside of the refrigerator with a disinfectant then wiped it out. She absent-mindedly stuck the flash drive into her jeans pocket and returned the in-date Italian salad dressing and a jar of dill pickle chips to the refrigerator.

"Want to go outside with me, Toby?" Riley said quietly.

She smiled when Toby scrambled to the breakroom from Maureen's desk, and the two of them went out. Toby explored the area while Riley hurried to the dumpster, tossed in the garbage sack, and shivered as she ran back to the door. "Come on, Toby. We can take a short walk after I eat lunch."

When they were back inside, Riley grumbled, "I'll wear a coat next time we go out."

While Riley ate her lunch and exchanged texts with Claire and Melissa, Doc Wesley came into the breakroom.

"How are you doing?" He joined her at the table.

"I'm afraid to say anything that might break the spell of a normal day because no telling what the afternoon will bring, but I've enjoyed being busy but not overwhelmed."

Doc snorted. "I agree. Your suggestion to find a retired veterinarian to work two or three days a week was brilliant, and we have one. Doctor Peterson will be here tomorrow then again next Tuesday. I hoped he would be missing the office after his long cruise, and he was. He agreed to work from ten until three on Tuesdays, Wednesdays, and Thursdays until we find a second veterinarian. I wouldn't mind having a second vet plus Doc Peterson, but we'll see what works out." Doc Wesley rose. "Now it's on Maureen to find us a good vet tech or two. I'd rather have two in the office, so people can actually take some time off."

"That's great news."

"One more thing. I got a call from a friend. A road construction crew found a man's body in a ditch four miles north of town. His throat had been cut. They identified him by his fingerprints. He was recently released from prison after serving his sentence for armed robbery and was the man who rented the car that was parked in the boutique parking lot."

Riley exhaled and furrowed her brow. *What is going on?*

"Are you going to be okay?" Doc Wesley asked.

"I'll be fine; I was afraid it was something like that. Is there any guess about motive?"

"His wallet was missing, so the current assumption is robbery." Doc shrugged then left.

After Riley gathered the remnants of her lunch, she threw away her trash and put on her coat; Toby joined her at the back door. When they stepped outside, Riley breathed in the cold air and coughed.

"So much for invigorating fresh air; it's downright cold."

Toby growled, and a man who had been crouched behind Maureen's SUV raced across the street and out of view.

Riley frowned. "Let's check Maureen's car."

Toby stood guard while Riley slowly circled the SUV as she surveyed it. "I don't see any scratches or any kind of damage. Maybe he took a shortcut through the parking lot and dropped something. You sounded ferocious, Toby. Maybe he was afraid you would attack him."

Toby puffed out his chest.

"You should be proud; I'm proud of you. He didn't have any business being on private property." Riley stamped her feet to warm her toes. "Let's go inside."

After she hung up her coat, Riley strolled to Maureen's desk.

"Did Doc tell you about Doc Peterson?" Maureen asked. "I have a phone interview for Doc Wesley with a vet tech at four thirty and a second one with another vet tech that I'll schedule after he tells me what would be the best time for him. Our four thirty appointment is for an immunization only, so that one's yours. If you need Doc after all, we have a plan; I'll take over the interview because I can ask process questions like describe your routine with a typical patient. Speaking of typical patients, here are your folders, and our first patient of the afternoon is due any minute."

Riley frowned as she read the folder. "There aren't any vet tech notes on the file. I'm not sure why the patient needs a standing weekly appointment."

"I forgot to tell you that Doctor Adams preferred to work solo with certain patients, especially the ones who came with wealthy clients."

Riley snorted. "As my grandma used to say, what a piece of work. Since we don't have any documented history, I'll do a new patient work up. Would you help me, Toby?"

Toby yipped.

When the client, who wore a form-fitting dress and four-inch heels came inside, she had an unleashed golden afghan hound that wore a jeweled collar and walked at the client's side.

"Hi, Theodora, I'm Riley, and this is Toby. Since I'm new, I'd like to make sure I have a complete record of you. We'll start with weighing. Have you been weighed before?"

Theodora stared at Riley then moaned.

"Really, you haven't? It will be easy for you because I can tell you have excellent balance. The scale is shiny; it's really pretty. I'll show you."

Theodora followed Toby and Riley.

The client turned to Maureen. "She talked to Theodora like she expected my sweet princess to understand her."

"She's the best," Maureen said.

Riley glanced at Toby, who winked.

The client joined them in front of the exam room as Riley recorded Theodora's weight. "I don't have any record of your weight, so it's nice to have a baseline. Thank you, Theodora. Next is temperature."

Theodora stopped in the middle of the doorway. Riley continued into the room. "Toby will tell you I'm fast and gentle."

Toby yipped, and Theodora hesitantly stepped into the room. Riley stroked her back, and Theodora relaxed as Riley quickly took her temperature.

"Your temperature is normal, but your coat is a little dry and brittle. Is anything special bothering you?"

Theodora moaned.

"I have a problem with feeling cold all the time too. I'm sorry you have so little energy. Will you wait in here with Toby while I find Doc Wesley to come see you?"

Theodora laid on the floor with her front paws crossed in front of her. Toby flopped down next to her and grinned.

Riley caught Doc Wesley on his way to the exam room. She gave him a quick rundown of her findings.

"Sounds like hypothyroidism. Is that what you're thinking?" Doc asked.

"Her symptoms definitely point to it. I can draw the blood we need while you examine her neck and abdomen and listen to her heart and lungs," Riley said.

"She's relaxed and sitting on the floor; Toby is sitting next to her."

"Let's do it."

While Doc Wesley listened to Theodora's heart, Riley said, "You'll feel a little poke, but it's just me, Theodora."

After Riley filled the four tubes, she said, "All done."

Theodora side-glanced at Riley.

Riley smiled. "Told you I was fast and gentle."

"Her heart rate is a little low," Doc said.

"Isn't that good?" the client asked.

"When a dog or a person is active, it is, but it's another symptom of a slow metabolism if they aren't, but we'll run some tests and let you know the results," Doc said.

"Do we keep our standing appointment next week?" the client asked.

"We'll leave it for now," Doc said.

As he rose to leave, Doc Wesley said, "It was nice to meet you, Theodora. We'll find the right medicine to help you get your energy back."

On the way to Maureen's desk, Riley asked, "Do you feel you're putting on weight?"

Theodora moaned.

"I'm the same way; it is annoying, isn't it? I'll let Doc Wesley know; we'll see you next week."

When Riley returned to Maureen's desk after cleaning the exam room, Maureen said, "You and Doc have two new fans. The client said she didn't understand why Doctor Adams didn't do anything except talk about himself and his big plans for his clinic. When she asked me who actually owned the clinic, she was genuinely pleased when I told her Doctor Cooper was the owner. She said he was brilliant, and you were magical."

Toby howled.

"Thank you, Toby. I thought it was kind of cool too." Maureen chuckled.

Doctor Cooper scowled as he strode to Maureen's desk. "We've got a problem. Hugo canceled the appointment to see a sick horse on Monday. I just got a call from the frantic farmer; we might have a horse that's dying. I have to leave now; I'd like for you to go with me, if you will, Riley. Maureen, call Doctor Peterson and beg him to come in. If he can't, reschedule all our appointments as early as you can. I'll work Saturday, if I have to."

"But Doc, you were supposed..."

"I know, but Samara will have to take the children without me. Hugo has left us with a big black eye in the community. We have to recover as quickly as we can."

"Doc, can't we work through lunch and until six or seven tomorrow to get everyone in?" Riley asked.

"I like it; Maureen, see what you can do. Are you coming, Riley?"

"Yes. Do I have time to change into my long johns? I need to grab my backpack and my work backpack."

"Good idea; go ahead. I have no clue what we'll find." Doc rubbed his forehead. "I'll grab a tote and toss in antibiotics and whatever else I can find. Riley, after you change, check behind me to see if there's anything I missed."

"Are you staying with me, Toby?" Maureen asked.

Toby barked.

"Thanks." Maureen picked up her phone.

After she changed, Riley hurried to Maureen's desk. "Do you have a shopping tote? Doc's grabbing meds; I want supplies."

Maureen slid out a large bookbag from under her desk and dumped the books on the counter. "Here; take this."

Riley raced to the supply closet and tossed in the gauze, bandaging material, a thermometer, first aid tape, sanitizer, a suture kit, a stethoscope, scissors, and two sizes of surgical gloves.

Before Riley left, Maureen gave her a slip of paper. "This is the farmer's phone number. Call on your way to see if you can get any more information."

When she reached Doc's truck, she tossed the tote and her backpacks in the backseat then climbed into the passenger's seat.

As Doc Wesley sped down the highway, he said, "I was going to ask you if you'd brought the x-ray equipment, then I decided it wouldn't be so bad if you did."

Riley side-glanced at him. "That's good, because I might have tossed it in at the last minute. I was pulling everything I could. Maureen gave me the farmer's phone number so I could call for an update."

She pulled out her phone and tapped the number.

When the farmer answered, she said, "This is Riley; I'm calling from the Jimson Veterinary Clinic for an update on your horse."

"This is a pleasant surprise," the farmer said. "She's doing fine."

"What?" Riley's eyes widened.

"What is it?" Doc asked. "Are we too late?"

CHAPTER SEVEN

"Doc, the horse is fine," Riley whispered quickly while the farmer continued talking.

"The horse is what?" Doc peered at Riley.

She shook her head and held up her hand for him to wait while she focused on what the farmer said.

The farmer continued, "I didn't think we needed to call back because Maureen said Doctor Adams had canceled all his appointments; I hope no one was inconvenienced."

"No, that was fine," Riley said.

The farmer continued, "Our youngest horse had a minor skin infection, and our niece who is visiting this week was worried. My wife thought Doctor Adams wouldn't mind stopping by to explain it was a minor wound. We're probably spoiled because Doctor Peterson never missed a chance to teach, but you probably knew that. My wife cleaned it up and put a little ointment on it; it's completely cleared up. Thanks for calling; we appreciate you." He hung up.

"Doc, turn around; we have to get back to the clinic. There's nothing wrong with the horse."

"What? Was it a prank call? The guy that called was very convincing." Doc Wesley slammed on the brakes and swerved into the ditch as he made a U-turn on the narrow country road.

Riley grabbed onto the arm rest to keep from being strangled by the seatbelt.

"I don't know if it was a prank or not, but it was someone who knew about the appointment that Doc Adams had canceled and wanted us out of the office."

"Call the sheriff."

Riley dialed nine-one-one.

"This is Riley Carter."

"Where are you, Mrs. Carter?"

"Doc Cooper and I were called away from the office on false pretenses; we're on our way back, but could someone check on Maureen?"

"I'm dispatching a deputy right now."

"Thanks." Riley hung up then called Maureen.

"Everything okay, Riley? I've got a client on hold," Maureen said when she answered.

"We're on our way back; I called the farmer, and the horse is fine. We don't know why we were called away, but lock the front door and stay away from the window. A deputy is on the way to check on you."

Riley exhaled as she listened to the squeak of the wheelchair as Maureen rolled across the floor then the click of a door lock.

"Door's locked. Did you lock the back door? I think I forgot to lock it after you left. I'll check," Maureen said.

Riley's hands were suddenly clammy.

"Are you okay, Riley? You're really pale," Doc said.

"Maureen couldn't remember if she locked the back door after I left; she's checking."

When Toby growled, Riley felt bile rise in her throat. "Toby said someone is in the back parking lot."

"I'll see who's out there," Maureen said.

"No! Run to the front, Maureen," Riley screamed. "Run!"

The explosion was so loud, Riley flinched and instinctively pulled away the phone from her ear.

Maureen coughed. "Toby's okay; I was knocked out of my chair, but I hung onto my phone." Her voice cracked. "Riley, something exploded behind the clinic and the back door blew open."

"Where are you? Can you get to the bathroom? Lock yourself in a room."

Riley's heart pounded until Maureen said, "I got back into my chair; Toby and I are in the bathroom. Riley, we have to talk sometime about how you thought I was supposed to run."

"What?" Riley shook her head. "I told you to run?"

"Is she okay?" Doc asked. "What's going on?"

"There was an explosion, and it blew the back door open. Maureen and Toby are in the bathroom."

"Did you even know you told me to run?" Maureen asked.

"I did not," Riley said.

"Did not what?" Doc asked.

"Told her to run; why would I tell her to run?"

Doc furrowed his brow. "I think you were trying to get her to move fast: I'm sorry, but you did tell her to run, Riley."

Riley bit her lip to keep from smiling. "Doc apologized because I told you to run."

"Hey," Doc said.

Maureen giggled. "You want to rephrase that?"

Riley shrugged. "Not particularly. Are you and Toby really okay? Was anyone else in the clinic?"

"No; Doc Peterson will be here in fifteen minutes. I hear a siren."

"Good; we'll be there in just a few minutes."

"I gotta go, Riley; I don't want anybody to bust down the front door." Maureen hung up.

"Maureen heard a siren, so she's going to unlock the front door."

"First the shooting, and now this. Why is the clinic being targeted?" Doc asked.

"It's more than just the clinic; John Winston's calves were poisoned, and another farmer's equipment was damaged."

"It's not like we're a critical infrastructure resource or industry like a power plant or water supply that are typical terrorist targets," Doc said.

Riley gazed out her window and furrowed her brow. *What was it Mrs. Thornton said?*

"Warped sense of farming," Riley said.

"What?" Doc rubbed his forehead with his fingertips. "I'm having trouble understanding anything today."

"Sorry, I was thinking and didn't realize I'd said it aloud; nothing is making sense." Riley exhaled. "Mrs.

Thornton declared whoever shot at her was a jealous wife, and we all laughed; but then she told me quietly the shooter had a warped view of farming."

"Well, at least you're as confused as I am, which is somehow comforting." Doc Wesley sighed.

When they neared the clinic, fire department vehicles blocked the road to the back of the clinic, and cars that were parked in the middle of the street blocked the road in front of the clinic. Two deputy cruisers, the sheriff's cruiser, and an ambulance were in the front parking lot; people stood in the middle of the road and milled around the parking lot while they gaped at the clinic. Onlookers gawked from the sidewalks outside nearby stores as still more people ran toward the clinic to see what was going on. The roar of the fire department engines and shouts added to the bedlam.

Doc double-parked in a furniture store parking lot half a block away, which was as close as they could get to the clinic. The two of them hopped out of the truck and rushed to the clinic. Riley jogged to keep up with Doc's long stride.

"Toby's okay, Riley," a woman said as they hurried across the clinic parking lot.

"Thanks."

When they went inside, Toby yipped and rushed to Riley while a paramedic took Maureen's blood pressure.

"Glad you're okay." Riley knelt next to Toby and hugged him as she stroked his back.

"My blood pressure's going to be elevated because y'all are annoying me. I didn't hit my head; my arm hurts because I fell on it, and it's only a little deformed. Give me a sling, if you must do something, or don't; I'll see my doctor tomorrow or whenever I feel like making an appointment," Maureen growled.

Gina stood next to Maureen. "Riley's here; I'll go back to work." She kissed Maureen's cheek. "I'm glad you're okay, Sis. Let me know when you're ready to go home, and I'll come get you."

Riley pointed toward the first exam room; Gina nodded and then headed to the hall. Riley, Doc, and Toby followed her.

After Doc closed the exam room door, Gina said, "Somebody set off an explosion in the back parking lot near the back door that was strong enough to blow the door open. Mo called me after she talked to you, Riley, so I got a quick peek at the back before everything was blocked off. Riley, the good news is that your car is fine; Mo's car has a broken windshield, but that's an easy fix. From what she's said, I'm positive her arm is broken, but she won't let anyone look at it; otherwise, she's fine. I'll remind her to call her doctor's office to make an appointment after I get back to work."

"Is there any damage to the building?" Doc asked.

"You'll need to replace the door because its hinges are a mess," Gina said.

Doc nodded. "Thanks; I'll see if I can get someone here before the end of the day."

When the exam room door opened, Doc Wesley glanced at the door and grinned as Doctor Peterson came in. "Maureen told me my patient was waiting in exam room one. What do you need for me to do, Wesley?"

"I'm not sure there's much we can do until all this hoopla clears out."

Doctor Peterson nodded. "I'll talk to the sheriff. I'm sure he's about ready to call a tow truck to clear the road. Maureen obviously won't go with the ambulance, so maybe we can take care of most of today's patients if Maureen can line them up for us."

"Let me know if you need me." Gina slipped out the door, and Doctor Peterson followed her.

"After I call a guy I know who will replace the back door for us today, I'll go to my truck and bring back as much as I can carry," Doc Wesley said. "We might as well restock while we wait for our patients."

"We'll go with you," Riley said.

While Doc Wesley called his friend, Riley texted Ben.

"Explosion behind clinic. Doc and I were headed to a farm visit. We're okay. My car wasn't damaged."

Her phone rang.

Riley cleared her throat before she answered, so her voice would be cheerful. "Hi, honey."

Ben growled, "Just a random explosion, and you're saying you and Toby aren't hurt at all. What caused the explosion?"

"I wouldn't call it a random explosion." Riley told him about the phone call to Doc Wesley and her follow-up call to Maureen.

Ben exhaled. "What does the sheriff say?"

"I haven't talked to him yet; he's busy."

"I'll call him. Babe..." Ben exhaled. "I loved you first." He hung up.

"Dang it, he hung up. Should I call him back, Toby?"

Toby peered at her.

Riley shrugged. "You're right; he's busy. I'll get even another time."

Doc Wesley cleared his throat. "You're braver than I am, Riley; I'll call Samara later. Do you still want to go? Are you ready?"

"Let's go."

When they stepped outside, Doc chuckled as people hurried to their cars and trucks. "Nothing like a deputy walking around with a ticket book to encourage people to move their vehicles. I wonder if the deputy borrowed a ticket book from the café? The sheriff's department uses an electronic, not paper, system for tickets. You'd think people would know that, wouldn't you?"

Riley smiled. "It's really effective, isn't it?"

On the way to the truck, she asked, "Who could have known about the horse appointment on Monday?"

"That is a good place to start. You, me, Maureen, and, of course, Hugo." Doc exhaled. "I'd like to say that Hugo is behind all this because he has really overstepped his bounds. I heard at the gas station this morning when I stopped to fill my tank that Hugo blamed me for canceling all his appointments because I wanted to take over the farm visits, but I forgot to check on the horse. Hugo was supposedly asking for advice on whether he should go himself, so the reputation of the Jimson Veterinary Clinic would remain unsullied."

"That's pretty slimy."

"You're right; so to answer your question, probably everyone in three counties knows. I called Hugo, and he told me he did check the horse and everything was fine after all. I'm really glad to be rid of Hugo Adams."

When they reached the truck, Doc said, "Let's take our chances and see how close to the clinic we can take the truck."

As he started the engine, Doc's phone rang. He frowned as he answered.

"Hello Kaitlyn. Yes, we're fine; no one was hurt."

While Doc Kaitlyn talked, Wesley rolled his eyes.

"What did he say his contributions would be to your practice?"

Wesley chuckled. "That's interesting, because I didn't see that at all. His opinion of himself and big ideas might be fine for a large practice, but he was not a good fit for us."

"I understand completely. We're stretched a little thin right now too, but we're better off without him; he's too much of a liability."

Wesley glanced at Riley. "Nope, not at all; she's a keeper. I didn't know that. It's definitely a small veterinary world in Georgia, isn't it? Julie Rae and I are old friends."

After Wesley hung up, he said, "Guess who called Kaitlyn and offered to help her grow her clinic."

"Nooo...not Doctor Adams? Seriously?"

"I guess his wife wasn't happy about leaving the area. Kaitlyn wanted to know what I thought, so I told her. I have more news. Doc Kaitlyn went to school with Thad Faraday; they're good friends."

Riley chuckled. "Doc Thad's wife is my best friend."

"Hugo told Kaitlyn you didn't work out well after all, especially with the rest of the staff at Jimson Veterinary Clinic, so he had to let you go. She called Thad. He told her to snap you up. She asked me if you were available; I hope it's okay that I told her no."

"That's great; I like where I am."

Wesley chuckled. "Good, maybe you can explain it to me because this is the wildest week I've ever had, and it's only Wednesday."

When they reached the clinic, the front parking lot had sheriff department cruisers and official GBI vehicles besides a few personal trucks and cars, and the fire department vehicles were gone.

"I'll park in the front lot as close to the door as I can. I'll bet the back lot is still blocked off, but you may want to sneak around the corner to check your car."

As Doc Wesley parked, Riley said, "Uh oh."

"What's wrong?"

"I think my husband is here to investigate the explosion."

"Isn't that good?"

"He'll be very thorough, but there may be a lot of glaring involved."

Doc Wesley laughed. "Not to make a value judgment or anything, but he might be entitled to a frown or two. Let's take everything to the trauma room, then we can put the items away. Actually, we may also be the targets of more disapproving looks when Maureen finds out we grabbed what we could, but didn't record exactly what we took."

"Good point; I'll do a quick inventory before I shelve anything."

Riley carried in her backpacks and the tote bag and hurried into the clinic with Toby by her side. When Toby yipped, she abruptly turned and rushed to the trauma room; she recognized the sound of footsteps behind her. After she set down her backpacks and tote on the table, she turned and smiled. "Hi, honey."

Ben's arms were crossed as he stood in the doorway with a scowl.

Riley raised her eyebrows and tried to look contrite; he strode across the room and hugged her. "You scare me all the time, and don't pull that cute look on me; I'm onto your tricks."

Riley sighed as she leaned against his chest and wrapped her arms around him. *I'm cute.*

"Maureen is convinced you and Toby saved her life, babe, but don't think that gets you off the hook."

Doc came into the trauma room and set two more bags on the table. "Don't mind me." He hurried out of the room.

Riley continued to cling to Ben. Her voice was muffled. "I have to take inventory."

When he loosened his hold, he stepped back and kissed her. "I'm the one in law enforcement; why are you the one who is always around when shots are fired or there's an explosion?"

Riley shrugged. *I'm not sure hazards of the job is the right answer.* "I guess I don't really know."

Ben exhaled. "I've got work to do; please don't make it even more complicated."

Riley watched his back as he left. *How would I make it more complicated? I suppose that would have been the wrong question to ask.*

Riley hurried to the supply closet then returned with an inventory sheet and quickly recorded all the items then returned them to their places.

After she put her backpacks in the breakroom, Riley returned the tote to Maureen and handed her the inventory sheet.

"This is what we took and what we returned to the supply closet. There's no change in the inventory. This is our list in case we need to pack for an emergency again," Riley said.

Maureen rolled her eyes. "Good cover story, Riley, but I'll let it pass because you and Toby saved me from becoming minced meat, and your husband was so relieved to see you. Is it true that things like this happen all the time with you? That's what he told the sheriff, and he asked the sheriff to keep an eye on you. I thought it was sweet, but isn't it a little over protective?"

"You'd think so, wouldn't you?" Riley cleared her throat.

Maureen snickered. "Want to hear the latest scuttlebutt? I heard we fired you but begged you to stay. The old rumor mill was pretty boring and actually even got a little rusty cranking out anything that was even remotely interesting until now."

Riley rolled her eyes. "I'm glad we got that clarified; when I went home Monday night, I wasn't sure if I was fired or I quit."

"You ready for your next assignment? Doc Peterson is in room one, and Doc Wesley is in room two. Check room one first; we'll let Doc Peterson have seniority."

Before Riley reached the first exam room, two patients came into the clinic.

"Reboot, Riley," Maureen said. "Take this folder and your patient to room three."

Riley quickly reviewed the folder then smiled at the black Doberman. "Hi, Sampson; I'm Riley, and this is Toby. We're new here. We'll make a quick stop at the scale then go to exam room three."

Sampson stepped onto the scale. "Thank you, Sampson. Got it."

When they were in the exam room, Riley said, "Your coat is so pretty." She stroked his back. "I'll take your temperature and check your ears before your rabies immunization, then you can be on your way."

Riley took his temperature. "Normal, as we all expected, right?"

Sampson grinned.

"Has anything been bothering you? Your ears? Have you been itchy?"

Sampson growled.

Riley nodded. "Okay, that makes sense."

"What is it? What's wrong?" The client asked.

Riley furrowed her brow. "Did his best friend stop going to the dog park?"

The client's eyes widened. "She did; they moved to Alabama. He was so sad, we quit going."

"It might be a good idea to pick it up again; he probably misses his other friends."

"I didn't even think about that; thank you, Riley."

Riley peered into Sampson's ears. "All clear. Quick injection, then we're done."

Riley cooed to Sampson. "You're so brave."

After his injection, she stroked his back again. "Good boy, Sampson."

"You really do have a way with dogs, Riley. We enjoyed meeting you, didn't we, Sampson?"

Sampson grinned.

When they reached Maureen's desk, Maureen said, "Here's your folder; Doc Peterson should be through in two or three minutes. I'll send him to you."

Riley quickly scanned the file then peered into the cat carrier as the middle-aged man rose when she approached them.

"Hi, Pedro. I'm Riley, and this is Toby. We're new here."

As the man carried the carrier to the exam room, he said, "Pedro is my wife's cat. She named him after an old friend of ours who is retired and lives in a condo near a beach. He captures feral cats to be immunized and spayed or neutered. He's a nice guy."

Riley nodded as she took the carrier from the man and put it on the table. She unzipped the carrier. "Pedro, I'd like to check your weight."

Pedro strolled out of the carrier. He was a small gray-striped cat and flipped his tail straight up with a slightly regal curve at the tip after he cleared the carrier. He sniffed Riley's hand that was on the table then peered over the edge at Toby and meowed.

"Nice to meet you too, Pedro; I love your manners. I'll put you on the scale then bring you back to the table. Toby can tell you I'm fast and gentle."

Pedro stared at Toby who woofed. Pedro relaxed; Riley put him on the scale.

"Up a little, but not much; that's excellent. Doc Peterson will be proud of you."

Riley stroked Pedro on his back from his head to his tail until he purred. "Temperature check," she said.

She scratched under his chin, and he purred again.

Doc Peterson came into the room. "I see you've met our Riley and obviously approve, Pedro. Let's see how you're doing."

Riley handed him the folder. "Weight's good."

Doc Peterson examined Pedro thoroughly.

"You're doing an excellent job caring for Pedro. When does your wife return from Switzerland?"

"Twelve days."

"Let's check Pedro again on Monday," Doc said. "Riley, ask Maureen to make the appointment."

"Will do; ready to go home, Pedro?" Riley asked.

Pedro marched into his carrier then meowed.

Toby grinned and yipped.

Riley laughed. "Yes, we'll be here next time you visit, but you're right, we won't be new."

"Does she always talk to animals, Doctor Peterson?" the man asked as he picked up Pedro in his carrier.

Doc smiled. "Sure does; always has from what I understand."

When Riley and the client reached Maureen's desk, Riley gave Maureen the file. "We need an appointment for Pedro next week on Monday."

When Riley returned to the exam room to clean it for the next patient, Doc Peterson joined her. "My old friend Ned told me you had a way with animals; when I told him that was great, he said I had no idea."

CHAPTER EIGHT

Riley put away the cleaning supplies. "When I was a kid, I thought everyone understood animals, just like they understood people. I felt sorry for the kids who didn't when they made fun of me because I thought they were missing out."

Doc chuckled. "I can see that. I bet Ned I wouldn't be surprised because I'm too old to be amazed by anything. But I've lost the bet, and now I owe him a bottle of his favorite whiskey. My wife has been hoping we could visit Ned and Lizzie, so she'll be happy when I tell her we have an excuse."

Doc and Riley strolled together to Maureen's desk.

Maureen said, "I have two more patients that are on their way in. We're in much better shape than I expected as far as catching up. Doc Wesley told me to schedule the vet tech interviews back to back, so I'm not counting on him for any patients the rest of the day."

"I'd like to put up my feet for a few minutes, Riley. I'll be in Doctor Adams's office. Doctor Adams definitely knew how to make an office comfortable. Do you mind coming to get me after you finish your assessments?" Doctor Peterson stretched his back.

"Not at all; that's how I'm used to working."

After Doctor Peterson left, Maureen said, "I didn't want to say anything in front of the doc, but do you think you could make me an ice pack for my arm? It's throbbing."

"I'll be right back."

Riley found a box of plastic storage bags in a cabinet in the breakroom. She filled one with ice cubes then refilled the ice tray with water. She found a box of clean rags and wrapped her improvised ice pack with the cloth.

When she returned to Maureen's desk, Maureen placed her right forearm flat on her desk and sighed. "The support feels good."

Riley carefully placed the icepack over Maureen's wrist. "You're going to be miserable tonight if you don't get a brace. Why don't you call your doctor to see if they can squeeze you in? Gina said she'd take you, and if you have the folders for our two patients, we'll get by."

"I'll do that, but first we've got a patient coming in that's really sick. Here's the folder."

Riley read the file. "I'll alert Doc Peterson and get a few things set up in the first exam room. Let me know when you see them in the parking lot."

Riley hurried to Doctor Adams' former office and tapped on the doorframe. "Doc, we have a sick patient on the way in."

"Who is it?"

"A chihuahua, his name is Murphy." She handed him the folder. "I'll get exam room one set up for a breathing treatment just in case. We'll let you know when they arrive."

"Thanks for the heads up, Riley." Doc rose to his feet and returned the folder to her. "Murphy is one of our fragile ones. I'll pull together the medications we might need if you'll take care of the equipment."

Riley hurried to exam room one and put the equipment they might need on the medical tray.

Maureen called out, "We have our patient."

Riley hurried to the front to greet the lethargic chihuahua the client carried in her arms. When the chihuahua coughed, Riley frowned at the harsh, dry, honking sound.

"I'm Riley, Murphy. We're going to take good care of you." Riley held out her arms, and the client nodded as Riley gently took Murphy from her and headed toward the exam room.

On the way, Riley said, "Doc Peterson will meet us there. I'll weigh you and take your temperature, Murphy, but I'm fast."

Riley stroked Murphy then gently placed him on the scale. "Doctor Peterson will want to know how much you weigh, so he can give you medicine for your cough."

After she took his temperature, Riley recorded it. "Your temperature is slightly elevated."

Doctor Peterson came into the exam room; Riley showed him the weight and temperature she had recorded.

Doctor Peterson gently examined Murphy's gums. "Let's give Murphy a little oxygen to go with his medicine."

Riley quickly finished setting up the blow-by treatment with the oxygen. She stroked Murphy's back while she held the small oxygen mask near his face.

When Doc Peterson alerted Riley with a nod at the medication as he drew it up into a syringe, Riley said, "Doc Peterson is going to give you some medicine that will help you breathe better. He's as gentle as I am."

While Doc Peterson injected the medication, Riley continued, "See if you can breathe in the extra air and hold it for a second or two, Murphy; that will help you relax and feel better."

As Riley continued to stroke his back and speak softly, Murphy breathed in and became more relaxed with each breath.

The client exhaled in relief. "He began coughing around lunchtime, so I gave him some of his cough medicine. When his cough became worse this afternoon, and he could barely lift his head, I called Maureen. She said to come in right away."

"We're glad you did," Doc Peterson said. "How was he yesterday?"

"He seemed a little tired. I didn't worry too much about it because my sister and her family spent a few days with us. In fact, I was tired myself when they left early yesterday morning. I think I let his routine slip, though. I was late on at least one dose of his medicine, which threw me off, and he was probably overstimulated with all the commotion. My sister and her husband have four children ranging in ages from three to nine, and of course, they brought their two dogs."

Doc nodded. "That's probably it; Riley, let's get some x-rays."

Riley gently scratched behind Murphy's ear. "I'll roll you to the x-ray room and take a few x-rays for Doc Peterson, and then we'll come right back. You'll be comfortable because I'll keep the mask close to your face; you'll still hear the air blowing, so you'll know it's working to help you breathe better."

Riley lifted him onto the rolling cart then wheeled him to the x-ray room. After she took the x-rays, she rolled Murphy back to the exam room; Doc Peterson left to review the x-rays.

Toby yipped; Murphy whined.

The client frowned. "Is everything okay?

Riley smiled. "Murphy's feeling better, but he'd rather be home."

"So would I, Murphy. I'm really sorry I forgot your medicine."

Murphy yipped.

"What did he say, Riley?"

"He should have reminded you, but he was having fun with the kids."

The client smiled. "They loved you, Murphy. They said you were the best dog, and my sister said you were a good boy."

Murphy smiled and closed his eyes.

"He's feeling much better, and much more relaxed."

Doctor Peterson came into the room. "The x-rays were good; his lungs are clear, and his trachea is fine.

I don't want to adjust his medication because it's been doing its job, except for this setback. I'd like to see him in a week to see if we do need to adjust his dosage."

On the way to Maureen's desk, Murphy growled. The client raised his eyebrows. "I thought you said you were ready to go home; what, you want Toby and Riley to go with you?"

Riley giggled. "That's exactly what he said."

Toby woofed twice.

"That sounded like 'boof' to me," the client said. "I guess I need an interpretation."

"Toby said we should have a Jimson Veterinary Clinic meet up day at the dog park sometime."

"I can arrange that," Maureen said. "I'll go along as the chaperone."

"Follow up in a week, please, Maureen." Riley placed the folder on Maureen's desk.

After Riley cleaned the exam room, she joined Maureen and Toby at the receptionist's desk. "Where's our second patient?"

"The client is an old friend of Doc Peterson's, so they're probably chatting over old times. They're in room two, if you want to check up on them."

"Have you called your doctor?"

Maureen picked up the phone and dialed. "Yes."

Riley cleared her throat as she sat in the chair next to the desk and crossed her arms. "I'll rest a minute before I check on Doc Peterson."

Maureen disconnected. "I'll call my doctor's office."

When someone answered, Maureen said, "I don't suppose you have any time for a last minute appointment, do you?"

"She broke her arm," Riley added in a loud voice.

"That was a nosy..." Maureen sighed. "Yes, we're pretty sure I broke my arm in the explosion."

"That's lovely." Maureen growled as she glared at Riley. "I'll be there."

Maureen hung up then made another call. "Gina, I have a doctor's appointment in ten minutes. You can't get away to take me, can you? Okay, bye."

"If Gina's not here in five minutes, I'll take you," Riley said.

"Maybe I got the wrong number," Maureen mumbled.

"Gina, you sound busy, so if you can't take me to the doctor's office in ten minutes it's okay." Maureen stared at her phone. "She hung up on me."

"I'll check on Doc Peterson."

Riley opened the door as Doc and the client shook hands.

"See you at church; thanks for the advice." The client slipped his elderly orange cat into the carrier.

When Gina rushed into the office, Maureen turned off her computer. "Riley, if you have any patients, just leave me the patient's name and your notes, and remind Doc Wesley to change the phone to after hours."

Riley sat at Maureen's desk, and Toby flopped down at her feet.

Doc Wesley strolled down the hall and stopped at Doc Adams' office. "Are you still here?"

"I was hanging around to hear the results of your interviews."

Riley rolled her eyes. *He was my bodyguard.*

Doc Wesley said, "If you aren't expecting a patient, lock the front door and join us, Riley."

When Riley returned, she stood in the doorway.

"Come on in," Doc Wesley said."

"I'm good right here," Riley said.

Doctor Peterson rose. "Now that you mention it, the room does have a foul odor. Let's go to the breakroom."

When the three of them were in the breakroom, Doc Wesley said, "I'll call someone to box up Adams' things and steam clean the room tomorrow."

"I appreciate it." Doc Peterson winked at Riley.

"Thank you," she whispered.

After they sat at the table, Doc Wesley handed each of them two sheets of paper. "I'll give you a minute to review their resumes."

When Doc Peterson said, "We have an experienced vet tech, and the other is fresh out of school. Are you leaning toward bringing in the one with experience?"

Doc Wesley nodded. "Based on the resumes, my first thought was that it would be nice to have someone who could hit the door running. What would you do, based on their resumes, Riley?"

"Call their references," she said.

Doc Peterson raised his eyebrows. "Where were you when we hired Hugo Adams?"

Doc Wesley nodded. "He's got you there, Riley. I talked to both candidates. The short version is that the experienced person is used to being in charge. Maureen would not be impressed, and from what I've seen so far, Riley, you are used to working as part of a team. The recent graduate, Micco, has three years' experience as a volunteer at a county animal shelter when he was in high school, which he neglected to put on his resume because someone told him that wasn't work experience. I'm leaning towards Micco, but I'll call his references right away since Riley mentioned it. I'll talk to Maureen in the morning because I would like to have two vet techs in the office."

"Maureen and I will have the new vet tech trained in a week," Riley said.

"Either trained or gone, am I right?" Doc Wesley smiled.

Riley shrugged and returned his smile.

"And what about replacing Adams?" Doc Peterson asked.

"That's not moving along as quickly as the vet techs," Doc Wesley said.

"If you are open to another recent graduate, I have some contacts," Doc Peterson said. "In fact, I wouldn't mind doing a little hands-on mentoring for a month or two."

Doc Wesley's eyes widened. "That would be perfect. I was shying away from someone straight out of school because I knew I wouldn't have time to provide any oversight at all, which wouldn't be fair to anyone."

Riley's phone buzzed with a text; she glanced at her phone and read the text from Ben. "On my way home; I'll pick up something for supper."

"Ben's on his way home," she said.

"Thanks for being here, Riley," Doc Wesley said. "I talked to Micco's references, and he's as good as we thought, so I offered him the position, and he'll start on Monday."

"That is great news." Riley rose to pick up her lunch bag and backpacks. "Doc, I'm supposed to remind you to change the phones to after hours."

"I'll do that right now; if I say I'll do it later, it won't happen."

After Doc Wesley left the breakroom, Doc Peterson asked, "Are you doing okay, Riley?"

Riley sighed. "My husband would claim this has been a normal week for me, except for the tornado. Toby and I are fine. See you in the morning."

His eyes twinkled, and his dimples deepened when he smiled. "I wouldn't miss it for the world."

On the way to the cottage, Riley said, "If we have time when we get home, I'd like to check Claire's recipes for simple things we can cook. I'd like to have a grocery list tomorrow, so Ben won't have to pick up something every day for our evening meal. We've got big shopping plans for Saturday, so maybe I should try to plan meals through Monday." Riley glanced at Toby. "After all, isn't that was normal people do?"

Riley rolled her eyes while Toby howled.

After she turned off the road at the short graveled driveway, she exhaled as she parked in front of the white cottage. "Welcome home to us, Toby."

When she opened the back door, Toby dashed around the house then waited on the front stoop for her. Riley frowned at her work backpack. "There's no reason to carry it in because I don't need it inside; I need it in my car," she muttered.

She picked up her backpack and lunch bag then went inside. After Toby ate, they went outside to watch for Ben.

While Toby sniffed the yard for any wildlife trespassers and Riley sat on a step, her phone rang.

"Hi, Maureen. What did the doctor say?"

"My arm is broken; she put it in a brace which is really nice because it doesn't hurt now that it's supported. After the swelling goes down, I'll see the orthopedic doctor for a cast. So far, this is not fun."

"I'm really sorry, but I'm glad it wasn't any worse."

"Thanks to you and Toby. Doc wants to hire one more vet tech for the office, so I better get busy. Are you doing okay?"

"Yes, Toby and I are home, and Ben's on his way."

"Good; I'll see you in the morning."

After forty-five minutes, Riley smacked her fourth mosquito as the sun hung low on the horizon. "I'm being eaten alive; we have to go in."

Toby followed her inside. "Ben should have been here by now. Do I text or call him or wait for him to call me?"

Riley called Ben, but his phone rolled to voicemail. She sent a text. "Are you okay?"

Riley stood at the window with her arms crossed. "What do we do, Toby? We could go look for him, I guess. What if..." Riley shuddered. "I can't think about what ifs. I'll leave him a note, and we'll drive to his office then come back here. Why don't I have a number I can call if I can't reach him?"

Riley scribbled a quick note: "Called and texted. Going to your office. Will come back here." She frowned then added the time.

She grabbed a bottle of water and a package of sliced Swiss cheese from the refrigerator, and a box of crackers from the cupboard then dropped them into a grocery sack. "Just in case...I don't know what, but just in case."

Riley and Toby hurried to her car. As she sped on the highway toward Ben's office, she glanced at the speedometer and eased up on the accelerator. "I should go slower so I don't miss him if he's broken down on the side of the road."

When her phone rang, Riley slammed on the brakes, and Toby slid on the seat and growled.

"Sorry."

She snatched up her phone. "Hello, sweetie. Where are you?"

Ben's chuckle was strained. "Halfway home. Somebody set a corn silo on fire and it blew. I was two miles away and saw the fire in the sky. When I pulled over as close as I could get to call it in, it exploded."

Ben's voice cracked, and he briefly paused. "There were cows in the field. Some of them didn't make it. Those that could run stampeded; the rest of them hid in the woods. The farmer and I have been hunting cows and herding them to the barn. My truck's on the side of the road; I left the keys in the ignition. Could you come pick up the groceries? I'd feel more comfortable if you'd lock the truck and toss the keys into the bed; it would be really embarrassing if my truck was stolen while I was chasing cows. I'm not sure when I'll be home, but I suspect it will be late."

"We can do that. I love you more."

"Maybe so, but I have seniority on bragging rights, babe, because I loved you first." Riley heard the smile in his voice before he hung up.

Riley exhaled. "He's okay, Toby, except he should have called earlier, and he knows it. We'll still leave him the snack we packed."

When Riley saw the line of cars and trucks alongside the road ahead of her and how many were leaving, she pulled into the next gate that led to a field and made a U-turn and parked on the shoulder facing home. "Ben's truck has to be in there somewhere. Ready for a walk, Toby?"

Toby yipped.

Riley zipped up her coat and grabbed the bag with snacks, then pulled out her flashlight and stuck it into her pocket. "I'm not sure I am."

When they neared a small group that leaned against the fence as they stared across the field, Toby quietly growled.

"I'm feeling like there's something a little off too," Riley whispered.

As Riley came closer to the group of three men who had their backs to her, a man said, "Boss told us he was going to give us a show, and he did. Aren't you next? Can you top him?"

A man removed his ball cap and exposed his bald head and a snake tattoo on the back of his right hand.

He grunted as waved his hat around his face. "What do you care? Let's go; skeeters are getting bad."

She stepped off the road and into the trees and watched until they left. "I don't think they saw me, do you, Toby?"

Toby yipped.

Riley nodded. "We'll stay in the woods until we see Ben's truck."

The next group was talking about the type of corn that was in the silo. "Good riddance," a man said. "How would you up the ante if you were next?"

"Looky-loos are leaving; we gotta get outta here too."

"Well, he's not all talk like we thought, is he?" The first man opened the driver's door of a car and climbed in.

When Riley and Toby reached Ben's truck, there weren't any other vehicles nearby, but the cloying odor reminiscent of burned corn tortillas hung like a cloud over the area.

Riley put the sack she had brought on the driver's seat of the truck then pulled out the three sacks of groceries before she locked the truck and dropped the keys in the truck's bed.

She trudged back to her car on the side of the road. "I wish I had gloves. I'm glad we didn't park any farther away; these groceries aren't only heavy, they are awkward to carry."

After she put the grocery bags on the front seat of her car and opened the back door for Toby, she sent Ben a text. "Mission accomplished."

He replied, "Hope to be home in an hour or less."

On the way home, Riley frowned. "It sounded like the silo fire was deliberately set to impress a group, like an initiation rite or something."

When they arrived home, Riley furrowed her brow as she put away the groceries. "I wonder what Ben had in mind for the pork chops."

She sent a text to Claire. "How do I cook thick pork chops for supper tonight?"

Clare replied almost immediately. "Baked. Add rice and a vegetable or salad. Here's a link."

Riley read the recipe and smiled. "We can do this, Toby. I just need to figure out my timing."

She assembled her ingredients and prepared the pork chops. She stared at the pan. "I don't want to put them in too early, but I don't want to wait until Ben gets here."

Riley tapped her fingers on the countertop, then turned on the oven to preheat and sent a text to Ben. "Let me know when you're close to leaving."

While she measured the rice, her phone buzzed a text from Ben.

"On my way to my truck."

After she put the pork chops into the oven, her hand shook as she put a pan of water on the stove to boil. She watched until the tiny bubbles became larger bubbles that danced.

When she added the rice to the boiling water, Riley exhaled. "I don't know why I'm so nervous about cooking. I just need to practice."

Riley set the table then put broccoli in the microwave to cook after Ben arrived. She inhaled the flavorful aroma of the pork chops. "At least it smells good."

When she heard the crunch of tires on the driveway, she ran outside, and Toby followed her.

Ben hopped out of his truck with a sack in his hand, and she tackled him with a hug.

He laughed. "Let's get you inside before you realize you're freezing."

When they went into the house with their arms around each other, Ben said, "Wow. The house smells amazing." He kissed her. "You're amazing."

"We have a few minutes; when the timer goes off, the pork chops have to rest."

Ben put the sack on the table. "Works for me; I have to change clothes. Do I have time for a shower?"

"Go right ahead."

When Ben turned off the water in the shower, Riley stirred butter into the rice and plated their food.

While they ate, Riley told Ben about the conversations she heard on her way to his truck.

Ben frowned. "Did you get a good look at any of the men?"

"I was trying to keep from being seen, and they had their backs to me, but one man took off his ball cap to shoo away mosquitoes. He was bald and had a snake tattoo on the back of his hand."

"I'm glad they didn't see you; I do need to document what you heard."

When Ben leaned forward to rise, Riley said, "Eat first; I'll repeat it all for you later."

Ben nodded and took another bite of his pork chop. "This is delicious, babe. Tell me about work; how was it? I mean, besides the explosion."

"Doctor Peterson agreed to work part time; I like him. He asked for Hugo Adams' office to be cleaned after it was cleared of Adams' things."

"Ah, fumigated," Ben said.

Riley giggled. "Exactly; Doc Wesley interviewed two vet techs and plans to hire the newly graduated one; he said he'd like to have two vet techs in the office, so I can go with him on farm visits. Maureen will find him more to interview. Doc Peterson offered to mentor a recent veterinarian graduate, so that opens up more possibilities for candidates."

"Sounds like your job will be what you had thought it would be."

"It really is; what about your job?"

"It's more challenging than anything else I've ever done, and I love it. I'll always be grateful to Uncle Seth for suggesting I get a degree in biochemistry in case law enforcement wasn't what I wanted to do after all. Turns out my degree is a big plus in law enforcement."

While Riley cleared the table and Ben loaded the dishwasher, Riley's phone rang.

She raised her eyebrows as she answered. "Hi, Maureen. Are you okay?"

"I hate to call so late, but we have two candidates that are available for interviews tomorrow morning at the office. One can be there at eight, and the other at eight thirty. Doc Peterson will be in at eight thirty; could you talk to our eight o'clock candidate then hand her off to Doc Peterson and talk to the eight thirty vet tech?"

"I could do that."

"Good; Doc Wesley is hoping you'll give each one a tour and ask some questions about their experience. He'll be at the office at nine and talk with them after they see Doc Peterson. You and Doc Wesley have a farm visit at four, so I'm overloading the morning after ten o'clock and the early afternoon until three thirty with patients. Please say yes."

"I'll be there before eight. Do you have resumes you can send me, so I can read them before tomorrow?"

"Seeing as how I've already set up an email to you with two attachments ready to send, I think I might be able to manage that." Maureen giggled as she hung up.

"Maureen scheduled two vet techs to interview tomorrow at eight and eight thirty, so I'll leave around seven thirty, which isn't that much earlier than we left this morning."

"I'll put chicken in the slow cooker in the morning and pick up dinner rolls on my way home," Ben said. "How about a fire in the fireplace with a cookie or two, a good book, good company, and a glass of wine tonight?"

"Sounds relaxing."

"I'll get the fire going then tell me what you heard and saw when you came to pick up the groceries from my truck so I can document it before we get too relaxed."

After Riley told Ben what the men said while he took notes, he kissed her. "Now wine and cookies; we don't have any books, do we?"

"They're all at your parents' house, but I could stop at the library before I come home tomorrow or Friday and pick up a couple of books for us. Any requests?"

"Nothing to do with my job or yours; surprise me." Ben opened a bottle of wine and poured two glasses, while Riley pulled out three cookies from the sack.

When Ben handed Riley her glass of wine, she gave him two cookies.

While she sipped her wine and finished her cookie, Riley giggled. "Surprise you? Is your brain too fried to think?"

Ben set down his wine glass, put his arm around her, and massaged her shoulder. "I can come up with an idea or two."

He leaned down and kissed the nape of her neck.

CHAPTER NINE

The next morning, Riley sighed as she sipped her coffee while Ben pulled out his favorite frying pan.

He frowned as he set the frying pan on the stove. "You seem a little down, babe; what's going on?"

Riley shrugged. "I don't know; I just have a bad feeling about today."

Ben rubbed her shoulders, and she put her hands on his. He nuzzled her neck then kissed her. "Last night was amazing."

"It was, wasn't it?" Riley sighed as she peered into her empty cup.

"Jump into the shower; you'll feel better." Ben opened the refrigerator.

"I'll at least smell nice." Riley's smile was weak as she rose from the table.

While Riley showered, Ben cooked breakfast.

After she was dressed, she hurried to the kitchen.

"How was it?"

"I smell better."

Ben smiled as he set their breakfast plates on the table.

After they ate, Ben showered while Riley fixed their lunches and put them in their lunch bags.

Ben hurried into the kitchen and reached into the refrigerator for bottles of water to go with their lunches.

When he turned, Riley stepped in front of him and clung to him.

Ben held her tight. "What's wrong, babe?"

"I wish we could stay home; it's not going to be a good day."

"Are you worried about me, Toby, or you?"

"No."

"Then we'll be okay." Ben gently lifted her chin with his fingertips so he could meet her gaze.

Riley exhaled. "We'll be okay."

Ben leaned down and kissed her. "Are you sure?"

Riley leaned against his chest and growled, "We have to be okay."

Ben patted her bottom. "Go to work, sweet thang, and put those vet techs through the wringer."

Riley giggled. "Like that's my usual technique."

"Actually, it is, babe; you're just so nice about it that nobody knows that's what you're doing. What about your long johns?"

"They're in my backpack." Riley secured her pistol in its holster, slipped on her cozy long-sleeved scrub top, layered with her thickest coat, and gathered her backpack and lunch bag. "Ready to go, Toby?"

As she started her car and waited for the defroster to clear the frost from her windshield, Riley said, "I know I told Ben we'd be okay; I'm not so sure what's got me so unsettled, but I'm worried about today. Do I tell him he should stay home?"

Toby yipped.

Riley scowled. "I don't care if his coworkers will call me the crazy Dog Lady. Is it Ben? Will he be safer at home?"

Toby growled.

"Fine; I won't let my feelings overrun common sense, but isn't it common sense if I have a feeling that someone is going to be hurt? I just need to know who."

On the road to the clinic, Riley said, "You know what's bothering me? It's those men from yesterday who talked like they were spectators at a sick, criminal competition to destroy property. One man said 'up the ante.' Their targets have seemed random, but are they really?" Riley groaned. "My stomach is turning over from thinking about it."

She lowered her window an inch for fresh air, and the frigid blast felt like an icy slap. After Riley caught her breath, she breathed in through her nose and exhaled with pursed lips until she shivered from the cold and closed the window.

When Riley reached the clinic, she peered at a lone, unoccupied truck that was parked at the edge of the front parking lot then shook her head. *Somebody must have had engine trouble or run out of fuel.*

After she parked behind the clinic, she said, "There has to be a reason for the senseless destruction; I just don't know what it is yet."

Toby rushed to the back door while Riley slung her backpack strap over her shoulder and grabbed her lunch bag. After she unlocked the back door, she and Toby went into the clinic. Toby dashed to the front while she put her lunch bag in the refrigerator and hung her backpack on a peg before she poured a cup of coffee and joined Toby and Maureen.

Maureen removed her headset. "I'm glad you're here early; there's a truck parked in front of the building that was here when I arrived. I'm worried that someone is casing the joint."

"I saw it; my first thought was somebody must have run out of fuel or had engine trouble overnight."

"I suppose you're right; it made me nervous, but everything is getting on my nerves lately." Maureen gave Toby a treat. "Except Toby, and maybe you."

Riley giggled. "Makes sense to me; I'm getting on my own nerves. Are we still a go for the two vet tech candidates?"

"Yes, we are; both of them have called to confirm, which is a huge plus as far as I'm concerned."

"You want me to check the truck?" Riley asked.

"I called the sheriff's office; you could check if you wanted to, but it's cold out there."

Riley grabbed her coat. "If it's somebody sleeping one off, they might want to take off before the deputy arrives."

When they went outside, Toby raced to the driver's side door, peered inside, then barked.

Riley stopped. "Are you sure? Anybody we know?"

Toby growled and dashed back to her.

"The bald-headed man?" Riley whispered. "Let's go back inside."

Riley and Toby returned to the clinic. "You were right, Maureen. It was too cold; we'll let the deputy be in charge of telling the driver to move on."

Riley hurried to the breakroom and hung up her coat. She kneeled beside Toby and hugged him. "Thank you, Toby. I'll let the professionals handle this one."

When Riley returned to Maureen's desk, she said, "Call our eight o'clock vet tech and tell her to park in the back parking lot. I'll meet her back there, and we'll go straight to the breakroom and chat for a bit before we tour the clinic."

"That's a great idea; you'll save at least a good three or four minutes. I'll tell both of them."

When Maureen picked up the phone, Riley went to the breakroom and texted Ben. "Time for a quick chat?"

She exhaled when her phone rang.

"Hi, sweetie."

"Hi, babe. You're not fooling me; this is not a casual call."

"There was a truck in the front parking lot when we arrived at the clinic this morning. Maureen called the sheriff's office. Toby told me the bald man from last night was in the truck."

Riley cleared her throat. "I didn't check; just thought you'd like a heads-up."

"Thanks, babe. Deceased, do you think?"

"That's what Toby said."

"I'll be ready to leave when the sheriff's department calls us." Ben paused. "Tell Toby thank you for me. I love you all the time." Ben hung up.

"I'll love you forever, sweetheart," Riley whispered.

While Riley waited for the first candidate, she reviewed the two resumes. "The vet techs have from one to three years of experience, so they should know what they are doing."

Five minutes before eight, Toby yipped. "Thanks for letting me know. Let's go meet Willa."

Riley opened the door as a tall, slender woman with her blonde hair pulled back into a ponytail approached the back door.

"Hi, Willa; I'm Riley, and this is Toby."

"Hi, Toby." Willa put out her hand for a sniff then scratched his ears. "It's nice to meet you, Riley."

"Come into the breakroom. Care for any coffee?"

"I've had my quota for the day," Willa said.

"Tell me about your current clinic," Riley said. "What's it like?"

"We're open Monday through Saturday. It's a fairly busy clinic. We have five veterinarians, ten vet techs, and twelve vet assistants. We also have four groomers, but they are a separate group."

"How does that work?"

"Each veterinarian has their own team of one vet tech and two vet assistants. The teams are kind of permanent, depending on vacations and illnesses; team members occasionally switch around for coverage as needed. The rest of the vet techs have specialties."

"Does that work well?"

"It does overall; the vets have different styles, which is why they are assigned their own team, and the specialty vet techs are highly skilled and cross-trained."

"We're a smaller clinic, but we may grow to two or three veterinarians. Ready for a tour?"

When they went into the x-ray room, Willa said, "This is newer equipment, isn't it? We have a tech who specializes in x-rays."

Riley nodded then continued to the exam rooms. "This is our trauma room."

"It's a little smaller than I've seen, but it's really clean," Willa said.

"The vet tech cleans the room and prepares it for the next patient," Riley said. "Right now, that's me."

"So, you do everything?" Willa asked. "What's your specialty?"

Riley furrowed her brow. "I guess you might say diagnosis and calming patients are my specialties, but I care for all aspects of each patient from the time they come into the clinic until they leave, except for scheduling and billing. What about you?"

"I do all the lab work, but I'm also cross-trained in splints and casts," Willa said.

Sounds boring. Riley side-glanced at Willa. "Do you miss the daily patient contact?"

Willa nodded. "Sometimes."

While Riley showed Willa the second exam room she asked, "Do you have a pet at home?"

Willa smiled. "No, I would, but my landlord doesn't allow pets."

"What interested you about the Jimson Veterinary Clinic?"

"Honestly, I wanted to see what the opportunities were, so I thought I'd shop around a bit."

When they approached the first exam room, Riley said, "I think Doctor Peterson is ready to talk to you."

Riley led Willa to the office that now belonged to Doctor Peterson. "You'll see Doctor Cooper after you and Doctor Peterson talk. Thank you for coming in on such short notice; it was nice to meet you."

After they shook hands and Riley introduced Willa to Doctor Peterson, Riley returned to Maureen's desk.

"What do you think?" Maureen whispered. "I think she's my favorite."

"She's very smart," Riley said. "Toby and I will wait for our next vet tech in the breakroom. That worked out fine."

When Toby alerted Riley, the two of them went to the back door. A slightly overweight young man who was above average height but not as tall as Willa climbed out of his truck. He smiled when he saw Toby, and Toby grinned.

"Hi, Owen, this is Toby, and I'm Riley."

Owen rubbed Toby's chin then strode to the back door with his hand out. After they shook, he said, "Thanks for taking the time to meet with me."

After they were in the breakroom, Riley asked, "Would you care for some coffee?"

"Heck, yeah. I have coffee in my blood."

Riley poured two cups.

"How long have you been here, Riley?" Owen asked.

Riley smiled. *Straight to the point.* "Today is my fourth day; my husband's job moved us here, and my previous employer recommended me to Doctor Cooper. What about you?"

"I've been at the clinic outside of Macon almost a year, and I love it, but my sister and her husband were killed in a crash a month ago. My parents have three small children to raise, and I'd like to help."

"They live nearby?"

"They own a farm about ten miles north of here."

"Tell me about the clinic where you work."

Owen smiled. "We have three veterinarians, four vet techs, and a brilliant receptionist. We take turns filling in for each other. The receptionist desk isn't my favorite because I can't bounce around, but I can do it and not mess up. Our receptionist keeps the flow moving. It's kind of a first-available system unless we get a sudden emergency." He shrugged. "I guess that's not for everybody. Some people like more structure, but it works, as far as I'm concerned."

"Ready for a tour?"

"Yes, ma'am."

She rolled her eyes. "Call me Riley."

"Sorry, ma'am. Riley."

When they stopped at the x-ray room, Owen said, "We have this same equipment. Have you used it yet? It's really easy and nothing like the old clunker I learned on in vet tech school."

"I have; it's a lot newer than I was used to, but you're right, it is easy to use, especially compared to vet tech school equipment."

Riley led him to the trauma room.

Owen surveyed the room. "You know my hands are itching to open drawers and cabinets to see where everything is."

Riley shrugged. "We have a little time; go ahead."

After Owen peered into drawers and cabinets and occasionally asked questions, he said, "I'd have to go through the room one more time, then I'd feel more comfortable. So, is there enough business for two vet techs? What's the plan?"

"The plan is to have two or three vet techs in the clinic. I'll be going on farm visits with Doctor Cooper after another veterinarian is hired."

"Wow, that's exciting to be on the ground floor of growth like that. Do you like farm visits?" Owen asked as they went into the second exam room.

"I love them," Riley said. "What about you?"

"I've never done any; I think I need more experience before I go into the field. How many years have you been a vet tech?"

"Now you're making me think..." Riley furrowed her brow. "It's been almost four years; might be getting close to five."

After Riley showed Owen the first exam room, she said, "It's time for me to hand you off to Doctor Peterson. I enjoyed talking to you."

"You too; thanks for your time. I know I asked a lot of questions, but I love to learn."

Riley led him to Doctor Peterson's office and introduced him to Doc. When she returned to Maureen's desk, Maureen said, "Deputy Contrero said a GBI agent would like to talk to you."

Riley glanced at the parking lot and whispered, "It's crawling with cops out there, isn't it?"

Maureen snorted-laughed. "Honey, you are so funny; I'm your alibi if you need one."

Riley giggled. "You never know; I'll grab my coat."

After Riley and Toby went outside, Toby dashed to Ben. Ben stroked Toby's back and talked to him then smiled as he met Riley's gaze.

He strode to her and saluted her with two fingers then put his arm around her. "Do you mind telling me if the deceased is the same man you saw last night? If you'd rather not, I understand."

"I don't mind if you're with me."

"Wouldn't be anywhere else."

He walked her to the car where two more GBI agents waited for them.

Riley glanced at the back seat and a few small tree limbs on the floor before she examined the body. "His bald head is the same shape as the man on the side of the road last night at the corn silo fire, and that's the same snake tattoo on his right hand as the man last night."

"Thank you, Mrs. Carter," one agent said. "We appreciate it."

Ben continued with his arm around Riley as he accompanied her to the clinic door.

She whispered, "Ben, I think there was a small branch from a cherry tree in the back seat of the truck."

"We finally have a link between at least one murder and one of our terrorist acts, thanks to you, babe." He put his hands on her shoulders and gazed at her. "Don't do it again."

Riley rolled her eyes. "Didn't you hear what I said?"

He kissed her. "Love you, babe. First and always. Go inside."

"Love you more," she muttered as she opened the door and Toby dashed inside.

When she joined Maureen at the desk, she asked, "Do you have folders for our farm visits? I want to put the addresses in my phone, so we don't get lost."

"I won't ask what that was about, but I saw you fraternizing with the enemy."

Riley flipped her hair. "It's my foolproof interrogation technique."

Maureen chuckled. "Here are your three folders."

"I'll be in the breakroom. Holler if you need me."

"You know I will."

While Riley saved the addresses to her phone, Doctors Cooper and Peterson joined her in the breakroom.

"What do we think?" Doc Wesley asked.

"I'll go first," Doc Peterson said. "Willa doesn't have the experience we need, but neither does Owen. Willa had beautifully manicured nails. Owen had dirt under his. I'm leaning toward dirt."

Doc Wesley smiled. "What about you, Riley?"

"Willa wouldn't be happy here and wouldn't stay long. She's used to a much larger clinic with a great deal of structure, which we don't have and never will. Owen is eager to learn and has family in the area. He'd be here for the long haul. I vote for dirt, but check references."

Doc Wesley laughed. "I agree. Dirt it is. I'll check Owen's references before we leave. Next, I need to find a veterinarian that can hold a candle to Owen."

Doctor Peterson rose. "It's a pretty high standard; good luck, Wesley."

"Hey, Doc Wesley," Maureen called out.

"We need an intercom system," Doc muttered.

"Coming."

"We'll back you up." Doctor Peterson motioned for Riley to follow Doc Wesley.

When the three of them joined Maureen at her desk, she said, "I'm glad all three of you are here. I just talked to Micco, and he'll be here tomorrow morning at nine thirty so he can meet everyone and get a tour of the clinic."

"That's a great idea," Doc Wesley said.

Maureen smiled. "It was Micco's idea; he called and asked if it was possible. I wish I'd thought of it first."

Doc Wesley cleared his throat. "While we're together, we have one more item to discuss. We all saw the truck parked in our front lot this morning. Maureen called it in, and a sheriff's deputy found a deceased man in the driver's seat. Georgia Bureau of Investigation assured me the incident has nothing to do with the clinic, so if any of our clients want to discuss it, please assure them we are safe, and so are they, and we don't have any inside information. Right, Maureen?"

"That's correct; thank you. I didn't want to bring it up, but I wasn't certain what to say to our clients."

Riley lowered her head and furrowed her brow to hide her skepticism. *Maureen wasn't sure what to say? Please.*

"Are you staying, Toby?" Riley asked.

Toby trotted to the back door.

"Are you sure, Toby?"

Toby yipped.

"I guess Toby's going with us. Is that okay with you, Doc?"

"I'll be outclassed by two experts, but I'll claim I was smart enough to bring them along, so let's get moving." Doc Wesley smiled.

Riley hurried to the breakroom to grab her backpack. After she changed into her long johns, she returned to the breakroom, put her lunch bag inside her backpack, put on her warm jacket, and zipped it. She picked up Toby's water bowl and bottled water then rushed to the back door where Toby waited for her.

After Riley pulled out her work backpack from her car, Toby trotted alongside her as she struggled with her load to Doc's truck. Riley opened the back door for Toby and tossed in her work backpack; when she set his water bowl and bottled water on the floor, she exhaled. *Doc's truck is almost warm.*

She hopped into the front passenger's seat, put her backpack at her feet, and fastened her seatbelt. "Ready when you are, Doc."

"Our first visit is back to the mules," Doc said. "Is that what you show?"

"Sure is. It's an annual checkup, so hopefully this is a simple vaccinate and check all the mules. Won't that take us a while?"

"Not if we split duties." Doc's eyes twinkled. "I learned that from you. How would we do that?"

Riley rolled her eyes. "The simplest would be if we started with the first mule together. After you've examined the mule, I'll vaccinate while you move on to begin the next examination, then I'll join you."

"I like that because if I've missed anything, you'll be my second set of eyes and ears."

While they were on their way to their first farm visit, Riley's phone rang. "It's from Maureen."

When she answered, Maureen said, "Lisa's husband called me. He said her medical team woke Lisa this morning to see how she was doing."

"Shall I put you on speakerphone so Doc can hear?" Riley glanced at Doc who nodded.

"Thank you. Nash said her doctor slowly decreased the amount of medication they'd used to put her into the medically induced coma, so she could wake up gradually. The doctor warned him she might be agitated when she woke, but he still wasn't prepared when she began screaming and thrashing as she tried to get out of the hospital bed. He said it was pretty rough until the medical team settled her down. He said she's lightly sedated and sleeping normally now. I knew you and Doc would want to know."

"Thanks; that's great news," Doc said.

"There's more," Maureen continued. "Nash said that before she fell asleep, she was almost inconsolable. She begged him to forgive her because she told them she had what they were looking for at the office, but now she can't remember what it was, or who she meant when she said, 'them.' I checked my files; someone has been through them. I can't tell yet if anything is missing because I haven't been through all the files, but a few are definitely out of order."

"What files?" Riley asked.

"I knew you'd want to know, so I'm making a list."

"I don't remember seeing any signs of a break-in this morning," Doc said.

"The thing is, I can't say the files were in order yesterday, though," Maureen said. "It's not something I have ever had a reason to check."

Riley furrowed her brow as Doc said, "Thanks for letting us know."

"We'll go over my list this afternoon, Riley." Maureen hung up.

"What do you think, Riley?" Doc asked as he slowed to turn at the farm's driveway.

"Lisa may have survived because she told them what they wanted to hear."

CHAPTER TEN

When Doc Wesley parked at the barn, Rachel hurried to join them from the house.

"Hi, Riley; I'm glad you're here. This is..." Rachel raised her eyebrows.

"Toby, our newest addition to the team," Doc Wesley said.

Rachel smiled when Toby nudged her hand; she rubbed his ears. "It's nice to see you, Doc. The mules are in the barn; I have the donkeys in the corral because they're almost as nosy as the cows." Rachel pointed to the far end of a pasture as the cows ambled toward the barn.

Doc Wesley chuckled as he put on his farm apron. "I guess I'd better do everything right, or word will get around, won't it?"

Riley shivered when a sudden icy blast of wind hit the back of her exposed neck; she quickly pulled up her collar then tied her apron around her neck to hold the collar in place.

Doc pulled out his medical bag; Riley grabbed the tackle box of medications and supplies.

When they stepped into the barn, Rachel said, "I didn't expect this much wind today; it's picking up a bit. I hope we don't get any more storms." Her chuckle was hollow. "I sound pessimistic, don't I?"

"What's your husband doing this morning?" Doc stroked the first mule's neck then gave him a treat from the pocket of his apron.

"He's working on the last piece of equipment that was damaged by vandals. He's almost back on schedule for his fall work, but I'm worried about him because he's under so much stress from the financial pressure and now the equipment breaking down."

Doc nodded. "Sorry to hear that; there are a lot of unknowns with farming, aren't there?"

After Doc Wesley and Riley examined and vaccinated all the mules, Rachel said, "Thanks for coming. I have the farrier scheduled next week, so at least the care for our animals remains on schedule." She rubbed her forehead.

Doc Wesley's phone buzzed with a text. "It's Maureen. I need to call her."

Riley picked up Doc Wesley's medical bag and the medication tackle box. Rachel strolled with her and Toby to Doc Wesley's truck.

After Riley put the bag and the box into the truck, Rachel furrowed her brow. "My husband heard that Doctor Adams is going to start his own online telemedicine and telehealth business. Have you ever heard of anything like that?" Rachel chewed on her thumbnail.

"I've heard of online vet care, but I know very little about it. If I was going to do something like that, I'd want to work with an established group for a while so I could see whether I was suited for it and to learn how they operated. It's a completely different business model than anything I'm familiar with, but I can see how the concept would be appealing to some people."

"But not you?" Rachel's smile was weak.

"Seems like the focus would be on the client, not the patient; definitely not me."

"I didn't think of it from that perspective." She stared at the sky, then cleared her throat. "I didn't want to say anything in front of Doc Wesley, but do you know if there is an organized group that is targeting farmers? One of our most trusted farm workers told my husband there's a growing group north of us that is harassing farmers because they see the huge cotton, corn, and vegetable fields, and the large farm equipment and think farmers are rich and have some type of protected status or underhanded deal with the government."

That's what has been bothering Rachel.

"I've heard that's what some people think, but I don't know about an organized group. Are you worried about your husband?"

"I really am, and whether it's true or not, it is taking a toll on him. I called his doctor; we have an appointment tomorrow for a checkup. I can't think of what else I can do."

"Everything okay?" Doc Wesley narrowed his eyes as he approached his truck.

Riley opened the back door for Toby, who hopped in.

"Everything's fine," Rachel said. "Just normal farming woes; I guess I needed a sounding board. I appreciate you, Riley."

On the way to the next farm, Doc said, "Maureen's worried that Doctor Peterson is overloaded. She said he seems near exhaustion and is pushing himself more than he should to keep up. This isn't ideal, but I'd like to drop you off at the clinic; I'll finish up the day solo."

Doc side-glanced at Riley. "Do you mind?"

"No, I'm disappointed, but I think it's the right decision."

Doc Wesley exhaled. "Thank you. I told Maureen I might drop you off. She said she'd let you be in charge of explaining why you're there, because she's afraid she'd say something wrong and hurt Doctor Peterson's feelings."

Riley's mouth quivered. "Dump it on the new girl?"

Doc Wesley laughed. "Something like that; just let me know, so I can back you up."

Riley gazed at the passing fields as they headed back to Jimson; when they reached the city limits, she said, "I might not know why I'm there until I tell Doc and Maureen, so I'll text you."

"You still have your apron on," Doc Wesley said.

"Good enough."

"What?"

"I can't take the cold; I tied the apron around my collar to protect my neck from the wind."

"That could be lame, except it really isn't. There's nothing worse than being chilled."

"I have a history of hypothermia, so I don't have to remember I'm more sensitive than most to being cold because I just am."

"I noticed that, which is why I insisted you had to return to the clinic."

Riley narrowed her eyes. "You're pushing it, Doc."

He chuckled with a nervous twinge in his voice. "I thought I could slip it past you, but down deep I was hoping you wouldn't take it wrong and quit on the spot."

"And drive home with the blast from the Arctic? Not hardly."

Toby yipped; Riley giggled.

"What did Toby say?"

"He's happy to return to Maureen's treat jar."

Doc nodded as he stopped at the clinic's back door. "You've got your priorities straight, Toby. Let me know if our story changes, Riley."

Riley opened the back door for Toby and grabbed her backpacks then closed the door and waved. When she realized Doc would not leave until they went inside, Riley and Toby hurried to the back door.

"Hi, honey, we're home," Riley called out.

"What's wrong?" Maureen rolled into the breakroom while Riley removed her apron, returned her folded apron to her work backpack, and hung up her coat.

Riley returned her lunch to the refrigerator. "I got bone-chilling cold. I had a very severe case of hypothermia and can't take the cold at all. Where's Doctor Peterson?"

Maureen nodded. "Well done," she whispered.

Maureen rolled back to her desk with Toby at her side. "He's in exam room two, but I think he's about to leave. There are three patients waiting to be seen."

"Don't give him a folder; ask him to meet me at his office."

"Hey, Toby; what are you doing here? Where's Riley?" Doc Peterson asked.

"She's in your office," Maureen said.

Doc Peterson hurried to Riley. "Are you okay?"

"I had a terrible exposure to hypothermia not long after I moved to Barton..."

"I'd forgotten about that; Ned told me about your experience."

"I can't take the cold at all, and the wind was really fierce at the farm. Doc Peterson brought me back to the clinic. He'll cover all the farm visits."

"He'll be fine. Do you need to go home?"

Riley shook her head. "No, I just want to work."

"Grab your folder from Maureen. I'll get off my feet for a while; come get me when you're ready for me."

"Thank you."

"No, thank you for coming back; don't tell anybody, but I discovered I'm not forty years old anymore."

Riley smiled. "Not a word."

Doctor Peterson exhaled. "I'm sorry you were cold, but I sure am glad you're here with me."

Riley held up a thumb when she went to Maureen's desk.

Maureen nodded. "Here's your folder."

After a busy morning of walk-ins interspersed with scheduled appointments, Maureen asked, "Do you have a concealed weapon permit, Riley?"

"Yes, why?"

"I was just thinking maybe I should get one."

Maureen exhaled. "No patients for forty-five minutes. Go eat lunch."

When Riley passed Doc Peterson's office, he called out, "Are you under orders to eat lunch? Okay if I join you?"

Riley returned to his doorway. "I'd love it."

While they ate, Doctor Peterson explained the disease process of the feline leukemia virus and what recent research had uncovered. After fifteen minutes, he paused and peered at Riley. "Aren't you going to finish your lunch?"

Riley stared at the napkin where she'd set down her half-eaten sandwich. "I guess I was busy concentrating, so I wouldn't miss a thing."

Doctor Peterson smiled. "I enjoy teaching. The University of Georgia veterinary college keeps asking me to teach a class or two every semester; maybe after Wesley hires his veterinarian, I'll take them up on it. What about you? Do you miss being a student?"

"I burned out." Riley described the years she attended night classes as a vet tech to complete her bachelor's degree while juggling a full-time job to support herself.

"That's impressive, Riley," he said.

"I don't know about that, but the following summer after I graduated, I doubled down again to take make-up classes while I worked so I could attend veterinary college with Ben."

"I'll bet you were burned out before you started."

"You're right. I completed the classes with top grades, but I was totally fried to a crisp. I was relieved when Ben realized he wanted a career in law enforcement, not the veterinary field. His decision removed the pressure I'd put on myself to take two more classes that fall so I could catch up and attend school with Ben at the University of Georgia."

"You were smart to take a break before you broke." Doctor Peterson chuckled, and Riley smiled.

Doc gazed at her. "Those classes are online, but you don't have to take both of them at once; you could take one."

Riley met Doc's gaze. "I hadn't thought about it like that."

"In fact, you could whittle down the online classes one at a time; so if you changed your mind later, you would have far fewer classes left to take and far less stress. It's an interesting topic for you and your husband to discuss over dinner sometime." Doc smiled.

"Riley," Maureen shouted. "Early arrival."

Riley stuffed her last bite into her mouth, threw away her trash, and hurried to the front.

Maureen handed Riley the folder, and Toby trotted to the door to greet the patient. Toby cocked his head when a man came inside with a sheet of paper in his hand, but no pet in sight.

"Miss Maureen, I was hoping y'all could help me. My husky Schubert ran away right after the tornado hit. We went outside to check the damage, and his eyes got all wild then he took off. I thought he'd come home by now, but he hasn't. Could I put up this poster on your door in case someone's seen him?"

"That's a great idea," Maureen said. "I'll bet Schubert's not the only one that was disoriented by the storm. Give me the flyer. We'll find a place where people will see it." Maureen looked over the flyer. "Add the date at the bottom and a phone number so people can contact you." Maureen's business face softened as she studied the flyer. "I hope he comes home soon; he looks like he's a good boy."

"He is." The man cleared his throat then hurried out.

"Sorry about the false alarm. We need a bulletin board," Maureen said.

"I could take down that picture." Riley pointed to a wall.

"Go ask Doc Peterson; it might be his; it's not my place to say what we put on the walls."

Riley stared at her. "Since when?"

Maureen snorted.

Riley found Doc Peterson in his office. "There's a print of a sailboat in the reception area. Is that yours?"

"Not at all; I took all my stuff home when I sold the practice to Wesley. Why?"

"We're going to put a bulletin board on the wall for lost pets."

"That's a good idea."

Doctor Peterson followed Riley to Maureen's desk.

"You need that wall with the sailboat? You go right ahead and take down that picture and use the wall space for lost pets."

Riley side-glanced at Doc Peterson, and he raised his eyebrows.

"I'll get the stepstool out of the breakroom," Riley said.

After Riley took down the picture, she asked, "Where's the bulletin board?"

"At the hardware store; I called Xavier, and he has one. You have to pick it up; he doesn't have anyone that can deliver."

"What about patients?" Riley asked.

"I can cover our patients while you're gone," Doc Peterson said. "Just don't take too long; I'm not getting any younger."

When Riley giggled, Maureen stared at her while Doc Peterson fake-hobbled to his office.

Riley rolled her eyes. "I'll grab my backpack and coat."

"They'll have it ready for you at the register; they'll invoice us, so don't let them tell you that you have to pay for it."

When Riley reached the back door, Toby joined her.

On the way to the hardware store, Riley said, "Let's surprise Maureen with some flowers; I think she could use a boost. If we find yellow flowers, we'll tell her the story about the peanut butter and jelly appetizers. She'll enjoy hearing about Mrs. Smythe."

After she parked in front of the flower shop, Riley opened the back door for Toby, then the two of them strolled to the hardware store.

"Hello, Riley. I've been expecting you and Toby." Xavier's gold tooth gleamed as he smiled.

He held his cell phone away from his ear. "I'm on hold with a supplier; I've been trying to catch this slippery character for two days. Maureen's cork board is in the back. I'll get it for you after I get off the phone unless you don't mind getting it yourself. It's near the back storeroom door and has a yellow note taped to it that says Maureen. She was really particular about making sure y'all got the largest one we had. What's it for?"

"Lost pets. We'd like to have a board in the reception area where people can post their lost pets."

Xavier furrowed his brow. "Lost in the storm? That's awful; I'll bet they're scared. I'll call Maureen and tell her to make sure people come by here too. The rest of the shops in our little strip mall will want to help; I'll pass the word."

When Riley and Toby went to the back, Riley found the large cork board with a packet of push pins taped to its back.

Riley grumbled. "This is going to be awkward to carry; I wish..."

Riley was interrupted by an angry male voice from up front.

"I had to park in front of your store; I never park there, and I thought you said you'd order me another box of flares. What if there's a road emergency?"

"They haven't come..."

Xavier was interrupted by a thud and a clatter. Toby growled then snarled.

"What was that? You got yourself a guard dog?" the angry man asked.

The front door slammed.

After Riley hauled the heavy bulletin board to the front, Xavier glanced up as he picked up boxes of tissues and stacked them on a cardboard display between the register and the door. "Thank you for being my guard dog, Toby."

"Who was that? Anyone you know?" Riley asked.

"I've known him for a while; he's the new accountant for the board of directors of the library. Arlo likes to say he's the head librarian, but he isn't. He's a royal pain, is what he is."

"Why does an accountant need flares?" Riley asked.

Xavier snorted. "Who knows? This is the fourth box he's ordered this month. He told me he gives them to people who are stranded on the side of the road."

After Riley placed the bulletin board in her trunk, she and Toby went into the flower shop. She smiled when a bell jingled as she opened the door.

Riley took a deep breath, savoring the fragrant scent of flowers that filled the shop, and her eyes widened at the vibrant display of colorful blooms adorning every available space.

A man called out from the back of the store, "We'll be right with you."

Riley examined an arrangement of yellow roses, daisies, and mini-carnations in a clear vase with "Fall

Y'all" hand painted across the front of the vase. "Isn't this perfect?" she whispered.

"What can I do for you?" A young woman hurried down the aisle toward the front. The name tag on her bright pink uniform shirt said, "Gabby."

"I'd like a bouquet of yellow flowers, and this one caught my eye. Is it already sold?"

"It is now." Gabby picked up the vase and carried it to the register.

"Which one did she pick?" the man called from the back.

"Fall y'all, Dad." She rolled her eyes.

"Excellent choice."

Gabby smiled. "Dad can't get around much and can't hear worth a hoot except when he wants to, but he's always interested in who buys his arrangements. He really is talented."

Her father shouted, "Thanks, honey."

Riley covered her mouth to stifle her snicker.

"Told you," Gabby whispered then cleared her throat. "We're installing a closed circuit TV security system next week, so he can watch from the back, but I've told him he can't yell at people because that would be creepy. Can you imagine buying some flowers and some random voice yells something like, 'Good choice; it matches your eyes.'?"

Riley nodded. "It definitely has the chance of being unsettling."

After Riley paid, Toby growled low. Riley glanced at the front door, and a man stood next to her car with his arms crossed.

Gabby glared at the man through the display window then handed Riley a gift card and envelope. "Put whatever you like on the envelope and the inside of the card; I'll be right back."

She stormed outside and waved her arms while she yelled, "It's not your personal parking space, Arlo. Now, move on before I call the sheriff's office."

"You'll be sorry," he shouted.

"Are you threatening me?" She pulled out her phone and held it up as she recorded.

"You don't have my permission to record me." The man kicked the front tire of Riley's car then stomped away.

Gabby's face was red when she came inside. "Sorry; he thinks the entire world should revolve around him and his interpretation of what's legal. Now, where were we?"

"I have the gift card you gave me; I think we're set."

"One more thing." Gabby tied a yellow ribbon around the vase. "It was nice to meet you; stop by any time."

Riley carried the vase to her car and placed it on the passenger floorboard with her backpack snugged against it to keep it upright.

When she parked at the clinic, she exhaled. "We made it, Toby."

She grunted as she carried the bulletin board inside and leaned it against the wall behind Maureen. "Here's the bulletin board."

Maureen furrowed her brow. "That's too heavy for you to put up; we'll let Doc Wesley take care of it in the morning."

Riley exhaled. "I think you're right."

Maureen opened a drawer. "There's a picture hanger already on the wall that is probably sturdy enough, but just in case, here are a few extras. They're left over from the supply I bought, so Doctor Adams could put up his certificates and pictures in his office. I'll create a notice to put on the door, so people know we have the bulletin board to post lost pets. Doctor Peterson is in exam room one, but he'll be finished in a few minutes. Are you ready for your next patient?"

The clinic door opened.

"I have to run out to my car; I'll be right back."

When Riley returned to the building, she hung up her coat in the breakroom then continued to Maureen's desk with the vase of flowers.

"Toby and I thought we all needed a pick me up in the office."

Maureen's eyes welled up, and she sniffled. "That is so sweet; you two make my day all the time, thank you."

Maureen handed Riley a folder.

After the patient and two women came inside, Riley smiled at the Golden Retriever. "Hello, Oona. I'm Riley and this is Toby. We're new. Let's start with weighing you."

One woman sat in a visitor's chair. Her voice was unusually loud. "I'll wait for you right here, sis."

Riley furrowed her brow. *She may be hard of hearing.*

Oona whined and limped as she followed Toby.

Riley giggled. "We might be new, but we're experienced and have seen all the tricks. You still have to step up on the scale."

The client said, "I'm glad you caught onto Oona's prank because I was about to say something. She pulls that helpless walk on everyone; how did you catch my sweet faker?"

"She didn't limp coming in," Riley said.

The client chuckled as the morose Oona snuffled then stepped onto the scale.

Riley recorded Oona's weight then opened the exam room door. "Thank you, Oona; we're in exam room two."

After they were in the room, Riley opened a drawer, and Oona promptly sat and grinned.

The client grumbled, "Oona; Riley can't take your temperature if you're sitting on your bottom."

Riley pulled out the thermometer. "I'm speedy and gentle. Do you want a belly rub?"

Oona flopped down and rolled over for a belly rub; Riley quickly took her temperature then gave Oona the promised belly rub while she cooed, "You're such a good girl."

When Riley stopped, Oona sighed, and Riley rubbed her chin.

When Riley pulled two treats out of her pocket, Oona scrambled to her feet. Oona watched while Riley slowly moved her hand higher to the left, lower to the right, and back to the middle. "Sit, Oona."

Oona plopped into her best sit, and Riley gave her and Toby treats.

"I'll get Doctor Peterson so he can check your eyes."

Doc Peterson waited for Riley in his office. When he saw her, he rose to his feet. "Maureen said you have Oona in exam room two. How's she doing?"

"Her weight is fine; her temp is normal. The chart said the client had reported the Oona's vision was worse, but when I moved a treat from side to side, she obviously tracked it. Oona pretended like she had a limp when they came in because she didn't want to be weighed. I wonder if there's a benefit to not being able to see very well."

CHAPTER ELEVEN

When Riley and Doctor Peterson walked into the exam room, Toby whined.

Riley raised her eyebrows then wrote "stairs" at the top of Oona's file before she gave it to Doc Peterson.

Doc Peterson read the file and nodded. "Tell me about Oona's vision; you wanted us to see her because it was worse. Can you tell me what you've noticed?"

"Her biggest problem is at night. She used to go upstairs with me and sleep outside my door. Now, when I say 'bed' she goes past the stairs like she doesn't see them. She goes into the living room and circles the area rug and paws it like she's not sure what it is before she finally lies down in front of the fireplace. I think she's trying to find the stairs."

While Doctor Peterson examined Oona's eyes, he asked, "Does she go upstairs any other time of the day?"

The client furrowed her brow. "No, there's no reason to go upstairs until bedtime."

Doctor Peterson gently palpated her Oona's joints. "She's got a little swelling on her left elbow. We'll give her an anti-inflammatory to see if that helps with the swelling. Let her sleep downstairs on the rug. You can bring her bed downstairs to see if she'd prefer sleeping on it. Circling and pawing before she settles down is normal, so I'm not worried about that. Let's check her in a month to see how she's doing."

After Doc Peterson left, Riley said, "I'll meet you at Maureen's office. I'll bring your medicine with me, Oona."

Riley pulled out the medication for Oona and closed the medical supply closet.

Before Riley reached the reception area, the sister said, "A friend of mine from Atlanta told me this farm trouble is all political and is being blown completely out of proportion."

When Riley turned the corner to Maureen's desk, the sister was at the door as she peered toward the exam room. "Sounds like they're about ready to leave; I better warm up the car. It was nice talking to you."

Maureen glanced up when Oona and the client headed toward her and casually removed her earbuds.

Riley said, "Doc wants to see Oona in a month."

While Maureen checked the schedule for an appointment, Riley reviewed the medication with the client.

After Oona and the client left, Riley asked, "What was the client's sister talking about?"

Maureen shrugged. "She picked up her phone after y'all were in the exam room; I turned up my music so I wouldn't be eavesdropping. Her voice certainly carries, doesn't it? Why?"

"She said something about political; I was just curious."

Maureen snorted. "Everything's political to that one."

After their last scheduled appointment for the day left at four, Maureen said, "I had already moved appointments from today to tomorrow. We'll go until six. Doc Wesley's last visit will be at three, so he should be in the office a little after four, so Doctor Peterson can go home. I cleared nine thirty until ten, so you can talk to Micco. Doc Wesley said it's up to you, but Micco mentioned he'd like to shadow you with one or two patients. I have paperwork for Micco to sign, so I can start him on the payroll tomorrow if he's training with you."

"That's a great idea."

"What is?" Doctor Peterson stopped in the hallway.

"Micco will work with Riley tomorrow as an orientation."

"I'll see you in the morning; what time is our first patient?"

"Your first patient is at nine," she said.

Doctor Peterson raised his eyebrows. "What time is Riley's first patient?"

"Eight," Maureen mumbled.

"See you in the morning." Doctor Peterson strode to the back door.

Maureen exhaled. "I can't sneak nothing past that man."

Gina tapped on the front door, and Riley hurried to unlock it. "Do you want me to go around to the back? I parked in the back to pick up Maureen then didn't know if anyone would hear me but came around front because the back door is usually locked."

Riley smiled. "No, come on in; I locked the door out of habit when the last patient left."

"Those are beautiful flowers; who are they from?" Gina asked.

"We needed something to brighten the day, so I picked them up when I picked up the bulletin board," Riley said.

"Bulletin board?" Gina asked.

"I'll tell you about that on our way to my house," Maureen said.

"Do you think the library is open?" Riley asked. "Ben and I left our books at his folks' house."

"I think it's open until five," Gina said.

"Toby and I will lock the front door after you leave, Maureen."

"That's our cue, Mo; after I drop you off, I've got a few more things to do at work before I go home," Gina said.

After Riley locked up, she headed toward the library. "During my conversation with Doctor Peterson about veterinary classes, I was so preoccupied with defending my stance of not wanting to affect Ben's career negatively that I neglected to consider the option of taking a single class to explore if it might be the right path for me after all."

Riley exhaled as she parked in front of the library. "I do enjoy learning; it wouldn't hurt me to learn to pace myself, would it?"

Riley glanced back at Toby. "Are you staying or going inside?"

Toby settled down on the seat and closed his eyes.

"I'll leave the window cracked just a bit for fresh air."

When Riley went inside, she stopped at the desk, but no one was there. She waited a few minutes.

"Pssst."

Riley turned; an elderly woman who sat at a large, round table with eight chairs motioned for Riley to come to her table.

The woman whispered, "They're in a finance meeting; it won't be a happy meeting because they're cutting staff. Do you need a library card? Apply for it online on your cell phone. If you have a local zip code, you'll have an online card and can self-checkout your books. I'm not a fan of fancy, shmancy technology, but sometimes, it's okay."

Riley smiled. "Thanks; We like to read."

"Is your dog going to be okay in the car by himself?"

"He'll be fine."

"I'm Edith. Stay clear of the accountant; his name is Arlo. He's what we used to call unhinged."

"I'm Riley."

"Ah, the new vet tech at the Jimson Veterinary Clinic. Good job getting rid of that snooty phony Doctor Adams."

"I didn't..."

"Well, according to him, he couldn't work with you. You must be very skilled to intimidate that blowhard so quickly."

Riley smiled. "I love your descriptions of him. You definitely have a way with words."

"Thank you, dear. There's one of those code things for your phone at the desk, so you can sign up. Do what you're supposed to do then sit with me while you get your library card."

"I'll be right back."

Riley grabbed the code then sat at the table and tapped information into the online form.

When the meeting room door opened, Riley glanced at a short, middle-aged woman with blue streaks in her hair who came out of the room with tears flowing down her cheeks. Edith pulled the scarf from around her neck and hissed, "Put this over your head. Put your hands in your lap and keep your head down. They're coming out of the meeting."

Riley covered her head then slumped over with her hands in her lap as Edith slid an open book in front of Riley. *This is bizarre. What's even more bizarre is that I'm doing what Edith said.*

Riley didn't move when a sobbing woman stood near their table.

"What are you blabbering about? You got yourself a nice pension; grab your things and get out of here. You're disturbing our patrons," Arlo growled.

The woman hurried to the main desk and opened drawers then rushed out the back door.

"Good riddance," Arlo said.

"You taking over, Arlo?" a man asked.

"Naw, it's all automated. We don't need no deadwood around here."

Arlo walked closer to the table and snorted. "I didn't know you had any friends, Edith."

"Thank goodness, my sister is deaf and didn't hear how rudely you spoke to a highly respected member of our community."

Arlo snarled, "You old biddies stick together, don't you?"

"Hey," an old man growled. "We can hear you back here, Arlo, and you're out of line."

Arlo knocked over the chair that was next to Riley then stomped out the back door. The library erupted with applause.

Edith tapped Riley on the arm. "Okay, dear, I'll take back my scarf now."

As Riley returned the scarf and righted the chair Arlo had pushed over, she exhaled. "It was extremely difficult to keep my mouth shut."

Edith smiled. "If Arlo hadn't left when he did, the entire assembly of refined, elderly folks in this library would have jumped him then sworn Arlo ran into a post and had a seizure."

Riley returned her smile. "I can see that; could I have been an honorary elderly?'

"Of course; in fact, consider it a permanent title; we'll make it Honorary Elderly in Reserve."

"HER?" Riley giggled.

Edith nodded, and her mouth twitched. "I'll pass the word; it will be the battle cry of the old folks, 'Remember HER is with us.'"

Riley furrowed her brow. "But seriously, how could Arlo force a long-term staff person into retirement?"

"He holds the purse strings and knows where all the skeletons are buried, and nobody is strong enough on the board to challenge him." Edith raised her eyebrows. "We have an election coming up on Tuesday for the library board. Are you up to being a write-in candidate?"

"Who are the other candidates? Are there any other write-ins?" Riley asked.

Edith exhaled. "I'm a write-in."

"Well, then, I'm your campaign manager."

The older woman put her hand on Riley's. "I'd love it, but it's going to get messy."

Riley rolled her eyes. "You were willing to toss me into the write-in ring, but now you've decided I might be a little delicate?"

"I suppose I let my natural proclivity for insincerity take over for a minute there. Forget I said anything, and I apologize for implying you might be a fragile flower."

"Fine; then what's my strategy?"

"Talk to Maureen; she's the best."

"Got it; I'll grab some books for our fireside reading and be in touch." Riley frowned. "How do I reach you?"

Edith scribbled a number on a scrap of paper. "This is my cell number. I text and answer the phone, but nobody calls me except my insurance agent; she's very gracious, and we chat several times a week. My so-called friends tell me she calls only to be sure I'm still alive, but they never call me, so what do they care?"

Riley sent a text to the number before she rose from the table. "Now, you have my number too. I'll talk to Maureen in the morning and get back to you before the end of the day."

"I'll hear from Maureen first; she'll take over."

Riley giggled then covered her mouth. "Sorry, it sneaked out; I think you're right. You really are brilliant, Edith. I didn't see it coming."

Riley strolled to the fiction section and found two books for Ben, two for herself, and two that either of them would enjoy.

After she checked out her books with the automated system, she hurried to her car and the sleeping Toby.

"I think we'll enjoy the books." She started the engine then texted Ben. "Toby and I are on our way home. Do I need to stop for any groceries?"

Ben replied. "No. Boil potatoes and stir fry carrots, celery, and onion and add to the slow cooker."

As Riley headed home, she snorted. "Ben's text read like he thinks I don't know how to cook. I'd be insulted if I actually did."

Toby whimpered as he laid his chin on Riley's shoulder; she reached back and scratched his ear. "Thanks for the sympathy, Toby; I know I'll learn. I'm just jealous that Ben is learning faster than I am."

After they were home, Riley prepared the vegetables for the chicken soup. She added the carrots, celery, and onion then set a timer for the boiling potatoes after she checked online recipes.

When Toby nosed the back door, Riley put on her warm coat. While Toby investigated the backyard, Riley's phone buzzed with a text from Ben.

"I might be home closer to six. Something came up."

Riley replied. "Thanks for the heads up. We're home."

After Riley declared she was cold, Toby followed her inside.

She lit a fire in the fireplace to take off the chill then sat on the futon to read; when the timer for the potatoes went off, Riley groaned as she rose. "It's not worth sitting for even five minutes because this pad is not the most comfortable seat for relaxing. I can't wait until it's Saturday, so we can go shopping."

While Riley drained potatoes, her phone buzzed a text from Melissa.

"Call when you have time."

Riley added the potatoes to the soup, then called Melissa. "You have perfect timing, Mom; Ben's going to be a little late, and our chicken soup is simmering in the slow cooker."

"Good to hear. So, catch me up on your news. How's the job?"

Riley told her about Doctor Adams leaving, Doctor Peterson filling in, and Doctor Cooper hiring new vet techs.

"Sounds like you're really busy, which I know you enjoy. What about farm visits?"

"Doctor Cooper's going solo until we're better staffed at the clinic; it makes sense to me, so I don't mind."

"What about your cottage?"

"The location is perfect for us. We're going shopping for furniture on Saturday. We have our bed and dining table with chairs."

"I thought the cottage was partially furnished."

"It had kitchen appliances, barstools for the counter that divides the kitchen and the dining area, and a futon in the living room."

Melissa snorted. "I've never heard of a comfortable futon."

Riley glared at the futon. "It definitely has lived up to its reputation. We're going shopping for a sofa and one or two recliners on Saturday."

"Is that all you need?" Melissa asked.

"That's it. We just need a place to read and relax in the evening."

"What about...sorry, Jake just came inside with the puppies, and evidently all of them are starving; I'll call you later." Melissa hung up.

Riley sighed. "I'll read at the breakfast bar."

CHAPTER TWELVE

Arlo pulled into his driveway then remained in his car while the neighbor across the street from him rolled his trashcan from the curb to the back of the house. When the neighbor glanced up at Arlo and waved, Arlo debated pretending that he didn't see the neighbor. *I went overboard and called too much attention to myself at the library. I need to be more social.*

Arlo exhaled as he stepped out of his car and waved then pulled out his groceries. When the neighbor took a few steps toward the street, Arlo put down his head and hurried to his front door. *I waved; that was good enough for social.*

While he waited for the oven to preheat, Arlo reviewed the list of events over the past month. *They're escalating.*

Arlo paced the kitchen until the oven signaled it had reached temperature. *If the boss found out I was tracking this stuff, I'd be collateral damage.*

After he put his frozen dinner in the oven, Arlo's phone rang. *Why is she calling me? I made sure the board fired her today. She needs to leave town.*

He sighed when his phone showed he had a voicemail. Feigning idle curiosity to avoid admitting concern, he listened.

"I know you're trying to protect me, Arlo, but you need to protect yourself too. Call me; I have some ideas about how I can help you."

Arlo deleted the voicemail.

After the timer went off, Arlo removed the foil tray and set it on the table. He absently stirred his steaming dinner with his fork as he thought about Linda. *She's the only friend I have.*

He slammed his fist on the table and called her.

"What do you want from me?" he growled.

"I want to help you," she said.

When Arlo didn't respond, she continued. "Edith is a write-in candidate for the library board. You can't protect everyone. You know I can help you."

"I don't need your help; I need you to leave town." Arlo hung up.

Arlo took two more bites of his dinner, then picked it up and threw it against the wall.

His phone buzzed with a text. "You need me to watch your back."

Arlo threw his phone against the wall.

CHAPTER THIRTEEN

When Toby yipped, Riley stuck the slip of paper with Edith's phone number into her book as a bookmark.

Riley threw open the front door. Toby dashed outside while she stayed on the porch, bouncing on her toes in anticipation as she listened to the crunch of tires on the driveway that became louder the closer they came to the house.

Toby danced alongside Ben's truck as it rolled to a stop, and Riley raced from the porch. Ben climbed out with his backpack and a grocery sack in his hand. He grinned, dropped his backpack, and rubbed Toby's face, then hugged Riley when she reached them.

Ben held Riley close. "Y'all sure now how to make a guy feel welcome. Let's go inside."

When they were inside the cottage, Ben inhaled and smiled. "I should have known you'd have a fire going. The soup smells amazing. I'll pop the dinner rolls into the oven; it won't take long for them to warm."

Riley smiled. "If you want to change out of your uniform, I'll take care of the rolls."

"Thanks, babe; that's a great idea. I'm definitely ready to be home and off duty."

While Ben changed, Riley preheated the oven, set the table, and put the rolls in the oven before she dished up the soup.

During dinner, Ben said, "I might be even later tomorrow; I'd rather put in the extra time on Friday, so I can focus on the weekend with you and Toby."

"That works for me; we're working until six or even seven tomorrow. Doc Peterson and I will cover the clinic while Doc Wesley visits farms until the early afternoon. After Doc Wesley comes to the clinic, Doctor Peterson can leave; we don't want to wear him out. Our goal is to take care of all the patients who had appointments this week. Micco is our new vet tech; he's coming tomorrow for what I think is supposed to be orientation. I'm hoping he can jump in and be more of a help than an extra task piled on top of everything else we have going on."

After Riley cleared the table and Ben loaded the dishwasher, he poured two glasses of wine and put cookies on a plate; Riley added more wood to the fire.

Ben gave Toby a treat before he and Riley carried their wine and cookies to sit on the futon in front of the fire. "Doctor Peterson and I had an interesting conversation about the University of Georgia veterinary program," Riley said.

After she told him about Doctor Peterson's suggestion to take one class at a time to see if she thought she might want to continue with the veterinary program and his offer to tutor her, Riley asked, "What do you think?"

"I think it's a brilliant idea, but what's important is what do you think?" Ben asked.

"When he first mentioned it, my immediate reaction was no way because I've convinced myself that I'm permanently burned out, but when Doc Peterson told me I obviously loved to learn, I realized he was right."

Ben munched a cookie. "What is particularly interesting about Doc Peterson's suggestion is that you aren't locked in. If you take three or four online classes and decide you don't want to continue, that's okay, but meanwhile, you studied under the guidance of a brilliant, highly respected veterinarian; nobody can take away what you will learn from Doctor Peterson."

Riley nodded. "That's it exactly."

"Why don't you sleep on it and see how you feel about it tomorrow, babe?"

"You're so smart." Riley leaned against Ben. "Aren't you glad we don't have to sleep on the futon pad? Isn't this the most uncomfortable thing you've ever sat on in your entire life?"

Ben chuckled. "It's definitely a winner, so far; I'm hoping there isn't a contender in the wings."

Riley sighed. "No kidding."

While they read, Ben's phone that he had left on the kitchen table rang.

Ben hurried to answer his phone. "Who would be calling at nine?"

He frowned as he picked up his phone. "This can't be good."

He answered then listened.

"Yes, sir; I'll be there in ten minutes." Ben glanced at Riley. "I understand."

Ben exhaled after he hung up. "I have to go into Jimson. There was a fire at the cotton gin. The fire marshal's on his way, but the sheriff asked for help to secure the scene. Will you and Toby be okay? I'm not sure how late I'll be."

"We'll be fine. Do you have time for me to make you coffee?"

"Not really; Graham asked me to leave immediately, but I'll change into a uniform first."

"Like you always tell me, dress warm."

Ben quickly changed. "Don't wait up."

After Ben left, Riley set up the coffee maker for the next morning then picked out a book to read. Toby joined Riley on the sofa while she read.

Riley's phone buzzed with a text. "I wonder what Ben forgot."

Her eyes widened when she checked the text from Melissa. "Is it too late to talk?"

Riley called her. "Hi, Mom. It's not too late at all. Ben just left to go into town to help secure a fire scene."

"I'm sorry he had to go into work, but I'm glad we can talk. I wanted to talk to you about furniture. The advantage of being part of a big family is that someone always has excess furniture that they love too much to give up except if someone in the family can use it. We've rounded up a sofa, a recliner, a soft reading chair, which is what Mugsy called it, two end tables for the living room, and not exactly matching bedside tables for your bedroom. I bought some sheets, towels, and a rug for Toby as a housewarming gift for your cottage."

A small tear slid down Riley's cheek. "Wow. I don't know what to say."

Melissa continued, "Dad and I would like to bring everything to you on Saturday. I already made reservations for us at a nice bed-and-breakfast for Saturday night, and it's not too far from you; Seth is going to look after Duffy and Finn."

"We really appreciate it, but I don't think that will work at all, Mom."

Melissa paused before she spoke. "Oh, I didn't even think to ask if you already had plans."

Riley cleared her throat. "You're going to ground me for teasing you, aren't you? Toby will be heartbroken if you don't bring Duffy and Finn; they can stay with us while you and Dad are at the bed-and-breakfast."

"But Riley, is your cottage big enough for three big, rambunctious dogs?"

"They'll wear themselves out. I'm not worried at all."

"Okay; in that case, you're grounded for making me panic. We'll bring supper, dessert, and evening snacks if you'll provide wine, beer, and sweet tea. Make your famous cinnamon rolls for breakfast on Sunday morning."

"That's a deal; thank you so much for everything."

After they hung up, Riley changed into her pajamas, stoked the fire then curled up on the futon with her book.

Riley woke when Toby whined. The lights were still on, but the fire in the fireplace had become ashes. She groaned when she sat up and peered at her phone for the time. "It's two o'clock. Let's check on Ben."

She texted him. "Are you at the cotton gin? We can bring you coffee and hot soup."

He replied, "I'm okay."

Riley snorted then pushed the button on the coffee maker and texted him. "Coffee's brewing. Shall I heat some soup for you?"

Her phone rang.

"Hi, honey."

"What are you doing awake?" Ben asked.

"I fell asleep on the futon if you can believe it. Thank goodness Toby woke me because I was cold. I'm going to add a blanket for the living room to our shopping list."

"I'd hate for you to come out in this cold."

"It's not that far, but I'll listen politely if you want to argue with me, then we'll come anyway, because I don't want to pour the coffee down the drain."

Ben snorted. "I knew that; so if you're going to be obstinate, would you mind bringing my warm gloves? I forgot them, and my hands are freezing. Let me know when you leave, and I'll meet you at the diner next door."

Riley poured soup into a pot to heat while she pulled out a small thermos for the soup, and the larger thermos for the coffee.

She raced to her bedroom and dressed in layers, including her long johns. After the coffee maker finished, she filled the thermoses. She dropped a soup spoon, paper towel, and three cookies into a sack then put everything, including Ben's warm gloves, into a grocery recycle bag.

After she zipped up her warm coat, Riley pulled up her collar. "I almost feel like I need to strap on snowshoes. I'm thankful you and Ben understand why I seem to overreact to the cold."

After they were in her car, Riley texted Ben. "On our way."

When they reached the edge of the town, Riley wrinkled her nose at the potent smell of smoke mixed with burned plastic and rubber.

After they reached the cotton gin, the air was so thick with smoke and the fumes from the fire apparatus that Riley's eyes burned. She stared at the sight of the still-smoldering building that was surrounded by law enforcement and fire department vehicles from cruisers to a hook-and-ladder truck.

She coughed as she pulled into the diner across the street from the gin mill. "Now I see why Ben said he'd meet us at the diner."

The lights were on at the diner, even though it normally closed for the day at three o'clock in the afternoon.

After she parked, Riley put her hand on her heart. "The diner must have opened to support the people who responded to the fire."

Ben opened the passenger's door, picked up the tote, then exhaled as he sat down and closed the door. "Honey, I really appreciated hearing from you." He pulled out the coffee thermos and poured coffee into the lid that doubled as a cup.

Riley stared at him as he gulped down the hot coffee. "We brought soup and cookies."

Ben reached into the sack and pulled out a cookie. "I have to get back. I'll have the soup a little later."

Ben furrowed his brow. "I don't know when I'll get home."

"Was there a fatality?"

Ben poured more coffee into the cup. "Why?"

"Because the fire's out, the fire crews are packing up their equipment, but it doesn't look like anyone is leaving any time soon."

"We don't know. There's a search team..." Ben shrugged and peered across the street. "I need to get back."

Riley leaned over with her lips puckered, and he smiled. "That's what I needed."

After a gentle kiss, Ben climbed out. Before he closed the door, he said, "Text me when you're home."

When Riley and Toby arrived at the cottage, she yawned. "I'll have to set the alarm on my phone so I don't oversleep."

After they were home, Riley texted Ben, set the alarm on her phone, dropped onto the bed, and fell asleep fully clothed.

Chapter Fourteen

When her alarm went off, Riley grabbed for her phone to turn it off before it woke Ben. She cringed when she dropped her phone, and it clattered to the floor with the alarm still beeping. She quickly rolled out of bed, snatched up her phone, and silenced it.

Riley held her breath but didn't hear Ben or Toby stir. She tiptoed to the bathroom for her shower. When she flipped on the light, she gaped at the wet towel on the floor. After she hung up the towel, Riley climbed into the shower. *I must have been out hard; I didn't hear Ben come to bed or even the water running.*

After she showered, she sighed as she dried. *I forgot to set up the coffee last night for this morning when we got back from taking coffee to Ben.*

She wrapped herself with her towel and crept to the kitchen to start a fresh pot of coffee. Toby raised his head then trotted to the back door.

"I hope you don't mind going outside by yourself." Riley opened the door for him then shook her head when the coffee maker gurgled. *Ben set up coffee for me when he got home.*

She quietly made her way to the bedroom and held her breath as she opened the closet door. After she grabbed a long sleeved T-shirt, a flannel shirt, and a pair of jeans, she paused and listened to be sure she hadn't disturbed Ben.

She held her breath to listen more closely, but didn't hear anything. The unexpected sound of loud scratching at the back door startled her. She snorted then peered closely at the bed. *Ben's not here.*

Riley flipped on the light and quickly dressed then hurried to let Toby inside. After she fed him, Riley saw a note on the counter that she had missed earlier. "Your lunch is in the refrigerator. Talk to you later. Love."

When she pulled out the heavy lunch bag, she peered inside. "Ben must think I'm a lumberjack. He packed two sandwiches, a banana, and four cookies." Riley exhaled. "I don't want to hurt his feelings."

When she picked up her coat, Riley frowned. "I'm supposed to work in the office all day, but things change on the fly sometimes, don't they?"

She tightly rolled her long johns then stuck them into her backpack.

On the way to the clinic, Riley said, "I can leave my leftovers in the refrigerator at work for lunch next week, or take them home for lunch tomorrow. I'll decide later."

As she neared the gas station, her phone buzzed a text. She shrugged. "We needed gas anyway."

Riley pulled up to a pump, and while she filled her tank, she read her text from Doc Wesley.

"Call me when you can."

After she returned the nozzle to the pump, Riley parked in front of the convenience store and called Doc Wesley.

"Thanks for calling me so quickly, Riley. Are you at home?"

"No, Toby and I are at the gas station. What's up?"

"Maureen called late last night; she won't be able to come in today, and maybe not for a while." Doc Wesley exhaled. "Have you heard about the fire at the cotton gin? Maureen said her sister was working late, and her car was still in the parking lot. There's no sign that Gina left, and no one has heard from her. The sheriff's department followed up with the surrounding hospitals but didn't find her or anyone that meets her description. Maureen is positive that Gina made it out, but the sheriff said there was little hope that she did."

"Gina was in the fire? That's horrible. How is Maureen going to manage without Gina? We'll have to cover Maureen's tasks at the office; I can call the receptionist at Doc Julie Rae's office for ideas."

"That would really help. I haven't heard whether Kaitlyn has opened her clinic somewhere yet, so I'll call her a little later to see if her clinic is open, and if not, would she mind if I ask her receptionist to work with us until Maureen returns? This is all..." Doc Wesley groaned.

Riley nodded. "Do you know where you are scheduled today for farm visits?"

"Maureen sent me the list before she left yesterday. I hate to cancel them. Do you think you and Doc Peterson can handle everything?"

"We'll be fine."

"I'm sure you will; Maureen completed all the paperwork, so we have Micco on the payroll if he can stay to help after his orientation."

"I'd forgotten about Micco, but we'll work it out."

"I know you will; this has been a week, hasn't it?"

After they hung up, a tear slipped down Riley's cheek as she backed out of her parking spot. *What is Maureen going to do without Gina?*

She slammed on her brakes when a car suddenly sped behind her. She narrowed her eyes at the driver. *Why is Hugo Adams in such a hurry?*

When she finished backing and turned toward the road, her eyes widened as Arlo sped out of the parking lot behind Adams. *Is Arlo chasing Doc Hugo?* She shook her head. *It's probably a coincidence.*

When she reached the clinic, another tear followed the first at the sight of the empty parking lot. *Another reminder of how things change so quickly.*

After they were inside, Riley locked the door behind them, hung up her coat, and put her lunch sack in the refrigerator. Before she started a pot of coffee, she texted Claire. "Call when you're available."

While the coffee brewed, her phone rang.

"Is everything okay?" Claire asked.

"Ben, Toby, and I are fine. Are you at home?"

"Yes. Thad's making our lunches because it's his turn, so I have plenty of time to talk. What's up?"

Riley told her about Maureen and her sister. "Doc Wesley plans to ask the receptionist from the other clinic in town to come in. Their clinic was closed because it was badly damaged by the tornado, so she may be available today, but none of us know anything about the computer system. Do you have any ideas on how we can track our patients?"

"I can send you a packet I developed as a backup in case we lost electricity, but you need someone to get into the computer system. I'll bet Doc Wesley knows the system well enough to get your temporary receptionist logged in, and I suspect the system is the same one that everyone uses, so she'll be fine. If you don't get the experienced receptionist and get her access to the system, you can track your patients today using what I'm sending you, but it's not ideal to go much longer than that. Keep me posted."

While Riley looked through the day's patient folders and sipped her coffee, she narrowed her eyes. "Why didn't Ben say anything when we took him coffee and soup last night?"

She drummed her fingers on the desk and fumed. "It's not like I would run around telling everybody. Since when do we keep secrets from each other?"

She stomped to the breakroom and refilled her cup then texted Melissa. "Call when you can."

Melissa called immediately. "Good timing. Dad and the pups have gone to town for some important piece of hardware. I hate to always ask this, but are you okay?"

Riley smiled. "Ben, Toby, and I are all fine."

She told Melissa about the fire, Maureen, and Gina. "We took him hot soup, coffee, cookies, and warm gloves, Mom. He didn't say a word. It's not like I'm a gossip who wouldn't have the sense to keep my mouth shut, which is obviously what he thinks."

"He doesn't think that," Melissa said.

Riley's eyes welled up, and her voice cracked. "Then why doesn't he trust me?"

"How much sleep did you get?"

Riley snarled, "What does that have to do with..." She slowly exhaled to calm herself. "...not much."

"Couple hours, maybe? How much sleep would you have gotten if he'd told you last night?"

"Oh. None." Riley bit her lip. "Are you saying he was protecting me?"

"Well, let's look at who we're talking about: a Carter man. What do you think?"

"I think he's gone overboard with that protective nonsense."

"You'd be right because you just described every Carter man I know, and we might as well throw in my brothers and Sheriff Dunn, too."

Riley smiled. "I think Sheriff Dunn scared Ben the first time they met."

Melissa chuckled. "Surrogate father?"

"Something like that; so, what do I do about Ben?"

"You won't cure him. I'd tell you to rattle his cage over it, but how much sleep has he had?"

Riley's eyes widened. "Maybe an hour. He sneaked out before I woke this morning."

"I wouldn't mention it until both of you have had a good night's sleep."

"That makes sense; thanks, Mom."

"You're welcome, honey. Are you working today?"

"Yes, Toby and I are in charge of the office today."

"I'll text you later."

After they hung up, Riley poured out her coffee. "I drank over half of that pot. Some people drink coffee to relax, but I'd have the jitters the rest of the day if I have any more. I'll make a fresh pot, so it will be ready when Doctor Peterson arrives."

While the coffee brewed, Riley hurried to the receptionist's desk, turned on the computer, and stared at the login screen. "I can't log into the computer to download the document Claire sent me."

She slammed her hand on the desk, and Toby barked.

"You're right." Riley slowly breathed in and then out. After she was more relaxed, she sent a text to Ben. "Please get some rest when you can. I love you more."

She glanced at the time on her phone. "Our first patient will be here in fifteen minutes."

Her phone buzzed with a text from Ben. "Needed to hear from you. I loved you first."

When she heard the back door unlock and open five minutes later, she caught a whiff of the lingering odor of smoke from the fire. She frowned when Toby snarled.

"Seriously? Adams is here?" she whispered.

Toby whined, and Riley sighed in relief.

Doctor Peterson said, "We hired professionals to box up your office, Hugo. They'll deliver your items to your house later today. Thanks for returning your key to the building. I'll take it now."

"But there are some things..."

"Everything is in the truck and on the way to your house. Thank you for the key."

When the back door slammed, Riley exhaled. "I didn't realize I was holding my breath."

Doctor Peterson called out from the breakroom, "Thanks for the fresh coffee; will you join me?"

Riley smiled as she followed Toby into the breakroom. "Are professionals really going to box up Doctor Adams' office?"

"They sure are; I have packing boxes in the trunk of my car; find me someone more professional than us. We'll toss his items into boxes in between patients, taking calls, dropping everything for emergencies, training Micco, making up computer entries, and any side quests we come across. I'll notify our professional delivery man, Cooper, that he's on the hook to deliver the boxes this afternoon. We wouldn't want to leave him out. While you take care of our first patient of the day, I'll bring in the boxes and tape."

Riley bit her lip. *We'll want the patient's name, the patient number from the folder, purpose of visit, procedures, and medications.* She grabbed a pad of note paper and a pen from the bottom drawer, set them on the desk, and unlocked the front door.

When a car parked in front of the building, Toby yipped.

"You're right; it will be a busy day."

Riley tensed when a man opened the door without a dog or a cat carrier. She exhaled when Mason, whose arm was in a sling, followed the man into the clinic. Mason's big grin was infectious. Toby grinned, and Riley smiled.

"Hey, Miss Riley. Dad brought me here so I could thank Toby for keeping me from getting too scared or hurt by the crowd."

Mason kneeled down, and Toby kissed his face. Mason giggled and rubbed Toby's face and under his chin. "Thank you, Toby. You're my hero."

While Mason cuddled Toby, Mason's dad smiled. "Today is Mason's first day to go back to school, but he wanted to stop by to see Toby. I thought you might like an update on my sister too. The doctors are really pleased with her progress and are talking about sending her to a rehabilitation facility for physical therapy. Her memory is slowly returning, just like her doctor said it would; she remembers the tornado but doesn't remember getting hurt. Lisa remembers you and told me if I saw you, to ask you to clean the refrigerator." He chuckled. "Sometimes it's hard to follow her thought processes, but it was evidently heavy on her mind, and she was so insistent, I promised I would."

When another car parked in front of the building, Mason's dad said, "Guess we better get you to school, Mason."

Mason's dad held the door open for the client who brought in two cat carriers.

The client smiled when the cat that was in the carrier on her right loudly meowed. "Cleo always wants Tito to go first."

She handed the other carrier to Riley.

"We'll start with your weight, Tito. Has anything been bothering you?"

When Tito meowed, Cleo hissed, and Riley giggled.

"He's right, you know; Cleo bothers him all the time, and of course, she denies it." The client put Cleo's carrier on a chair and sat next to her.

After Tito, Cleo, and the client left, Riley stared at her notes she had jotted down from their visit. "There has to be a better way."

She joined Doctor Peterson in his office; he sat in his chair next to the bookcase and tossed books into a box like he was playing cornhole.

He smiled. "I'm probably enjoying this much more than I should. How are you doing?"

"I need a better way to document the patient visits. Can you log me into the computer system? I'm struggling with how to record the patient's vitals and immunizations so we'll have the information later, and how to make sure Maureen will have what she needs for invoices."

"Sure can; I wish I'd thought of it earlier."

"If I document like I always do and set the files aside for billing, then Maureen, or maybe even Fiona, if she comes to help, will have the information they need."

"You're right." Doctor Peterson turned on his computer and logged in. "Okay, the system's up. You can log in anywhere just like normal. Maureen's computer requires a screen login because it's in a public area. The password is work is fun, except it's all one word. I think there's a story behind that, but she denies it."

Riley exhaled. "This is an enormous relief; thank you, I'll get the first visit into the system before our next patient arrives."

Riley quickly recorded Tito's and Cleo's information.

After their nine o'clock patient left, Doctor Peterson said, "I just heard from Wesley that Fiona will be here after lunch. Kaitlyn has found a building and will move her equipment this weekend, so we'll have to come up with someone else next week, but at least we'll get through today. Fiona's willing to stay late with us, so we won't start next week with a backlog."

"That is great news."

A tall, dark-skinned young man with his straight black hair pulled back into a single braid came inside. Toby whined and trotted to the man, who reached down and stroked his back.

"It's great to see you again, Micco," Doctor Peterson said. "How's your mama doing?"

"She's well, Doctor Peterson."

After they shook hands, Micco turned to Riley. "You're Riley?"

"Yes, and you've met Toby. I'll give you a quick tour."

As she led Micco to the first exam room, Riley asked, "Do you know about our staff shortages?"

"Yes, Doctor Cooper called me this morning and asked if I could start today. I was afraid I might slow you down, so I told him I'd talk to you first."

Before she opened the exam room door, Riley paused. "I go really fast; is it okay if I don't wait for you to catch up with me?"

"I'd rather you didn't."

"Don't coddle him, Riley," Doctor Peterson called out.

Micco rolled his eyes. "Thanks, Doc."

"Maureen set aside thirty minutes for your training, so ask questions as we go along. We have three exam rooms, and they are all set up the same except for the trauma room."

Micco scanned the room. "Is it okay if I open drawers and cabinets first?"

"Go right ahead."

Riley sat in the client's chair while Micco examined each drawer and cabinet.

Micco turned to Riley. "Are there any supplies kept somewhere else that might be needed?"

Riley nodded. "I'll show you the supply and medication closets."

Micco examined the contents of the supply closet. "This was helpful."

After Riley showed him how to access the medication cabinet, they continued to the lab section then the x-ray room.

Micco exhaled. "I know this machine. It isn't what my class was trained on, but we visited a large practice that had this machine. During a break, the vet tech showed those of us who were interested in how to operate it. There were only three of us, so it was like a private lesson."

Micco followed Riley down the hall.

"This is our breakroom. I should have brought you here first so you could hang up your backpack. Did you bring your lunch?"

When Micco nodded, Riley pointed to the refrigerator.

After Micco put his lunch sack in the refrigerator and hung up his backpack on a hook, Riley asked, "Do you drink coffee or hot tea?"

Micco furrowed his brow. "No, should I?"

Riley smiled. "Not at all. I was asking because Doctor Peterson and I drink coffee, but if you don't, then you aren't responsible at all for making coffee."

"I could learn," Micco said.

"Don't you dare," Doctor Peterson called out from his office.

Micco's mouth twitched into a small smile. "Got it, Doc."

As they returned to the receptionist's desk, Micco asked, "What else do I need to know before the patient arrives? Is there anything I can do to help?"

"Did Doctor Cooper tell you that Fiona, the receptionist for the other veterinary practice in Jimson, will be here this afternoon to help us?"

"He did; I don't know Fiona, do you?"

"No, but Maureen mentioned her earlier this week and said she was good." Riley glanced at the bulletin board. "Maureen planned to put the bulletin board on the wall, so we can use it for community announcements. We'll have people coming in today to put up notices about lost dogs and cats from the storm. Maureen thought the picture hanger that is on the wall would be sturdy enough, but if it isn't, she has more we can use."

After he hung the bulletin board, Micco examined it. "We might want to replace it with hangers on the corners. It will be steadier."

"I agree; let's take it down for now. If anyone comes in with flyers, we can tape them to the side of the front counter for the time being."

"I can fix it; do you have any more picture hangers?"

Riley opened the drawer where Maureen kept them. Micco took two then while he hung the bulletin board, Riley pulled out a small packet of colorful push pins.

Micco opened the packet then pinned it to the bulletin board. "We're in business now."

Riley pinned the notice about Schubert on the board then taped the notice about the board on the front door.

She smiled as a client opened the door, and a large St. Bernard came into the office. Toby trotted to the St. Bernard to greet him. Riley glanced at the folder then handed it to Micco.

Riley smiled. "Hi, Sebastian. That's Toby. I'm Riley, and this is Micco. We're new here, but we're really fast and gentle."

Sebastian cocked his head and grinned.

Riley motioned toward the scale. "You've been here before, so you know where the scale is."

Sebastian ambled to the scale then stared at Riley.

She smiled. "Go ahead; it's just a tiny step up."

Sebastian sneezed and backed away. When Toby yipped, Sebastian stepped on the scale.

The client giggled. "He likes to balk at the scale. Did Toby just call him out?"

"Something like that," Riley said. She glanced at Micco, who had recorded Sebastian's weight in his file.

When they went to the first exam room, Riley said, "Remember I said I'm fast and gentle?" Riley stroked Sebastian's back, and he relaxed. "I'll take your temperature."

Riley showed the thermometer to Micco, who recorded the temperature.

"Is anything bothering you, Sebastian?" Riley asked.

Sebastian moaned.

"I'm really sorry your stomach doesn't feel good. We'll let Doctor Peterson know. I'm going to touch your stomach, but I'll be gentle."

Riley carefully palpated Sebastian's stomach. "No bloat; that's good, Sebastian. We'll be right back."

Micco followed Riley out of the exam room. "I have questions, but I'll save them."

Riley nodded. When Doc Peterson met them in the hallway, Riley said, "Sebastian's here. He said his stomach bothers him after he eats the new dog food, but I didn't find any sign of bloat."

Micco handed the file to Doc, who quickly reviewed it.

"Did you ask the client about the new dog food?" Doc asked.

"No, I'll let you ask."

Doc chuckled as he went into the room.

"Well, Sebastian," he said, "Your weight is down a little more than I would have expected, but your temperature is fine."

While Doc Peterson examined Sebastian he said, "Is anything new with Sebastian? New people, rug shampoo, or dog food?"

The client smiled. "My neighbor told me about this new brand her dog likes; it's a little more expensive, but it's supposed to be specifically formulated to be good for their bones."

She showed him a photo she had on her phone. "I knew you'd want to know about it so you could tell the rest of your clients. It's the latest thing."

Doc Peterson peered at the photo then frowned as he shook his head. "St. Bernards tend to have an allergy to the ingredients in that brand. How is he doing on it?"

"It's taking him a while to get used to it; my neighbor said that's very common. So far, he eats only half of it. I leave it out a while, but he's not interested."

"It's probably triggering an allergy; let's return to feeding him his standard food. How was that going for him?" Doc Peterson asked.

The client rubbed Sebastian's ear. "He loved it; I should have realized that was the issue. Thanks, Doc. We'll stop by the store on our way home and pick up a large bag of his regular food. Do you think I could donate what's remaining in the bag to the animal shelter?"

"No, they can't accept opened bags. Send them a generous donation instead. I understand they're overloaded with lost pets."

"We'll do that."

After the client left, Micco said, "Riley, my grandmother's like you; she talks to animals all the time then tells me what they said. She said I understood the animals too before I went to school, so I wasn't surprised when you asked Sebastian if anything was bothering him, and I knew he hurt somewhere when he answered you, but how did you know it was his stomach?"

"My grandma and I understood animals, so I thought everybody did. When I went to school, the other kids teased me, but I thought there was something wrong with them and felt sorry for them. Grandma told me they'd forgotten."

"Did you tell them there was something wrong with them?" Doc Peterson asked.

"Of course. What are friends for?" Riley glanced toward the door. "Here's our next patient."

Doc Peterson laughed as he headed to his office.

CHAPTER FIFTEEN

After their third patient of the morning, a middle-aged woman came into the clinic with a stack of papers in her hand. "I heard you had a bulletin board for lost pets. Quite a few of the folks in my neighborhood are elderly, so my best friend and I checked to see if any of them had lost pets. We recorded their information then created flyers for them. We don't have any pictures, but we have wonderful descriptions."

Before she left, the woman smiled. "Would you believe all the pets are good boys or good girls?"

After Riley and Micco posted the flyers, she said, "Here's the file for the next patient, Micco. Do you feel comfortable taking the lead? I'll back you up."

Micco exhaled. "Comfortable isn't the word I would have picked, but if you're there with me, I'd like to take the lead."

"Do this your way, not my way," Riley said.

"I might borrow some things," Micco whispered.

When the elderly white and brown pit bull came into the clinic, Toby greeted her.

Micco smiled. "Hello, Phyllis. That's Toby. I'm Micco, and this is Riley. I'm new. Riley is my teacher, and she's very smart."

After Phyllis looked them over, she grunted.

"We'll start with getting your weight."

Phyllis moaned as she followed Micco down the hall.

Micco said, "I hear you, Phyllis, but it's all part of the process, and like Riley says, we're fast and gentle." Phyllis picked up her speed to walk alongside Micco.

Micco has a fan. Riley glanced at Toby, who grinned.

After Phyllis stepped onto the scale, Micco recorded her weight. "Good job, Phyllis. You're down a half pound, and it shows."

Phyllis held her head high and cocked to the left as she sashayed into the exam room.

"Temperature is next. We'll let Riley do that because she is amazing; I'm still learning."

Riley rolled her eyes then quickly took Phyllis's temperature.

"How you doing, Phyllis? Is anything special bothering you?" Micco asked.

Phyllis whined and lifted her front right paw.

Riley rolled her eyes. *What a ham. There's nothing wrong with her paw.*

"Did you go to the groomer recently? Your nails look nice, but what about your ear that was infected?"

Phyllis stared at Micco then snuffled.

You nailed it, Micco.

"Riley and I will remind Doctor Peterson to check your ear. He'll be here in just a few minutes."

After Riley left the exam room with Toby and Micco behind her, she almost bumped into Doctor Peterson, who stood near the door where he could listen. "You three are a good team. Give me your report, Micco."

"Phyllis's weight was down half a pound and her temperature was normal. Her left ear may not be cleared up from the infection; she tilted her head so she could hear me with her right ear."

"What about her front right paw?"

"A diversion, but if you check it, she'll save face."

"Good job, Micco. You learn fast." Doctor Peterson headed to the exam room.

"Go with him, Micco," Riley said. "He'll prescribe another course of antibiotics. Bring Phyllis and the client to the desk. I'll wait for you there and will update the file while you get the antibiotics."

Riley poked around different screens on Maureen's computer then paused. *I haven't smelled the smoke from the fire since early this morning. Did it dissipate that quickly?*

After Micco led Phyllis and the client to the receptionist's desk, he handed the file to Riley. "I'll get your medicine, Phyllis, and be right back."

Riley smiled. "We'll send you a bill for Phyllis's visit today. I'd like to verify your address to be sure we've recorded it correctly. Did you want us to send it to you by email or postal mail?"

"Email, please."

After Riley jotted down the email on her notepad and repeated it to the client, who verified it, Micco joined them with Phyllis's medicine.

"I enjoyed meeting you, Phyllis. Doctor Peterson would like to check your ear in two weeks," Micco said.

"Give me a minute; I think I can schedule that for you now, if you like." Riley clicked onto the scheduling screen. "How is two weeks from today at the same time?"

The client checked her calendar on her phone. "That's perfect."

Riley smiled. "We'll send you the usual reminder."

After Phyllis and the client left, Riley recorded the information about the appointment on the note pad and exhaled. "I can view appointments, but I can't add or edit them."

"I was impressed because after I saw you couldn't add it, I thought we'd have to tell the client to call us next week, or maybe it would be better to say someone would call her later."

"Maureen or Fiona will still have to put the information into the system, which is extra work for them, but a phone call would add even more time and effort." Riley stared at the computer screen. "I have an idea..."

"I'll clean the exam room," Micco said.

Riley nodded as she clicked on the menu labeled "Receptionist." When she came to the login screen, Riley typed "Maureen R" for the user name and "workisfun" for the password.

She groaned at the error message, "account name or password is incorrect."

"I know I'm right," she muttered. She refreshed the screen and typed "Mo R" for the user name and "workisfun" for the password.

"I did it!" she squealed.

"Good for you," Doctor Peterson said.

Micco strode to the desk. "Did what?"

"I cracked Maureen's code. We can enter the appointments. I won't tackle the bills, but we can set up appointments. I'll show you."

Doctor Peterson joined them at the desk while Micco pulled up a chair next to Riley.

She logged out, then showed Micco the main screen and the menu item, Receptionist.

When she clicked it and came to the user name and password screen, Riley said, "My username is Riley C; Yours is Micco O."

Micco rolled his eyes. "I've just been haunted by my ghosts from first grade."

Riley smiled. "Her sister called Maureen, Mo, so I typed in Mo R as the username. The password for screensaver lock is workisfun, with no spaces, so I guessed that Maureen's password would be the same as the screen lock."

"That was good detective work," Doc said.

"Not really; it was just the only thing I could think of, and thank goodness Maureen isn't as security conscious as she should be. I'll add Sebastian's appointment to the schedule. You can enter the next follow-up appointment, Micco."

"I'd like that. The exam room is clean; is there anything else I can do to help?"

Doc Peterson nodded. "Help me finish packing up Adams' stuff, then when you have time, take the boxes to the breakroom. Doctor Cooper will deliver them this afternoon; he just doesn't know it yet."

"We have about ten minutes," Riley said as she added Sebastian's appointment.

Micco followed Doctor Peterson; Toby stayed with Riley.

Riley's phone buzzed with a text. "This is Edith. Heard about Gina. Call when you have time to talk."

Riley replied, "Will call at my lunch break."

When the client opened the door, Riley asked, "Ready for your next patient?"

Micco hurried to the desk and quickly reviewed the file. "You'll be with me, right?"

Riley nodded. "As long as you like."

A few minutes before eleven, the clinic phone rang. After Riley hung up, she said, "Micco, we have a change to our morning schedule."

Micco exhaled. "I knew our smooth schedule was too good to be true. The eleven o'clock patient will be late, right?"

Riley smiled. "The client said they'd be about fifteen minutes late. I didn't want to reschedule the patient, so we might run into a time crunch for lunch. If you take the eleven o'clock, I'll take the eleven thirty patient. You can go to lunch after your morning appointment, and I'll join you. If I haven't finished my lunch by one, you can take the first afternoon patient."

Micco furrowed his brow. "Can we review the three files?"

"That's a good idea."

After they read the files, Riley asked, "What do you think?"

When Micco hesitated and avoided her gaze, she continued, "The eleven thirty patient might be the best patient for your solo."

Micco exhaled. "Thank you. I eat fast, so I'll probably be ready for the one o'clock patient at the same time as you. What about Fiona?"

"I almost forgot about her; you know what I know, so I think either of us could get her started. If she needs any more help than logging in, she might have to ask Doctor Peterson or wing it."

Micco chuckled. "I'm interested in seeing whether Fiona is the wing it type."

Riley smiled. "I would think she would have to be, but now I'm curious, too."

Riley's patient arrived at eleven twenty-five. When the client opened the door, Riley whispered, "Want to race?"

"No way," Micco said.

As she greeted the patient, Riley's mouth twitched as she unsuccessfully suppressed a smile. *He'll try.*

"Is it okay if I don't go back?" The client asked. "I haven't slept well since..." her voice trailed off.

"That's fine," Riley said. "We won't be long, will we, Molly?"

The white, British shorthair cat purred.

"Why thank you; I love your golden eyes too," Riley said.

After Riley weighed Molly and took her temperature, she asked, "Are you having any trouble breathing when you walk or climb stairs?"

Molly growled.

Riley nodded. "I'm not a fan of stairs either, but otherwise, are you breathing okay?"

Molly meowed.

"I'm going to take a listen." Riley pulled out a stethoscope and listened to Molly's heart and lung sounds. "I'll let Doctor Peterson know what you said. I'll slip you back into your carrier while I find him."

Molly marched into her carrier.

"Thank you; you are such a sweet girl."

The client came into the exam room. "I hope it's okay that I came in, Riley. Thank you for letting me rest a few minutes."

"Any time; we want you to be comfortable too."

Molly purred, and the client smiled.

Riley went into Doctor Peterson's office and handed him Molly's file to review. "Molly is not only avoiding stairs, she's also staying in the kitchen near her food and water dishes because she runs out of breath after taking only three steps. The client has always kept Molly's litter box in the mudroom that is next to the kitchen, but even going that far leaves her out of breath."

"Did you listen to her chest?"

Riley nodded. "Her lungs sounded a little wet; I haven't heard her heart murmur before, so I don't know if there's any change there."

Doctor Peterson frowned at the file. "There's no mention of a heart murmur in Adams' notes, and she didn't have one the last time I saw her; I might not have listened as carefully as you did. Good catch, Riley."

When Doc Peterson walked into the exam room, he smiled at Molly and the client. Riley unzipped the carrier, and Molly strolled out of her carrier.

"Let's see how you're doing, Molly."

Doc checked her ears and eyes then listened to her chest. He glanced at Riley and gave a slight nod.

"Molly has developed a slight heart murmur. We'll just keep an eye on it. She has a little lung congestion, so we'll increase her medications a bit. We want her to be comfortable enough that she's roaming the house."

"She pretty much sticks to the kitchen. I moved her bed there because I thought she might be cold."

Doc Peterson nodded. "That was a good way to help her feel more comfortable. I'd like to see her again in two weeks. Our goal is to help her feel strong enough to roam the house."

After Doctor Peterson left, Riley slipped out and then returned with Molly's medicine. On the way to the receptionist's desk, Riley said, "We'll schedule the return visit now, and bill you for today's appointment and medication."

After they made the appointment, the client's eyes welled up. "Thank you, Riley."

A few minutes later, Micco came out of the second exam room with his patient and client.

"No follow-up needed, Riley."

"That's great news. We'll bill you for today's visit."

The client chuckled. "Computer glitch? They always happen at the worst possible time, don't they?"

Riley smiled. "They sure do."

After the client left, Riley exhaled. "Ready for lunch, Doc?"

"Toby and I are on our way."

Riley picked up the files for the rest of the day then she and Micco went to the breakroom. Doctor Peterson glared at the files in Riley's hand. "We're on our break."

"These are for our staff meeting after lunch. Micco and I reviewed the last two patients and our first patient of the afternoon and made some adjustments to our assignments. I thought we'd do the same thing for our afternoon patients."

Doc Peterson raised his eyebrows. "Maureen, Lisa, and I used to do that all the time; I didn't realize I missed it. Let's eat and talk about conspiracy theories."

While they ate, Riley asked, "Do we have any conspiracy theories to talk about?"

"I heard one at the gas station this morning that was new to me," Doc Peterson said. "I heard someone was creating crises for the farmers to change the way they vote."

"How are they doing that?" Micco took a big bite of his sandwich.

"I don't know; of course, any good conspiracy theory worth its mettle would never have details." Doc Peterson peered over his coffee cup.

"A client mentioned politics yesterday in a conversation with Maureen, except Maureen wasn't listening to her," Riley said.

Doc Peterson chuckled. "Maureen told me once that her job description did not include suffering with prattle, so she was getting earplugs. I'd forgotten about that; I guess her earbuds replaced them."

"Halloo," a woman called from the front desk.

"That's probably Fiona. I'll bring her back," Doc Peterson said.

Fiona waddled as she followed Doctor Peterson into the breakroom. She was as short as Riley, but far outweighed her. Her white hair was clipped short and spikey, and her artfully applied makeup rivaled any social media influencer half her age.

Riley glanced at Micco and whispered, "Wing it."

Micco nodded.

Doctor Peterson introduced Fiona to Riley and Micco.

Fiona nodded. "Nice to meetcha. Somebody get me set up on the computer; I'm sure I've got at least two days' worth of work ahead of me before I can go home this evening."

Micco said, "I've finished eating; I'd be happy to show you, Miss Fiona."

"Call me Fiona, Micco, unless you want me to call you Mr. Micco; it's your choice."

"Yes, ma'am." Micco threw his trash into the trash can.

"It's Fiona, sir, not ma'am," she said.

"Yes, Fiona."

After they left, Doc Peterson said, "That Micco is quick to roll with the flow; he's a keeper, isn't he?"

"If he shows up on Monday, and we know he will, so yes."

Doc Peterson left while Riley finished eating.

She called Edith.

"Give me a second to put on my coat," Edith whispered.

Riley waited.

Edith loudly said, "I'm going for a walk to clear my head. I need a breath of fresh air. I won't be long in case anyone needs me."

When Riley heard the click of a closing door, she asked, "Too many listeners?"

"That's it." Edith sighed. "Okay, I'll be quick. I'm going to drop out of the board race. I've been getting a great deal of hostile pressure to remove my name from the ballot, so I'm going to withdraw."

While Edith talked, Riley strolled to the women's restroom and went inside.

"Really?" Riley locked the restroom door.

"I'm doing it to step out of the spotlight. A group is circulating a petition for farmers to sign that states they will support and vote for Kenneth Gleason, the challenger of our district's state senator race because the incumbent, Dennis Johnson, has not done enough to protect farmers and their property. The kicker is the signers are also requested, which means required, to donate at least one thousand dollars, and farmers are paying it. If you donate and sign, the implication is that you will get preferential treatment for extra protection from the state. There's a little sleight of hand going on here. Gleason's campaign states the agriculture programs must be trimmed back because ninety-five percent of the farm money goes to foreign investors. The library board came out as a major backer of Gleason and is encouraging, in a very intimidating way, farmers to donate. It's obvious I would be in the way because I would ask questions."

"Where is their data coming from?" Riley frowned.

"The library board claims it's from an obscure economic impact research paper that I can't find, but I quit looking after the not-so veiled threats started. I've written what I've found so far in my gardening book. Unfortunately, when I first started digging into it I was more curious than anything else; I wasn't careful, because I didn't expect it to be as dirty as it is. I cannot believe that no one is questioning the data; in fact, some people claim they've suspected the foreign investors were wiping out our state agricultural resources all along."

"Do you think this is related to anything else?" Riley asked.

"I think it's related to that man being killed, the shooting at the clinic, the gin fire, the calves being poisoned, and the sabotage of farm equipment. The attack on Lisa must be related too, but I don't know how or why. I can't do any more research at the library because I was certain I was being monitored; I was limited to my slower than usual home internet, but I decided it was being monitored too, which is why it became even slower, so I switched my research to gardening and garden pests."

"Can I help?"

"No." Edith exhaled. "Well, maybe. The only person I trust in town besides Doctor Peterson is Xavier at the hardware store. I'll drop off my gardening log with him and tell him you'll pick it up later. He'll understand. The hardware store is open until eight tonight or you can pick it up tomorrow. There's no rush; it will be safe with Xavier. If I'm off track, tell Xavier, and he'll let me know; otherwise, I'll stay low for a while." Edith has a catch in her voice. "Riley, I have to know; do you believe me?"

"Yes; keep working on that gardening project."

"Thank you; you could consider a butterfly bush for your cottage. Ask Xavier which one he recommends."

"Okay, is this code?"

Edith laughed. "If it was, it isn't any more, is it?"

As Riley headed toward the receptionist's desk, she muttered, "When is code not code?"

"I don't know." Micco stood in the hallway. "When it's misinterpreted?"

"Exactly." Riley's eyes twinkled. "What if it's deliberately intended to mislead?"

"Am I in trouble?" Micco asked. "I'm almost following what you're saying. Is there any way I can help?"

"Maybe. What do you know about butterfly bushes?"

"They have a delicate bluish purple flower; they're a fairly hardy perennial plant, and they do attract butterflies, except they're considered invasive in some places. I don't know much more than that. I don't see what butterfly bushes have anything to do with code, though."

"That's exactly right," Riley said.

"Now, I am lost," Micco said. "We have a patient, and Fiona suggested I might want you to mentor me. Actually, she said hold my hand, but I decoded it."

Riley giggled. "Well done; let's go decode."

While Micco greeted the patient, a male French bulldog, Riley mulled over what Edith had told her. *Why does she trust Doc Peterson?*

Riley followed the client, the patient, and Micco into the first exam room.

Riley snapped out of her musings when Micco said, "I'll bet this is uncomfortable, Pierre. What do you think, Riley?"

Riley examined the area where Micco pointed and nodded. "We'll ask Doctor Peterson to check it; I'll bet he has some medicine that will help you feel more comfortable, Pierre. How long has it been bothering you?"

Pierre grunted.

Riley's eyes narrowed as she leaned down and sniffed the wound. Her lips tightened. "That is definitely a long time...you're very strong, Pierre."

Riley washed her hands and pulled out a sterile cotton swab from a drawer. "Doctor Peterson might want to take a peek."

Micco followed Riley to Doc Peterson's office. "A long time? How long?"

"Since yesterday," Riley said.

"Yesterday? It shouldn't have looked that bad."

"Are you talking about the slight abrasion that is close to the open boil??"

Micco's eyes widened. "His open wound is so bad that he's not feeling any pain? So, that's why you sniffed it then swabbed it. What can I do to help?"

"Do want to take the file to Doc Peterson or run the swab?"

"I'll take care of the swab. I'll have results as soon as I can."

Riley went into Doc Peterson's office and handed him the file.

After Doctor Peterson read the file, he furrowed his brow. "Did you smell infection?"

"Yes; we did a swab; Micco has the swab in the lab."

"Do we wait for him?"

"Waiting is hard, but yes." Riley exhaled. "I talked to Edith recently; she told me the only people in town she trusted were you and Xavier. Why is that?"

Doc Peterson raised his eyebrows. "If I told you, wouldn't I be betraying her trust?"

Riley narrowed her eyes. "That's the most polite and effective deflection I've ever heard." Riley said.

Doc chuckled. "Thank you; I was rather proud of it myself."

Riley glared at him.

Chapter Sixteen

Micco joined them. "Am I interrupting something?"

When Riley turned her glare to him, he cleared his throat. "Pierre has a staph infection, but it isn't MRSA."

Doc Peterson exhaled. "That's good. We don't have the facilities to take care of a staph infection that is resistant to antibiotics. Doctor Cooper and I need to talk about that because we need a plan in place. Meanwhile, let's go see Pierre and get that fella on some antibiotics."

"I'll stay here," Riley said.

Doctor Peterson nodded. "We'll call you if we need the big guns."

Riley rolled her eyes as the two men went into the exam room.

As she headed toward the receptionist's desk, her phone buzzed a text from Ben.

"Call when you have time."

Riley whirled around and went to the breakroom and called Ben.

"Hi, honey."

"Do you have any plans to go out anytime soon?" he asked.

"No, is there something you wanted?"

"Just curious."

Riley exhaled. "There's more than that. What?"

Toby trotted to Riley and leaned against her.

"How well do you know Edith?"

"She's a good friend; is she okay?" Riley's head spun, and she grabbed onto a chair to keep from fainting.

"She's fine, but you'll hear that she was arrested for attempted murder, babe. It's going around we have evidence that she set fire to the gin, but we haven't found Gina's body yet."

"Who's going to believe that? She's a frail, elderly woman." Riley rubbed her forehead.

"Right, but it doesn't take much to strike a match."

After he hung up, Riley raised her eyebrows. *It sounds like it's just a rumor, but if Edith is under arrest, she's safe. Did you implicate yourself? Smart move, Edith.*

Riley frowned. *I need to talk to Maureen.*

Riley called Maureen.

"Riley? Is something wrong?" Maureen asked.

"I'm checking up on you; are you okay?"

"I'm worried about Gina and annoyed about breaking my arm; did you know they put on a cast? I could sneak and take off my brace to take a shower, but if I get the cast wet, they'll have to remove it and put on another one, which resets the clock. To top it off, I'm still waiting for my car to be fixed. I should be at work."

"Wasn't the windshield the only damage?"

"You're right...I'll call them as soon as we hang up."

"Good; call me back."

Riley hung up and exhaled.

Toby trotted into the breakroom and whined as he nudged Riley.

"You're right; I certainly don't want to be the reason we get behind."

When Riley joined Fiona at the receptionist's desk, Fiona was on the phone. Fiona handed Riley a folder and drummed her fingers on the desk while she rolled her eyes.

"I don't mean to interrupt, but I have work to do. All I know is that your items are out for delivery, and no, I don't have a tracking number. What's so all-fired urgent about the stuff you had in your office? Is there something in particular you can't live without between now and this evening?"

Fiona set down the phone and shook her head. "Doc Adams hung up on me. He must have had something really important in his office."

"Maybe he's leaving town soon and wants to be sure to take all his office memorabilia with him."

"We could only wish, but I doubt it; I heard his wife doesn't want to leave the area because of her folks. He's burned bridges in Jimson, so he's put himself in the position that he can't stay. I'd feel sorry for him, but it's his own doing. Besides, what kind of weasel hangs up on a kindhearted person like me?" Fiona cackled.

After the four thirty patient left, Doc Peterson asked, "How many patients do we have left to see today, Fiona?"

"We have six more; at a normal pace, which is how the appointments are scheduled, that would take us until seven thirty. Our pace is faster, so I'd like to call clients and invite them to come in early, so we have a tighter schedule. What do you think?"

"I'm willing," Doc Peterson said. "What do you think, Riley?"

"We have an efficient system in place; I say go for it."

"So do I," Micco called out from the first exam room where he was cleaning.

Fiona stretched her arms, wiggled her fingers, and motioned for them to move away from her desk. "Give me room."

As Riley walked her next patient to the scale, she smiled as she heard Fiona say, "We can squeeze you in earlier..."

When Doc Wesley came into the clinic at six, Riley was leading their last patient of the day to exam room two while Micco cleaned room one.

After Riley had examined the patient and headed to Doc Peterson's office, Fiona said, "Doc Wesley will take your patient."

Riley nodded and changed direction. Doc Wesley met her in the hallway.

"What do you have?"

"Wrigley is a male German boxer with tapeworms. He ran away during the hurricane, but he has a history of exploring, so he's probably had the tapeworms for a while. They took him to the groomer's after they found him yesterday and got him cleaned up."

"Anything else?"

"The groomer complained about how dirty his ears were, but I checked, and they did a good job of cleaning them. No sign of redness, so I think the tapeworms are all that need to be treated."

Riley handed him Wrigley's file. Doc Wesley reviewed it and nodded. "While I examine him, pick up his medication, and I'll meet you at the desk."

After the client and Wrigley left, Doc Wesley locked the front door.

"Your folders are on your desk, Doc Wesley. I talked to Maureen," Fiona said. "She'll be here on Monday at her usual time; I explained how I did everything, and I'm leaving her documentation in case she has corrections and needs a paper trail. Y'all were a joy to work with."

Fiona shook hands with everyone then headed to the back door.

Doc Wesley said, "Doctor Peterson is waiting for us in the breakroom. We'll have a quick debriefing then call it a day."

After the four of them sat at the break table, Doc Wesley said, "I have several things. I called Owen's three references, and they spoke highly of him, of course. I'll call him this evening and offer him the position."

"That was relatively painless," Doc Peterson said.

Doc Wesley nodded. "I'd like to open the clinic tomorrow just in the morning for walk-ins. Are either of you available?"

"My in-laws are bringing us furniture in the afternoon, so I could work with you in the morning. I'll have to check with Ben first."

Riley texted Ben. "Doc Wesley wants to accept walk-ins tomorrow morning only. Is that okay with your schedule?"

She sent the same text to Melissa.

Melissa replied, "We won't be there until three at the earliest. Fine with us."

The text from Ben buzzed while she read Melissa's. "I have follow-up in the morning, so works for me."

"All clear," Riley said. "I'll be here in the morning. What time?"

"Let's say eight, and we'll have a hard stop at eleven-thirty," Doc Wesley said.

When Micco opened his mouth, Doc Wesley said, "Micco, you'll have plenty of chances to put in extra hours, won't he, Doctor Peterson?"

Doc Peterson chuckled. "Oh, yes; we all pitch in."

"One more thing, then we'll be done for the day. Maureen called me, and her car was fixed. She'll be here in the morning with us, Riley," Doc Wesley said.

"That's great news." Riley smiled.

"One more thing, then that's it from me. Maureen sent me five resumes from new veterinarians. Fiona printed two copies of each before she left." He handed Doc Peterson a folder. "We can discuss our next steps tomorrow. Anyone else have anything?"

"What time do we open on Monday?" Micco asked.

"Our first patients are scheduled for eight thirty; be here at eight, so you'll be ready to take a breath before the rush hits, or if our first appointment shows up early. Doc Peterson will be here; I arrive around nine. If that's it, y'all have a great evening and weekend. I'll shut down the system and be right behind you."

Riley glanced at Micco, who gave her a knowing nod. "Micco and I will stay until you leave. It's not a good time for anyone to be alone."

Doc Peterson rose. "That's no surprise to me, Wesley. I almost forgot to tell you that you're delivering Adams' office contents to him. We boxed up everything today. See y'all on Monday."

Doc Wesley shrugged. "I guess we start with loading boxes into my truck."

"One of my best skills," Micco grinned.

After the boxes were loaded, Doc Wesley shut down the clinic data system and turned off the laptops, while Riley checked the exam rooms, and Micco organized the lost pets on the bulletin board.

When Riley joined him, she stood back and admired his work. "It was smart to put the dates on them, Micco. We have a few that are missing contact information. I'll stick notes on them in the morning asking for phone numbers."

Micco had a small stack of flyers in his hand. "These are duplicates, Riley. There must be several people taking flyers around for the same pet."

"Probably, but we don't need the clutter. Leave them on Maureen's desk; we'll ask her in the morning what she'd like to do with them."

"I'm ready to leave," Doc Wesley called out.

After Riley and Toby were in her car, she sent Ben a text. "Leaving work."

When he didn't reply, Riley said, "He might be a lot later than he planned. I'll stop at the grocery store and pick up a premade meal that I can warm up when he's on his way home."

As she neared the hardware store, Riley said, "I almost forgot my hardware stop."

Riley parked in the middle of the parking lot because all the spots in front of the hardware store were taken.

"The store is busy; I didn't expect that, but I guess I should have because almost everyone must have repairs to make," Riley said. "Hopefully, I won't be long."

While people came inside the store, picked up what they needed, paid for their items and left, Riley roamed the aisles.

Xavier appeared next to Riley when she stopped in front of the plants.

"Can I help you with something, Riley?"

"Is now a good time to plant butterfly bushes?"

"Where we are, it is, as long as they're planted before the first frost. Butterflies, especially monarchs, seek nectar in October, and the butterfly bush attracts them; however, the butterfly bush overall doesn't support the life cycle of butterflies, which is a major reason some consider the butterfly bush to be an invasive species. A better choice is milkweed, especially for monarchs. Where we live, the best time to plant milkweed seeds is after the first frost."

"I have a lot to learn about gardening," Riley said, "but I'd like to have some milkweed seeds."

"I have an old gardening book you might enjoy reading for research; it's especially fascinating if you're looking to replace an invasive species."

I wonder if I can report this correctly to Micco? Riley rolled her eyes as she followed Xavier. *I wonder if I'll remember this after I reach the parking lot. It's definitely code that isn't. The butterfly bush is viral, and it draws attention away from the milkweed that supports the lifecycle of the monarch.*

As Riley left the hardware store with the sack that had the milkweed seeds and Edith's gardening book, she dropped the sack into her backpack. *Maybe the gardening book will help me identify the viral butterfly bush and the supportive milkweed.*

Her thoughts were still swirling when she reached the grocery store. *Who is a butterfly bush and who is milkweed?*

Riley stood in front of the refrigerator case of meal kits and stared at the plastic trays of raw chicken and uncooked broccoli. *I could pull this together with spices we like.* She shook her head. *This is my butterfly bush. It looks good, but it won't save me any time.*

She wandered through the store and stopped in the frozen food section. As she reached for a box of frozen breaded shrimp, she heard a familiar voice.

"Are you looking for something that doesn't take a lot of prep work or time?" Fiona asked. "If you stir a little creamy horseradish into some catsup, you'll have cocktail sauce. It's one of my go-to meals when I forget to thaw something or got home from work later than I planned. I like to throw a bag of those steam-style vegetables or risotto in the microwave and warm up a couple of dinner rolls."

"That sounds good; I don't know what time Ben will be home tonight, and I have a feeling that's how it's going to be more often than not."

"My husband does equipment maintenance for the county, but he's the same. I switched to less time-sensitive meals early in our marriage; it's been less stress on me, and he's just happy to sit down to a hot meal."

While Riley put the large box of shrimp in her cart, she asked, "Will you be working all weekend?"

"Looks like it." Fiona rolled her eyes. "Doc Kaitlyn hired movers. We're moving into a larger building that has been empty for a while, so I'm going to be cleaning at the new clinic while Doc supervises the movers while they load what's left at the old clinic and what's in storage. I'll set up the computer equipment as soon as it's unloaded, so there won't be any surprises on Monday. Doc and I have big plans to have everything done in one day. My husband's working tomorrow too. Somebody's been stealing stop signs, and there have been several horrible crashes with injuries, but no fatalities yet, thank goodness."

"That's awful."

"He said it started this week and from the number they've found missing so far, it's not just a couple of obnoxious kids being bored after school; the county commissioners are flooded with calls complaining about the county road maintenance not keeping the roads safe. I hear that Kenneth Gleason, the challenger for our district's state senator race, is riling up folks about it, too, which doesn't help at all."

After Riley reached the front checkout lanes, she sighed with relief when she found a lane with only two people ahead of her.

When the line didn't move, the person in front of her turned to her and whispered, "I apologize because I should have warned you I always make a line stop. I hope you aren't in a hurry."

Riley smiled. "It's usually me."

"You're Riley, the new vet tech, aren't you?" the woman asked. "My yellow lab, Daisy, has an appointment on Monday. Doctor Peterson told me long ago that no one in the office would remember my name, so I should always tell them I'm Daisy's mom."

Riley giggled. "He's not wrong. Nice to meet you, and I look forward to meeting Daisy."

While the woman in front of Daisy's mom checked out, Riley shuddered at Arlo's voice when she heard him two rows away.

"The roads are unsafe because they're shifting the improvement money to pay off those corporate farms. It's been going on for ages, but we finally have somebody who will stand up to the foreign investors and take back what's ours."

"I don't know about that," a woman said.

"Well, you should; you lost your job because of them." Arlo stormed out of the store.

Daisy's mom shook her head. "I heard Arlo was the one who asked the board to fire her; he's got a lot of nerve blaming someone else."

"He was talking to the librarian?"

"Yes, and it's so hurtful because they used to be such close friends; she'd do anything for him when the rest of us had no patience at all with Arlo. He might not be wrong, but he sure is one angry man."

"Not wrong?" Riley asked.

"Not at all; there's just too many bad things happening, and nobody's doing anything about it." Daisy's mom moved forward to replace the woman in front of her who left.

After Riley paid for her groceries and rolled her cart out of the store, she followed the short, middle-aged woman with blue streaks in her hair.

When the woman stopped at a car and opened the trunk, Riley slowed when she neared her.

"How are you doing?" Riley asked.

The woman turned and smiled. "Just fine; you're Riley, aren't you? I've heard wonderful things about you. You certainly have a way with animals."

"Thank you; I love working at the Jimson Clinic. Everyone is so nice here."

The woman's face saddened. "They are, for the most part."

"You're the librarian, right? Sorry, but I remember animals' names, but not people's names."

The woman's eyes twinkled as she chuckled. "That's why you're such a good vet tech. People call me Linda, but I'm Greta's mom. Greta's not with us anymore, but my second cousin's husband always said vet people think of humans by their animal's names."

Riley smiled. "Somebody's telling trade secrets. I can help with your groceries."

Linda nodded. "He is a kindhearted man and loves the community; he's always telling me I need another dog, but I don't know."

As Riley handed Linda sacks from the cart, Linda set them inside the trunk. Riley's eyes widened briefly at the box of flares.

After Linda finished putting her groceries into the truck, she folded the flaps on the box. "I'm glad I ran into you; everybody tells me I should take an extended vacation, but I think I'll stick around for a while. There are some things I can do to help the community like Edith is doing. I've updated my journal and just need to find a place where it will be safe for a while until things cool down for me."

She gazed at Riley. "I'll walk with you to your car and help you with your groceries. Edith told me she trusted you, Doctor Peterson, of course, and Xavier. She's not what people are saying, you know."

"I know." When Riley reached her car and opened her trunk, Linda handed her the grocery sacks one at a time.

After they were loaded, the woman pointed at the road. "Was that Maureen?"

Riley turned her head to look at the road. "I don't see her."

Linda sighed. "You're right; it's a man driving a car like hers. I guess that was wishful thinking on my part. It's such a shame that she's so despondent over Gina."

"She really is sad. It was nice to meet you, Greta's mom." Riley watched as Linda slowly walked back to her car with her shoulders slumped and her head down.

On their way home, Riley said, "I took longer than I expected, but I have something decent for supper, a treat for you, and cookies for Ben and me."

After Riley fed Toby, she put on her jacket, stuck her phone in her pocket in case Ben called or texted, then she and Toby went outside. As the sun slowly slid below the horizon, Riley said, "I'm officially cold; let's go inside."

She hung up her coat. "I'd planned to do laundry tomorrow, but I wonder what I thought I'd wear. The clothes basket is practically overflowing."

Riley gathered up their dirty clothes; she went through Ben's pockets of his jeans and uniform pants and shirts. She pulled out two pocket knives, some change, and gas receipts before she tossed his clothes into the washer.

"I'm not the packrat Ben is," she chuckled as she went through her pockets.

She raised her eyebrows when she pulled out an object from her jeans and cocked her head. "I'd forgotten about the flash drive that was in the refrigerator."

She furrowed her brow. "Mason's dad said Lisa wanted me to clean the refrigerator."

After Riley started the washer, she started a fire in the fireplace. "Ben's probably been outside all day."

She set her laptop on the table and plugged in the flash drive and saved the files on her computer in a folder she called 'Fridge' then ejected the flash drive.

The first file she opened was a spreadsheet titled 'Donations'; the columns on the spreadsheet were date, name, address, total amount, cash amount, check amount, and reference number. She scrolled down until she reached the last row with data.

"There are almost three hundred donors. Cash amounts are frequently more than the check amounts."

She sorted the data by the amount of the check. "The smallest check is five thousand dollars."

Riley opened the next file titled 'Friends of G.' "This is a list of bank accounts with the bank names, account numbers, deposit amounts, and reference numbers."

She compared the reference numbers to the ones on the Donation file. "They match."

The next file she opened was titled 'Cross Ref Donations and Friends of G.'

"Lisa must be a spreadsheet whiz, but at least we had the same idea, Toby. I wonder if G stands for Gleason." She shook her head. "I don't have any evidence to support any wild speculations even though I'm certain I'm right; I'll let the professionals investigate."

Toby opened his eyes and padded to his water bowl for a drink.

"The next file is 'Payments', but I'm sure it's more of the same. I'd almost forgotten about the laundry." Riley rose from her seat, stretched, then moved the clothes from the washer to the dryer.

After she poured a glass of sweet tea, she scanned the rest of the files. "These are the source documents for the spreadsheets."

Riley's phone buzzed with a text from Ben. "On my way home."

Riley shut down her laptop and turned on the oven to preheat. After she read the directions on the box of shrimp, she returned it to the freezer. "I'll wait until he gets home, so he'll have time to change clothes or have a glass of sweet tea or a beer."

When Ben came inside, he strode to Riley and hugged her. She sighed and leaned against him. After a sweet kiss, she said, "Supper will be ready in about twenty minutes, if you'd like to change or shower."

"Both." He kissed her and pulled off his shirt then hopped on one leg then the other on his way to the bathroom as he removed his pants and undershorts along the way.

"Cute buns there, sexy cowboy," Riley said as she quickly put ten shrimp on a baking sheet and popped it into the oven.

She smiled as she picked up the clothes he'd scattered on his way to the bathroom. She opened the bathroom door and was greeted by a face full of steam. "Do you want sweet tea or beer?"

"Will you have a beer with me? I'm ready to be off duty."

"Best idea I've heard all day." She tossed his clothes into the washer to add to the towels after her shower for another load of laundry.

When naked Ben came out of the bathroom, Riley whistled; he grinned and swaggered to the bedroom to dress. Riley put the risotto with peas and mushrooms into the microwave while Ben opened two beers.

"You want yours on the table, babe?" Ben tipped up his bottle and took a long drink of beer.

"Yes, please." Riley placed the dinner rolls in the oven on top of the shrimp.

While they ate, Riley said, "It's been so frantic the last couple of days, I can't remember if I told you we don't have to go shopping for furniture because the folks are coming here tomorrow with family donations of furniture."

Ben chuckled. "I should have thought of that; it's a family tradition. Are we going to give them our room?"

"No, Mom made reservations at a bed-and-breakfast for tomorrow night. Duffy and Finn will stay with us."

"We'll have wall to wall dogs; what time do we expect them?"

"I think after lunch some time; Mom will let me know. What time are you leaving in the morning?"

"Probably about seven thirty. What about you?"

"About the same."

After they finished eating and the dishwasher was running, Ben said, "That was a wonderful meal, babe."

Riley emptied the dryer; Ben hung up his uniforms while she folded the rest. "I'm going to shower, but first, I have some files to give you. I'll let you look at them if you promise you won't start working until tomorrow."

"Sounds like something I'd want to work on right away."

"Not really; I'll show you in the morning."

"Okay, I promise I won't start working until tomorrow."

Riley set up the computer on the table and inserted the flash drive. Ben pulled his chair around so he could see the screen.

"What am I looking at?"

"A flash drive I found at the clinic in the refrigerator earlier this week when I cleaned it. I stuck it into my jeans pocket and forgot about it until I checked my pockets before I put clothes into the washer. Lisa left early on Monday so she could send her husband a report for his farmers' meeting near Atlanta; she said she had all the backup data on a flash drive, but the report he needed was on her computer at home. Her brother told me today that Lisa asked him to tell me to clean the refrigerator, but he thought she was confused."

Riley pulled up the first spreadsheet. Ben peered at it. "This is very incriminating."

"I thought so."

"Can I look at the files while you shower?"

"Sure."

When Riley rose, Ben pulled the computer in front of him and began scouring the spreadsheets.

Riley returned from the shower with their wet towels and wearing her favorite flannel nightgown and her fluffy bedroom slippers. She sashayed past Ben and dropped the towels into the washer then started it.

When she turned with one hand on her hip, Ben smiled and raised his eyebrows as he looked her up and down.

She giggled. "Just pretend it's sexy. I'm cold."

He closed the computer. "Let's go warm you up."

Chapter Seventeen

While Riley poured coffee into the large thermos for Ben, he fed Toby then the two of them went outside.

Riley opened the washer to move the clothes to the dryer, but it was empty. *That sneak beat me to it.*

After she removed the laundry from the dryer, she hung his uniform shirt and pants in the bedroom closet, then quickly folded the rest of their clothes and the towels and put them away.

When Ben opened the back door, Toby dashed inside for his after breakfast treat.

"Are you going to be in the office all morning?" Ben asked.

"Yes, but I'll have my long johns in case anything changes."

"Thanks; I worry about you. I'm taking the thumb drive." After a quick kiss, Ben put on his jacket and rushed to the door.

"Loved you first." He closed the door.

Riley snatched up her phone and texted him as he started his truck's engine. "Love you more."

She giggled at his reply. "Too slow. I win."

"It never gets old, Toby." She exhaled then gathered her backpack and put on her warm jacket.

Riley smiled when she pulled into the parking lot behind the clinic. "It's not quite seven thirty, and both Doctor Peterson and Maureen are already here. I wonder if they compete over who gets to the clinic first, and I wonder who wins."

While she hung up her backpack and coat, Toby dashed to the receptionist's desk and yipped. Riley smiled when Maureen giggled and cooed to Toby.

Doctor Peterson came into the breakroom carrying a platter. "My wife keeps pastry dough in the freezer for special events. She made a blueberry pastry for us because we're working on Saturday to take care of walk-ins."

Maureen called out, "I heard blueberry pastry."

Doc Peterson put two pieces on a paper plate. Riley took the plate and the coffee pot to Maureen's desk.

Riley set down the plate and refilled Maureen's cup. "Thanks, Riley. I see you put up the bulletin board and organized it."

"Micco did that. We found duplicate flyers; we left them on your desk."

"I wondered about that. Take down the ones with notes and put them on my desk, and I'll work on contact information for them. I'll try to cross reference them with our files since they listed the pet's names. Maybe later I'll have time to call the ones who have phone numbers to see if their pets are still missing."

Riley smiled. "It's great to have you back in action."

"I talked to Fiona yesterday; thank goodness she's experienced."

"We would have left you a mess if she hadn't been here."

Maureen rolled her eyes. "I can only imagine. Eat your pastry before I unlock the door. I've already had two calls asking if we're open."

When Riley returned to the breakroom, Doctor Peterson pointed to the two plates of pastry and a folder on the table. "Pour yourself a cup of coffee and join me. Read the resumes; I'm interested in your thoughts."

After they sat at the table, Riley took a bite of the blueberry pastry. "Mmm. This is absolutely delicious. How does she get the crust so flaky?"

Doc Peterson chuckled. "It's all kitchen magic."

Riley read the resumes. "All of them have outstanding academic records." She set two of them aside then pointed to the three remaining. "These three look a little more promising."

"Why is that?"

"I was just thinking about Micco. One of them volunteered at a county shelter while she was in high school, one worked as a vet tech for three years before he began the veterinary program, and the third one currently works at a fast-food restaurant."

"I understand the first two, but why the third?"

"He must need the extra income, but he still kept up his grades and is as strong academically as the others. He's determined to be a veterinarian."

"That's an interesting observation; I would have missed that. Now I can't wait to hear what Wesley has to say."

Doc Peterson frowned as his phone rang. "Wesley's calling me."

He rose as he answered the phone and strolled toward his office. "You're kidding me. Do we close the office?"

Doc Peterson closed his door. When he opened it a few minutes later, he said, "Maureen, I need to talk to you and Riley in the breakroom."

Riley shuddered at the seriousness on his face.

"Wesley called me. Hugo Adams was shot in his front yard. Arlo has been arrested and charged with murder."

Riley stared at him; Maureen's face paled.

Doc Peterson continued, "Wesley said it's up to us whether we open the clinic this morning."

Maureen cleared her throat. "It's a shock, but we're here to serve our patients. It's up to you two, but I'd rather work."

Riley nodded.

"I agree; I'll let Wesley know." Doc Peterson went to his office and closed the door.

Maureen exhaled. "I feel bad for his wife." She left the breakroom.

A few minutes later, Maureen called out, "We have patients in the parking lot."

Riley hurried to Maureen's desk as Mason and his dad came in with an Australian Shepherd that was muddy and had a matted coat and a flea collar, but no dog collar or leash.

"Oh my goodness," Maureen said. "That baby has been outside for a while, hasn't he?"

Mason said, "We don't know what his name is, so I call him Buddy; he came to our house yesterday afternoon. I found him still on our back porch this morning when I took out the trash; he was excited to see me and jumped all over me until I told him he had to stay down. We gave him some water and some canned chicken. He waited on the back porch for me while we ate breakfast then hopped into the car when I opened the door for him."

Mason's dad added, "We thought we'd check the bulletin board and would like for you to check him out. We'll take him to the groomer's after this if we don't find him on the board."

Maureen and handed Riley a new folder with a sheet inside to record her findings.

"Let's weigh you, Buddy," Riley said.

Toby yipped and led Buddy to the scale; Mason and Riley followed them while Mason's dad examined the bulletin board.

Buddy sat on the scale and grinned at Mason.

"Good boy." Mason beamed.

"His weight is a little less than what it should be, but it's not bad." Riley jotted it down.

After they went into the first exam room, Riley said, "I'm going to take your temperature, Buddy."

Buddy leaned against Mason while Riley stroked him and took his temperature.

"Thank you, Buddy. Your temperature is normal. Next, I'll you for fleas and ticks then check your ears."

"Dad went to the store last night and got a flea collar for him and pulled off all the ticks he could find. We put a sheet on the back seat in case he had fleas," Mason said.

"That was a smart idea because he does have a few fleas, but I don't see any ticks. Doc will prescribe medicine that will protect him from fleas and ticks. The groomers will probably use a flea comb to remove the eggs, so you don't end up with fleas in the house."

"That's good, because Mom was worried about that."

"A few more tests, Buddy," Riley said.

While Riley looked at Buddy's ears, Mason said, "I didn't tell Dad, but Buddy followed me home. My friend and I went bike riding..." Mason bit his lip when Riley raised her eyebrows.

He stared at Buddy. "I have an old bike with no gears. I rode it pretty good with only one arm, and I didn't fall. We were riding on the old highway, so it was pretty smooth; there wasn't any traffic and almost no houses. We rode past Miss Gina's house. There aren't any houses close to hers. We saw a ghost and got scared, so we turned back and rode as fast as we could. That's when we heard Buddy huffing behind us. I don't know how long he'd been chasing us. My friend is kind of afraid of dogs, so when I stopped, he rode off. I just rode normal, and Buddy trotted along with me. I didn't say nothing when I got home, then when I took out the trash, Buddy was still there."

"Buddy could have come from anywhere then."

"That's right; you aren't going to bust me, are you?"

"You should tell them yourself."

"They're going to ground me."

"Is that unfair?" Riley asked.

"No, but I won't tell them about getting scared," Mason muttered.

Riley nodded. *A man's entitled to a little dignity.*

"I'll get Doctor Peterson. Should I ask your dad to come in with you?"

Mason exhaled. "Yes, ma'am."

"Doc Peterson will give you and your dad a few minutes to talk, then he'll tap on the door."

Mason nodded and straightened his shoulders.

Riley left the room and stopped at the bulletin board where Mason's dad was still examining the flyers.

"Would you like to go in with Mason and Buddy while I brief Doc Peterson on our patient?" Riley asked.

"Sure thing." Mason's dad went into the first exam room.

"What do we have?" Doctor Peterson asked when Riley stood in the doorway of his office.

She handed him the file. "Mason and his dad brought in an intact, one-year-old, mostly Australian Shepherd male, who is most likely a stray. He came to their house yesterday and had fleas and ticks, so they put a flea collar on him and removed the ticks. Mason calls him Buddy. His ears were filled with dirt, so I couldn't tell much there. He has tape worms. I'll let you know about the heartworm in a few minutes. They're planning to take him to the groomers to get cleaned up if he's not on the board. Mason and Buddy have bonded."

Doctor Peterson nodded. "Are we killing time with this in-depth report on purpose?"

Riley grinned. "Yes, sir, we are. Mason and his dad are having a man-to-man conversation."

"Is Buddy on the bulletin board?"

"No, and I think he has traveled far from home. He was most likely in the storm alone."

"Do you think he'll be hard to train?"

"I don't think so at all."

Doc Peterson smiled. "Do you think Mason is ready to be rescued?"

Riley returned his smile. "I told Mason you'd tap on the door. I'll check on the heartworm test and be there as soon as I have the results."

Riley checked the test results and exhaled. When she walked into the exam room, she said, "Buddy's heartworm negative."

"Excellent," Dr. Peterson said. "We discussed immunizations; I gave Buddy the full round, so that's done, too. Next up is a bath. We'll leave it up to the groomer whether they want to comb him or if they think it would be better to shave him."

"Dad called Mom, and she said it's okay if Buddy stays in the house after his bath, if he's a good boy and goes potty outside," Mason said.

Mason's dad nodded.

Riley glanced at Buddy's file. "I'll meet you at Maureen's desk with Buddy's medications while

Maureen makes Buddy's followup appointment for us to take care of his boy surgery and check his ears."

When Riley took Buddy's medicine to Maureen's desk, a husky puppy and a woman with tears overflowing onto her cheeks stood outside near the window and away from the door.

After Mason and his dad left with Buddy, Maureen said, "Go see your patient outside without your coat, even though it's cold." Maureen handed her a jar of mentholated ointment. "And rub a little of this under your nose." ,

"A skunk encounter?" Riley rubbed a little ointment under her nose.

"Exactly, at a distance of about four feet, so there was no physical contact."

"So the client wants to know what to do about the smell."

"Right. Your patient's name is Fearless."

Riley snorted. "How embarrassing. I won't be long."

When Riley went outside, she said, "Hello, Fearless; I'm Riley."

The client sniffled. "What do I do about this? My neighbor said to wash him with tomato juice. Is that right?"

"The idea is to wash the poor guy with something acidic to counter the odor. There are commercial products you can buy, but I'd recommend white vinegar diluted with water. Add a little dish soap or baby shampoo for a fresher smell than vinegar then rinse with water. If you don't have any vinegar, buy a gallon jug from the grocery store on your way home. After you've washed

Fearless as well as you can, you could see if any of the groomers can work him in today."

The woman sighed. "When I opened the door, he ran inside and rubbed his face on the carpeting."

"I am so sorry. You can try a mild solution of vinegar, maybe try it first in a corner, or the grocery store might have a rug shampoo for strong odors."

"Thank you so much, Riley. My brain was fried by the skunk smell. I pulled him away so he wouldn't get sprayed a second time, so I'm stinky too." She sighed. "They're going to love me in the grocery store." She giggled. "Of course, I'll have a checkout line, and maybe the entire store, all to myself. Fearless and I will become town legends, won't we?"

Riley's smile turned into a shiver.

The woman said, "Thanks for your help. You're freezing; go back inside."

"Thank you; call us if you have any more questions."

When Riley went back inside, Maureen said, "She called me and I asked her to wait outside; she understood. I'll bill her for a tech visit; the client should have named her sweet puppy Reckless."

"I need to clean Buddy's room," Riley said.

"You probably need to change your clothes too; you still have a whiff of skunk lingering."

"I have spare clothes in my backpack. I'll change real quick."

"Before you go, you might not have heard that Edith was released yesterday; they said she was completely cleared."

"That's good news; I didn't understand how they could have arrested her in the first place."

"She was obviously framed, but I don't know why," Maureen said.

When Riley pulled out her clean shirt and jeans, Edith's gardening book fell on the floor. She picked it up and flipped through it. Riley stopped in the middle and stared at the pages. *This is a list of banks with account numbers and passwords. Lisa and Edith must have been working together. I have to tell Ben.*

Riley sent Ben a quick text. "I have a booklet with a list of banks, account numbers, and passwords."

He immediately replied, "On my way."

After she changed clothes, Riley put her stinky shirt and pants in a plastic bag and dropped the bag outside the back door then hurried to clean Buddy's room.

When she returned to Maureen's desk, a man sped into the parking lot and slammed on his brakes in front of the clinic. He jumped out of the car and ran around to the passenger side of the car. Riley raced to the door and opened it as he carried in a limp, brown, long-haired dachshund. A weeping woman followed them inside.

"Tell Doc we'll be in the trauma room," Riley said.

"Doc, trauma," Maureen shouted.

The man's forehead and temples were soaked with sweat despite the cold weather. "He just ran in front of me; I slammed on the brakes, but he hit the side of the car, and the car knocked him into the ditch across the road. He landed in the dirt, not on the hard surface of the road. Maybe that's good."

The man laid the dog gently on the table in the trauma room. "We're pretty shook up. Is he going to be okay?"

"Why don't you wait with your wife in the reception area?" Doc Peterson hurried into the room. "We'll take it from here."

The man nodded and left as Riley leaned over the dog and gently ran her hands along his body.

"He's breathing. I can't tell if anything is broken; I'll take him in for x-rays."

"One second." While Doc Peterson pulled out a stethoscope to listen to the dog's chest, Riley turned on the oxygen tank and set up blow-by oxygen for the dog.

"His heart rate is a little fast, but regular. Lungs are clear. I'm particularly interested in his ribs and hips." Doc gently slid his hand along the dog's chest and abdomen. When he palpated the dog's legs, the dog whimpered as Doc touched his right rear leg.

"You got that?" Doc asked.

"Yes; I won't be long." Riley eased the dachshund onto the gurney and rolled him into the x-ray room. She snugged a strap over him then quickly took the x-rays.

She and Doc Peterson examined the x-rays.

"All I see is the break in the right rear leg here." Doc pointed. "Check his abdomen again; your touch is gentler."

Riley palpated the dog's abdomen and watched his face. "It's soft, and he didn't react to any pain."

The puppy stirred then whined. When he opened his eyes, he tensed his muscles.

Riley said, "His pupils are a little dilated, but they're equal, so he might just be scared."

Riley hummed a calming tune and felt the dog's muscles relax.

Doc exhaled. "He might have a mild concussion. It's times like this that I wish I could ask how many fingers."

Riley opened the trauma room door. "Toby."

He trotted into the room.

Riley leaned close to the dachshund. "Sweet boy, do you feel okay?"

When the dog moaned, Toby whimpered.

"We know your leg hurts, and we're so sorry. We'll take care of that. Anything else?"

The dog whined.

"I'm so sorry. After we put a splint on your leg, I'll tell the people you're thirsty and hungry."

"I'll splint it, if you'll go talk to the people who are waiting," Doc said.

Riley whispered to the dog, "Doc likes dogs better than people."

Toby grinned, and the small dachshund's smile was barely discernible.

"What's your name?"

The dog yipped, and Toby grinned.

Riley laughed. "I know it isn't Mighty Warrior, but that's what I'll tell the people."

When Riley went to the reception area, both the man and the woman immediately rose from their chairs.

"How is he?" the woman asked.

"He has a broken leg. Doc is putting a splint on it. He was probably stunned by being thrown across the road, but he's alert now. Do you know anything about him?"

"When he ran out from the side of the road, we thought he was a survivor of that horrible car fire out our way last night, then I saw the rabbit he was chasing," the man said.

"While my husband ran across the road to the ditch, I found this in the middle of the road." The woman handed Riley a small metallic disc. "If this is his, his name is Max. I called the number, but it's disconnected."

"I'll be right back."

Riley went into the trauma room. "Is your name Max, Mighty Warrior?"

When Max barked, Doc jumped.

"Didn't expect that," Doc mumbled.

"Thanks, Max. I think the people might want to take care of you."

"We heard him bark," the man said. "It sounded pretty strong."

Riley smiled. "He's doing great. We definitely know his name is Max, and he's completely aware."

"What's going to happen to Max?" the woman asked. "Can we go see him?"

"As soon as Doc splints his leg. Did you want to take care of him? If you don't, it's okay, because we can call animal services. They're a little overcrowded, but they'll try to put him with a dog that isn't too big."

"Max is going home with us," the woman said.

"I promised him water and food; pick up dog dishes and food on your way home, and he might enjoy a soft dog bed and a few toys. If you schedule an appointment for Max to return on Tuesday, we can check his splint and get him established for regular care," Riley said.

"That's exactly what we want to do," the man said.

After the man made the appointment, he carried Max to their car. Max curled up on the woman's lap, and she smiled.

"What was all that about Mighty Warrior?" Doc asked.

"That's what Max first told me was his name; he's a smart, lighthearted guy, and a jokester," Riley said.

After Riley cleaned the trauma room, she went to Maureen's desk.

Maureen side-glanced at Riley. "I didn't know whether to laugh or cry when you told those sweet people we'd call animal services."

"Did I go too overboard, or was it okay that I gave them a little nudge?"

"I'm glad they took Max, because I agree with you. They really wanted him to go home with them," Maureen said. "I hadn't heard anything about a car fire, so I texted a friend of mine who knows everything."

"Do we have anyone else coming in?" Riley asked.

The office phone rang. "Not yet." Maureen answered.

Riley turned toward Doc Peterson's office, but paused when Maureen gasped.

"That's horrible; thanks for letting me know."

CHAPTER EIGHTEEN

After she hung up, Maureen gazed at Riley. "The car that burned belonged to Linda; it was completely engulfed in flames when the fire department arrived. Arlo is beyond devastated; my friend's word was berserk. I knew they were close friends, but I guess that wasn't common knowledge."

Riley sat down. "Are they sure? Is there any chance..."

"I don't know; my friend said the fire was so hot that the only thing left was the car frame and smoldering tires."

Riley frowned. *Greta's mom had all those flares in the trunk. Would they have made the fire even hotter?*

Ben texted Riley. "At the back door."

Riley said, "I won't be long. I'm going to put my stinky clothes next to my car."

She hurried to the breakroom and pulled out the gardening book from her backpack and threw on her coat before she rushed outside.

Ben ambushed her with a kiss. When he released her, she giggled.

"Here's the gardening book. It's really odd that Lisa had the files with detailed transactions, but Edith had the passwords for the bank accounts. Do you think they got together to break up the conspiracy, or whatever it is?"

Ben stared at her. "A good conspiracy fighting a bad conspiracy?"

Riley rolled her eyes. "Sounds far-fetched, doesn't it?"

"Absolutely, so stay out."

Riley raised her eyebrows.

"Please." Ben kissed her. "Gotta go, babe, before I say anything else that gets me in trouble."

He jumped into his GBI cruiser and left while she ran to her car to drop off the stinky sack next to it then hurried back inside.

As she headed back inside, Riley muttered, "Conspiracies like a butterfly bush and milkweed."

After she hung up her coat, Maureen called out, "Patient on the way."

When Riley reached the desk, Maureen said, "It's a snake encounter. I told them not to bring the snake with them and asked for a photo instead. I learned that the first week I worked here and refuse to make that mistake again." Maureen shuddered.

"Did they send you the photo?" Riley asked.

"No. I don't want to see it." Maureen closed her eyes.

"There are excellent online resources to identify snakes. I'll show you when they get here."

"No, thank you. Snakes are not listed in my job description. Here's the file."

Riley read over the file before she strolled to the door to watch for the patient and client. When the client arrived, he was carrying a yorkie.

Riley smiled at the smiling yorkie. "Hi, Lucy. I'm Riley, and this is Toby. We're new, but we know what we're doing. I'd like to see the photo of the snake. Let's go into exam room one."

After they were in the room, the client put Lucy on the table and pulled out his phone. Lucy walked to the edge of the table and peered at Toby.

"Did the snake bite you?" Riley asked.

Lucy growled then snarled.

"Sounds like you were very brave."

Also, sounds like the snake is my patient, but I don't think Maureen would approve.

The man continued scrolling on his phone.

"Where did the snake go after you bit it?" Riley asked.

Lucy lay down on the table then yipped.

Riley stroked Lucy. "Let's get your weight and temperature real quick."

After Riley recorded Lucy's weight and temperature, the client exhaled. "Here it is, finally."

Riley looked at the photo. "It's a rat snake. It's not venomous and is actually a great snake to have around."

"But it bit Lucy."

"Did you see it bite Lucy?"

"No, but she yelped like she'd been bitten."

"I think she bit the snake and told it to go away before she got mad."

"Really? That actually sounds exactly like something Lucy would do."

Riley nodded. "I examined Lucy, and she doesn't have any bite marks. How did you get the photo?"

"Lucy was barking at a bush; when I got close to see what was there, the snake slithered out and disappeared in the grass. I snapped the photo right before it disappeared."

"You more than likely won't see it again because it will probably avoid Lucy, but maybe it will stick around to hunt rats and mice."

"I didn't know what kind of snake it was," the man said.

"I appreciate you brought in a picture; it really made a difference for Lucy. That's actually a remarkably clear photo of a rat snake; you should post it on social media."

The man straightened his back and raised his head. "Really?"

Riley nodded as she glanced at Lucy's file. "Lucy is due for her annual check-up. Since you're here, we'll ask Maureen to schedule it."

While the client checked out with Maureen, Riley went into Doc Peterson's office. "Rat snake, but Lucy bit the snake."

Doc rose from his chair. "Did the client have a photo?"

"Yes, he did."

Doc hurried past Riley to Maureen's desk. "I'd like to see your snake."

The client pulled up the photo.

Doc smiled. "What a beauty. This is a great photo."

The client beamed. "Thanks."

After Lucy and the client left, Maureen glared. "Y'all are weird."

"What time are we shutting down?" Doc asked.

"Doctor Wesley said we had a hard stop at eleven thirty," Maureen said.

"That's only fifteen more minutes, and we've had a full morning." Doc smiled.

"I'll double-check the rooms, so they'll be ready for Monday," Riley said.

"You know that will bring in a flood of patients, don't you?" Maureen chuckled.

While Riley cleaned and restocked the last exam room, her phone buzzed with a text. She raised her eyebrows as she read it. "Call me, please. Thank you, Edith."

Riley called her.

"Thank you for calling me back so fast; I need a big favor."

"Of course; what can I do?"

"One of my old friends had ordered campaign posters for me when I was running for the library board, and Xavier has been keeping them for me at the hardware store because they were too big for the trunk of my compact car. Unfortunately, Xavier's annual inventory is scheduled tomorrow, and the crew will be showing up at eight in the morning. He told me they're careful, but I'm afraid my posters will be damaged. Xavier told me the posters would fit inside a normal-sized trunk, and I really hate to ask, but would you mind picking them up and bringing them to my house?"

"We'll be closing the clinic soon. Text me your address, and I'll stop by the hardware store and bring them to you."

"I'm really sorry to bother you, but I appreciate your help."

Edith hung up; Riley headed to Maureen's desk.

When she glanced at the bulletin board, Riley smiled. "We're had a few more reunions. That's great."

Maureen nodded. "The front door is locked, and Doc Peterson just left. I told him we'd leave together; are you ready?"

"I just need to grab my jacket and backpack on my way out."

After they were outside and the back door was locked, Maureen rolled to her car.

"Care for any help?" Riley asked.

"Nope; I'm not overly coordinated, but I'm proud to be self-sufficient. See you on Monday," Maureen said.

Riley opened her car's back door and Toby hopped in.

As she backed out of her parking space, Riley said, "We're going to the hardware store to pick up Edith's campaign posters." Riley shrugged. "It made sense when she asked me. I'm getting used to odd requests; what about you?"

She glanced in the rearview mirror. Toby grinned.

"Want to go in with me?" Riley asked after she parked.

Toby trotted to the hardware store and waited for Riley at the door.

"There you are, Toby, and you brought Riley." Xavier chuckled at his own joke.

Xavier glanced toward the back then cleared his throat. His voice was loud when he spoke. "I'll get those items you ordered and load them into your car for you, Riley. I assume you'll want them in your trunk."

"Yes, please," Riley said. *I wonder who is here that we're doing this little dance for.*

While Xavier headed to the back of the store, Riley casually checked each aisle then narrowed her eyes when she spotted a woman who seemed to peer around a corner as she watched the back of the store. Riley shrugged as she returned to the cash register. *I wonder who that is. She seemed awfully interested in what Xavier was doing.*

When Xavier brought the posters to the front, they were wrapped with brown craft paper.

Riley spoke as loudly as Xavier had earlier. "Thank you so much for getting these so quickly. I have a presentation at the school on Monday."

Xavier's eyes twinkled. "The children will love hearing about your experience with animals. You've become a celebrity."

Riley chuckled. "I don't know about that, but I'm happy I can be a positive role model for the children."

"You certainly are one of the best. I'll carry them out for you," Xavier said.

When they reached her car, Riley giggled as she raised the trunk. "Who were we annoying?"

"From what I hear, Doc Kaitlyn's vet tech, Bonnie, has been saying unkind things about the staff at Jimson

Clinic. I can't tell you how tickled I was that you picked up on my attempt to give her a reason to be jealous; I was honored to be a part of such a devious plot to put her knickers in a knot."

Riley laughed. "I haven't heard that since Grandma mentioned someone we didn't like at all. Thank you."

"You be safe; if you need anything, text Edith, and you'll get what you need. We have a heavy duty support network in place."

Riley gazed at him then held out her hand. "Thank you so much, Xavier."

"You belong here, Riley. We're proud to call you one of our own." Xavier strode back to the store.

"Wow. Grandma would say, 'Don't that beat all.'" A tear slipped down Riley's face as she opened the back door for Toby. "I'm sorry you didn't meet Grandma. She would have loved you and Ben."

Riley copied Edith's address into her GPS and followed the directions to the edge of town. She turned onto a dirt road then arrived at a small house with clapboard siding and a wide veranda. There were two cars parked in the driveway.

"That's odd; it looks like Edith has company."

As Riley headed toward the front door, Toby whined and dashed to the corner of the house. Riley followed him.

When the front door opened, Riley's eyes widened.

"Come on in, Riley," Gina held a gun in her hand; it was pointed at Riley. "This is a welcome surprise."

"Sorry, Riley, she burst into the house before I realized she was here." Edith sat on an overstuffed chair with a stack of books on the table next to her; Linda sat across from her on a sofa.

Mason said he saw a ghost at Gina's; he must have seen her. I'm glad she didn't see him.

Toby growled.

Gina snarled as she pointed her gun at him. "Put him outside, or I'll shoot him."

Riley turned and opened the door for Toby. "Wait outside, boy."

Gina's eyes were dark with hate. "Arlo was supposed to have gotten rid of the librarian, but he double-crossed me. I stole a gun from his house and shot the nosy veterinarian who thought he'd freelance as a blackmailer. Nobody double-crosses or blackmails me."

Linda shifted forward on the sofa and stretched out her leg, and Gina glanced at her.

"What are you doing?"

"I have a leg cramp; I have to stand up."

Gina wheeled to the side to face her. "I'll fix your leg cramp."

Gina aimed her gun at Linda, and Riley pulled out her pistol from its holster and aimed at Gina.

"Drop it, Gina." Riley growled.

When Gina turned to fire at Riley, Edith swept off the books from the table onto the floor.

Gina jerked as she fired; Riley fired at the same time.

Riley kept her pistol aimed at Gina, who dropped her gun as she clutched her chest and fell to the floor. Gina grunted as she reached for her gun.

Linda picked up the gun and pointed it at Gina. "Give me a reason to pull the trigger, Gina."

"I'm on the phone with nine-one-one," Edith said.

Toby was frantically scratching the front door and barking; Riley hurried to the door and opened it. He raced inside and snarled as he stood over the bleeding Gina who was cursing all of them.

"Shut up, Gina," Edith said. "I can't hear what the dispatcher is saying."

"You heard her," Linda growled and pointed the gun she held at Gina's knee.

Gina gritted her teeth and glared at Linda.

While they waited for law enforcement and the ambulance, Linda said, "Riley, you have the journal that lists Gina's activities for the past two years. Arlo gave it to me for safekeeping because Gina was getting suspicious of him, and rightly so, because Arlo was undercover. She owns Kenneth Gleason; all the details are in the journal, including information about her backers."

Riley furrowed her brow as the sound of sirens seemed to come from every direction. "Arlo was undercover? I have his journal?"

The sound of a siren roared to the front of the house then abruptly halted.

"Ben's here. He'll be interested in hearing that I have Arlo's journal."

Ben burst into the house with his pistol drawn then scanned the room. "Would you two please put your guns down?"

Linda put Gina's gun on the sofa behind her where Gina couldn't reach it, and Riley set her gun on the floor to her side away from Gina.

"Honey, I just learned I have Arlo's journal," Riley said.

"He'll be glad to hear that; where is it?"

"You know Arlo? Linda, where do I have Arlo's journal?" Riley asked.

"I panicked and dropped it into your car's trunk in the grocery store parking lot when I thought I saw Maureen. I was afraid she was working with Gina; for the record, she isn't, but I didn't know how to get the journal back from you until Edith and Xavier made up the poster story."

"Poster story?" Ben asked.

"I'll tell you later. It was an excellent subterfuge, Edith; I'm impressed."

"Thank you; Xavier will be proud to hear that."

The house was suddenly swarmed by law enforcement officers; Ben retrieved Arlo's journal and the fake posters from Riley's car then gave the journal to another GBI officer.

The ambulance crews brought in their gurneys. While the first ambulance crew removed Gina to transport her to the hospital, the second paramedic checked Edith then Linda. After Edith and Linda refused transport, the ambulance crews left.

Ben kept his arm around Riley, and Toby leaned against her on her other side while she repeated what had happened to a GBI officer.

After Riley was released from the scene, Ben walked her and Toby to her car.

"Go straight home, babe," he said.

"Bossy," she muttered as she drove away from Edith's house.

CHAPTER NINETEEN

After Riley and Toby arrived home, Riley parked her car out of the way near the woods, so there would be plenty of room for Jake's truck and the trailer.

She texted Ben. "I'm home."

He replied, "Ten minutes; I picked up lunch."

When Ben arrived, he strode into the house. "Ready for tacos? I saw a food truck on my way home and had to stop."

Riley inhaled the aroma that floated in with Ben. "I'm definitely ready for tacos. They smell amazing."

She put plates on the table. "Do we need salsa?"

"Not at all, but you could pour some iced tea while I prepare our gourmet meal by ripping open the sack. We have fresh tortilla chips, salsa, guacamole, and tacos."

While they ate, Ben asked, "Tell me something about your day that won't upset my stomach."

She told him about Mason and Buddy.

"Do you think Buddy's original people will show up?" Ben asked.

"I have a feeling they won't, but I can't explain why. Maybe it's because Buddy and Mason bonded so quickly. We've heard stories about dogs that ran away because they were looking for their humans. I think Buddy and Mason have been looking for each other."

"I love an exciting dog and his boy lived happily ever after story."

Riley told him about Lucy and the rat snake.

Ben laughed. "Poor snake. I'm amazed you and Toby didn't decide to go on a quest to find the snake to be sure he, except maybe it was she, was okay. Were you surprised by Doc Peterson's reaction?"

"Actually, I decided he was an authentic old school veterinarian. If Toby and I had gone on a snake rescue, I'm convinced he'd have tagged along as senior advisor and our voice of respectability."

Ben nodded. "You definitely would need him to cover the respectability side. You're cute, but you've got this wild, edgy side that doesn't seem to line up with regular rules."

"That's strictly personal opinion." Riley sniffed.

"How about a cookie?" Ben's eyes twinkled.

"Are you changing the subject because I win? Yes, to the cookie."

Riley's phone buzzed a text from Melissa. "Five minutes out."

She showed her phone to Ben. "I'm looking forward to seeing them."

"I'm glad we have a one-bedroom cottage. Don't you know they're looking forward to a night alone without the puppies or any other responsibilities?"

"I hadn't thought of that. They'll have a one-night vacation because the puppies will be here with Toby."

"We'll be the dog hotel hosts, won't we?" Ben put his arm around Riley and nuzzled her neck as he unbuttoned the top two buttons of her shirt.

"We are highly qualified." Riley giggled as she scrunched her shoulder to protect her neck from being tickled.

Toby yipped.

"Dang; busted by the parents," Ben said.

Riley kissed him then buttoned up her shirt as they headed to the door to greet their company.

"Are we going to tell them about our day?" Riley asked.

"Absolutely; they'll love hearing about Mason and Buddy and Lucy and her snake."

Riley giggled as Ben put his arm around her and opened the door.

NEXT TO READ:
ELUSIVE EMBEZZLER
JENNA ROSS MYSTERY, BOOK 1

When Jenna Ross inherits a charming bed and breakfast from her deceased husband's family, she sees the opportunity as a path to heal from her loss.

She settles into a comfortable routine that is abruptly upended when the trail of a bold embezzlement in

Atlanta leads to the sleepy town of Paisley, Georgia, and a guest disappears.

Jenna clashes with her landscaper and steps on the county sheriff's toes as she stubbornly persists in unraveling the mystery that leads to a killer.

https://barrettbookshop.com

Let's Stay in Touch
SUBSCRIBE to the Judith A. Barrett Newsletter!
https://judithabarrett.com/newsletter

About the Author

Judith A. Barrett, award-winning author, lives on a farm in Georgia with her husband, two dogs, and a dozen chickens. She writes series for her readers: romantic mystery, cozy mystery, thriller, and survival fiction novels. All are stories with a twist: not your typical characters from not your typical author!

When she isn't writing, Judith is working on farm chores, hiking or camping with her husband and dogs, or rocking on her front porch while she wonders what the characters are plotting in her book she is writing.

Her motto: You keep reading; I'll keep writing!

Find your next book at her online store. Buy direct from the author!

BARRETT BOOK SHOP

BarrettBookShop.com

Browse, shop, read, enjoy!

Subscribe to her eNewsletter!

JudithABarrett.com/newsletter

Let's keep in touch!

www.ingramcontent.com/pod-product-compliance
Lightning Source LLC
Chambersburg PA
CBHW020856020726
47497CB00005B/1427